The Coast Connection

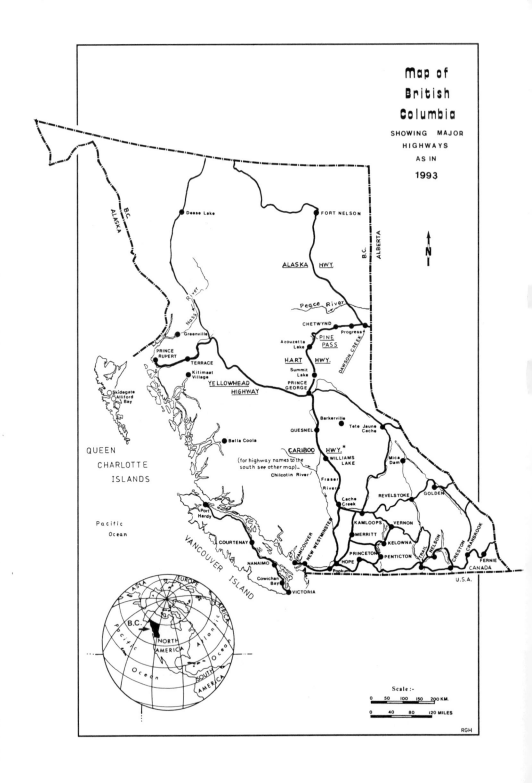

Map of
British
Columbia

SHOWING MAJOR
HIGHWAYS
AS IN
1993

N

Dease Lake

FORT NELSON

B.C.
ALASKA

ALBERTA
B.C.

ALASKA HWY.

Peace River

CHETWYND

Progress

Azouzetta Lake

PINE PASS

DAWSON CREEK

Greenville

Nass River

PRINCE RUPERT

HART HWY.

TERRACE

Summit Lake

Kitimaat Village

PRINCE GEORGE

YELLOWHEAD HIGHWAY

Skidegate
Alliford Bay

Barkerville

Tete Jaune Cache

QUESNEL

Bella Coola

QUEEN
CHARLOTTE
ISLANDS

CARIBOO HWY.*

(for highway names to the
south see other map)

WILLIAMS LAKE

Mica Dam

Chilcotin River

Fraser River

Pacific
Ocean

REVELSTOKE

GOLDEN

Cache Creek

Port Hardy

KAMLOOPS

VERNON

COURTENAY

MERRITT

KELOWNA

VANCOUVER

NEW WESTMINSTER

PRINCETON

PENTICTON

TRAIL

NELSON

CRESTON

CRANBROOK

NANAIMO

HOPE

Popkum

FERNIE

VANCOUVER ISLAND

Cowichan Bay

CANADA
U.S.A.

VICTORIA

ALASKA

EUROPE

AFRICA

B.C.

Pacific Ocean

NORTH AMERICA

Atlantic Ocean

SOUTH AMERICA

Scale:-

0   50   100   150   200 KM.

0   40   80   120 MILES

RGH

The Coast Connection

A History of the Building of Trails and Roads
Between British Columbia's Interior
and its Lower Mainland
from the Cariboo Road
to the Coquihalla Highway

by R.G. Harvey

oolichan books
Lantzville, British Columbia, Canada
1994

Canadian Cataloguing in Publication Data

Harvey, R.G. (Robert Gourlay), 1922-
The Coast Connection

Includes bibliographical references and index.

ISBN 0-88982-130-5

1. Roads—British Columbia—History. 2.Trails—British Columbia—History. 3.Transportation and state—British Columbia—History. I.Title.

HE357.Z6B7 1994   388.1'09711C94-910375-6

Publication of this book has been financially assisted by The Canada Council and by the Province of British Columbia Ministry of Small Business, Tourism and Culture through the British Columbia Heritage Trust.

HISTORIC COVER PHOTO: BCARS 10224 A-3868
COLOUR PHOTO BY THE AUTHOR

Published by
Oolichan Books
P.O. Box 10
Lantzville, B.C.
Canada V0R 2H0

Printed in Canada by
Morriss Printing Company
Victoria, British Columbia

About the Author

Bob Harvey first saw the Coquihalla Pass on his way to the Interior from Vancouver when he started working for the Department of Public Works in the spring of 1948. After travelling by bus to Hope because the railways were flooded out, he continued eastward to Nelson by the Kettle Valley Railway. Only later when he knew the history of these railways did the irony of his situation strike him: here was the lowly Coquihalla line—the handmaiden of disaster—fully operational, while the CNR and the CPR idled helplessly. Bob Harvey did not forget the rare daylight trip by passenger train through the rocky chasms of the Coquihalla, the train trundling across high trestles over racing snowmelt torrents below while a speeder probed ahead for washouts.

Mr. Harvey went on to become District Engineer at Nelson in the Kootenays, then at Nanaimo on Vancouver Island. He served as Regional Highway Engineer headquartered in Prince George, where he was responsible for all routes in the northern half of the province: seven thousand miles of wilderness roads in an area twice the size of Italy. Major projects completed while Mr. Harvey served as Regional Highway Engineer include the rebuilding of the Cariboo and Hart Highways and the improvement of the link from Prince George to Prince Rupert on the northwest coast.

In 1967 Bob Harvey came to Victoria, where he occupied several senior positions before becoming Assistant Deputy Minister (Operations) for the Highways Ministry. He served as B.C. Deputy Minister of Transportation and Highways from 1976 until his retirement in 1983. Bob Harvey is a life member of the B.C. Association of Professional Engineers and Geoscientists and the Transportation Association of Canada. He is a graduate in civil engineering from Glasgow University. His wife, Eva, comes from a pioneering Kootenay family; they have five children.

Acknowledgements

Especial thanks to Al Rhodes, Acting Deputy Minister (1983-86), and Tom Johnson, Deputy Minister of Transportation and Highways (1986-87), for their help and patience. Not only did they provide access to Ministry files, annual reports, PABC material and so on, but they also condoned my badgering of their staff when without doubt all were extremely busy. Others in the Ministry similarly helpful are too numerous to mention but my appreciation is no less. I must also thank those unidentified authors whose work has appeared throughout the years in the Department files.

My sincere gratitude to Frank Clapp, who has done so much for the Ministry as a historian, especially with his booklet on Ministry ferries. Frank generously offered his manuscript on the history of the Hart Highway, which has been of great benefit in preparing this book.

My thanks to the late Hon. Alex. Fraser for being a Minister who was kind and easy to work with during my seven years as his Deputy, and to my wife and family for their patience and encouragement.

Finally, none of this would have seen the light of day without the editing of Alison Gardner and Rhonda Bailey and the courage of Oolichan Books in taking on an engineer as an author.

—R.G. Harvey,
   Victoria, B.C.

Contents

Maps and Drawings

Lists and Schedules

Photographs and Personality Profiles†

† The source acknowledgements for personality profile
photographs include the biographic material.

9

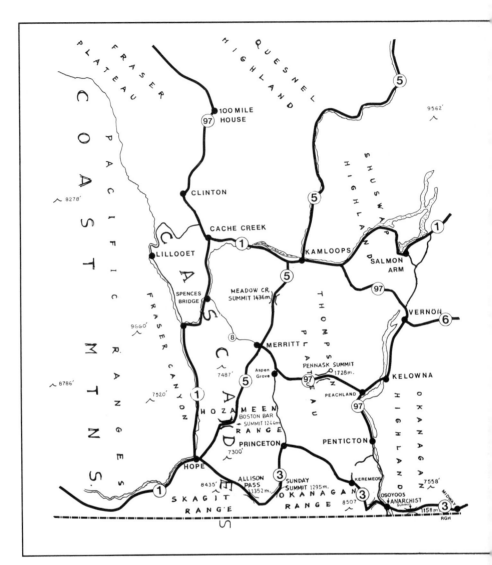

1   The Trans-Canada Highway goes around the Cascade Mountains by the Fraser and Thompson Canyons and then crosses the Thompson Plateau by way of the Thompson and South Thompson valleys. It then climbs over the Monashee Mountains by Eagle Pass and the Selkirk Mountains by Rogers Pass at 4534 ft. It passes through the rocky Mountains by Kicking Horse Pass at 5405 feet elevation.

3   The Crowsnest Highway crosses the Cascades by Allison Pass, 4436 feet, and Sunday Summit, 4250 feet, the Okanagan Highland by Richter Pass, 2250 feet and then again by Anarchist Summit, 3800 feet, the Monashees by Eholt Summit and Bonanza Pass, 5036 feet, the Selkirks by Kootenay Pass, 5820 feet, which is the highest point of a major highway in Canada, the Purcell Range by Goatfell Summit, and the Rockies by Crowsnest Pass, 4580 feet.

10

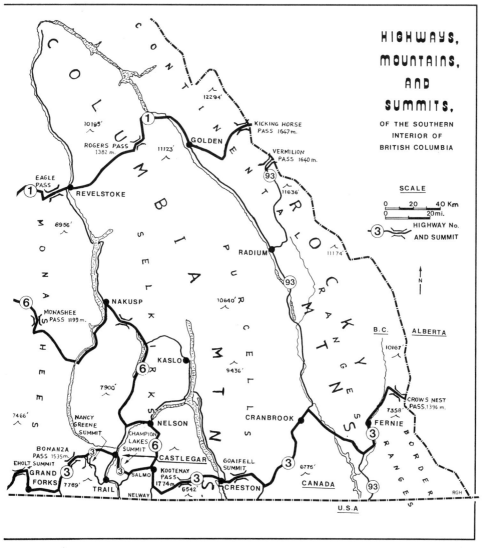

HIGHWAYS,
MOUNTAINS,
AND
SUMMITS,
OF THE SOUTHERN
INTERIOR OF
BRITISH COLUMBIA

SCALE

HIGHWAY No.
AND SUMMIT

5   The Coquihalla Highway crosses the Cascades by Boston Bar Creek Summit, 4081 feet, and then the Thompson Plateau by Meadow Creek Summit, 4711 feet. After Kamloops it becomes the Yellowhead South Highway, which was formerly the North Thompson Highway, and crosses the rockies by Yellowhead Pass, 3760 feet (off the map).

6   Highway 6 crosses the Monashees by Monashee Pass, 3935 feet, between Nakusp and Vernon.

93   The Kootenay Columbia Highway crosses the Rockies by Vermilion Pass, 5382 feet. It was a Coast Connection (Seattle to Banff) prior to 1926.

97   The Okanagan, then Cariboo, then Hart Highway, crosses the Rockies by Pine Pass, 2850 feet (off the map). This is the lowest crossing of the Rockies of any of the passes.

"The Missing Link"

This view shows the first trunk road—between Spuzzum and Lytton in the Fraser Canyon—built in British Columbia to suit the internal cumbustion engine. The road lies on the same ground as the original Royal Engineers' Cariboo Road, which fell into neglect after the CPR main line was opened in 1885. In the intervening forty-one years, the only direct route between B.C.'s lower mainland and its interior was by rail. The road shown here also lies on the site of the province's magnificent Trans-Canada Highway, which was finished in the 1960s.

The Coast Connection

*T*HE TRANSPORTATION systems of any region are crucial to its ability to develop in terms of communication, economic growth, and human settlement. As the development of western Canada has unfolded over the past 150 years, British Columbia has been fortunate to attract a colourful and determined cast of characters who pushed the visionary limits each in their own way, with technology, financial means, and difficult weather and terrain as the only stumbling blocks to their enthusiasm and energy. During this time period, the southern coast of British Columbia has been the heart from which the lifegiving arteries and veins of transportation and commerce—ranging from primitive fur brigade trails to sophisticated super highways—have spread to create the Coast Connection.

The story of the Coast Connection is one of men and mountains, roads and rivers, and the inevitable bridges, tunnels, and ferry links that bind the most challenging geographical features together. Three of the major mountain chains of North America press forcefully into the province: the Canadian Rockies, the Coast Range, and the Cascades. Between the Rockies to the east and the Coast Range and Cascades to the west lie a series of lesser ranges giving way to highlands and plateaus in between. These ranges are grouped into the Columbia Mountains, named in honour of the river they surround: they are the Cariboos, the Purcells, the Selkirks, and the

Monashees. The Okanagan, Shuswap, and Quesnel Highlands and the Thompson and Fraser Plateaus bridge these ranges in massive sweeps of remote geography that would each encompass many a small country in another part of the world. (For a detailed map of these landforms, see Chapter 7.)

Two pioneers are most notable for translating vision into action during the earliest phases of colonial development in this distant corner of Britain's farflung empire. Sir James Douglas, first Governor of the combined colonies of Vancouver Island and mainland British Columbia, had the remarkable foresight to realize that a wagon road through the lowest and largest canyon of the Fraser River was the key to unlocking the treasure chest of British Columbia's interior region—this despite almost overwhelming difficulties of construction and very little support from his superiors in Britain. When he was sent a contingent of Royal Engineers and little else, Douglas harnessed the skills of these remarkable military frontiersmen and urged them on to ever greater challenges. Far from their familiar English surroundings, the Royal Engineers painstakingly educated the rough and ready colonists in how to build timber cribs and trestles, how to drill and blast rock, and how to build that rock into walls to support their narrow but stable roadways, in areas "where no sensible roadbuilder should venture."

Sir Joseph Trutch was another influential visionary, an entrepreneur, road and bridge contractor, and a respected civil engineer. Arriving in British Columbia in 1859, Trutch took a contract to build part of the road through the Fraser Canyon as well as a bridge over the Fraser River. Later, as B.C.'s first permanently resident Commissioner of Lands and Works, Trutch conceived the idea of a transcontinental highway and sent his assistant, Walter Moberly, to find a way through the mountains lying at the eastern border of the newly created colony. Moberly did identify Eagle Pass, which ironically had to wait for a much longer period of time to become the route of a usable road than it did to become the route of a commercially successful railway.

After his appointment as B.C.'s first Lieutenant-Governor, Trutch continued to crusade for the preservation of potential and actual road routes in the face of the voracious appetite of the railways, which were consuming all possible avenues through B.C.'s mountains during the late 19th century era of railway euphoria.

The connection of the lower coast of British Columbia to the interior valleys and plateaus by road has never been simply the logical creation of a system of geographical arteries. Throughout the history of the province, the Coast Connection has required the channelling of the energies, skills, and aspirations of our very best leaders—Premiers, Ministers of the Crown, pioneers and engineers. Many have tried with varying degrees of success.

First, there was Joseph Trutch, who saw the Fraser Canyon road completed in 1865, only to witness its destruction by the Canadian Pacific Railway within twenty years. Then Premier McBride and his Minister of Public Works, "Good Roads" Taylor, were enthusiastic supporters of a road to the coast. Together they tried—prematurely—to build a connection from Hope to Princeton, an effort overwhelmed in midstream by the world's first global conflict. Finally came the most diffident and unlikely roads champion: Premier Bill Bennett. His Coquihalla extravaganza sparked the greatest effort of them all but produced the least credit for its creator.

Sir Joseph Trutch would, no doubt, be proud of today's network of highways and railways from the central and southern interior of British Columbia to the densely populated mouth of the Fraser River and the city of Vancouver, a network traversing some of the most challenging terrain found anywhere in the world. Criss-crossing the province's plateaus, highlands, and mountains for a distance of over two thousand miles, these various routes represent a challenge to roadbuilders that even today defies the most sophisticated of engineering techniques and the most modern of construction equipment. Yet these hard-won routes are consistently taken for granted by B.C.'s citizens. (See road map following.)

In today's dollars, it is almost impossible to calculate the value of this transportation system. Recently the Coquihalla Highway and a section of the Trans-Canada Highway leading to it were completed at a cost of nearly a billion dollars. Yet this section represents only one-tenth of the system's total mileage. Even at that, the economic value of their Interior routes to the citizens of B.C. is far in excess of any initial building costs each year, no matter how they are calculated.

As a civil servant and engineer in British Columbia over a period of thirty-five years, I became intimately involved in the existing and projected transportation network of the province—from the Kootenays to Vancouver Island, from Prince George to Victoria. As a perpetual student of history and with my retirement looming in 1983, I could find no comprehensive account where the focus was entirely on the transportation history of the Province. Indeed, much of the transportation lore has been spread thinly through the works of worthy historians and biographers focussing on pieces of B.C.'s colourful past, but much else has been left unsaid from a road transportation perspective.

However, history cannot be flooded onto a plate, letting it run off

A Sea of Mountains

A line of ridges that seemed to stretch forever faced Hudson's Bay man A.C. Anderson in 1848 when he looked over his task of finding a way from Fort Hope inland to Fort Kamloops and Fort Colville. The photograph shows the view from a trail in Manning Park.

Hard to get through—and hard to forage

Anderson's challenge was not only to find suitable trails to move through with the fur brigades, but also to find areas of grassland where the horses and mules could forage. There could be as many as 200 animals in one brigade.

The Ice Age comes to the rescue

Strange but true—in the last ice age, the grinding action of the ice cap, which moved as far south as Puget Sound and covered the sharp peaks and ridges of the Cascades to a depth of 6000 feet, caused the landform

by its grinding action. Above that altitude matterhorn-type peaks still exist. This is shown in the photograph above. The rounded hillside is sparse in trees, and quickly grows ground vegetation in the spring snow melt, and that fed the fur trader's animals, as shown below.

17

in all directions; it must be channelled into a coherent story with limitations in order to make sense and present a clear focus. For this reason, I have chosen to concentrate on an account of the transportation routes linking the lower coast to the B.C. Interior, spanning the near century and a half between the construction of the Yale-Cariboo Road and the Coquihalla Highway. To readers whose roads and historical interests are represented elsewhere in the province, I can only say there is certainly another story to be told in due course.

Over a period of five years, I have taken upon myself the task of drawing together as much material from public and private sources as I could find to track the Coast Connection. I have used many of the primary sources to which I was privileged to have access as well as many of the living, breathing sources who each had much to share from personal observation. With the completion of this volume, I leave it to the reader to decide if the gap has been filled and the story of the Coast Connection told fully and fairly.

I hope you will enjoy this journey into the world of trails, roads, and bridges. To help you with the language, the book has a glossary of technical terms; like any traveller you will require maps, and these are provided; and finally, you will find some snapshots taken from the car window.

Bon voyage!

CHAPTER ONE

1793–1864

After the trails for the fur brigades were blazed, British Columbia's transportation system really got under way. A road to the Interior region of the colony was built in order to accommodate the flood of goldseekers.

THE MEN of the fur brigades were hardy souls travelling in bands up to two hundred in number, on foot or horseback, leading their packhorses laden with furs. A single line could stretch over half a mile of tortuous trail, slowly wending its way through forest and grassland, across river and over rock slide. The choice of route was usually dependent more upon suitable grazing areas for the animals than on the steepness or directness of their travel. The pace was agonisingly slow, often only ten to twelve miles a day in mountainous country.

Their banner, when they struck out from Kamloops bound for Fort Langley on the lower Fraser River, was that of the British-based Hudson's Bay Company. Not only were the fur traders the first non-native travellers of commerce in British Columbia, they were also the first explorers of the Coquihalla Pass as an on-going transportation route for the company. After deliberate exploration for this route in 1846-47, the first brigade "business trip" set out from Kamloops for the southwest in 1848. The fur brigade trail through Coquihalla Pass might well be called the first all British Columbia Coast Connection!

This whole transportation era began in 1793, when Alexander Mackenzie led the way for the fur traders from what is now Alberta into British Columbia, using the Peace River as his route through the Rocky Mountains. Mackenzie was soon followed by fellow explorer Simon Fraser, who in 1805 established the first trading post east of the Coast Range and west of the Rockies, at McLeod's Lake in central British Columbia.

That settlement was never entirely self-supporting, for it relied upon supplies and food brought in from the east, mostly provided by the buffalo herds that were abundant on the Prairies at that time. Hides for pack saddles and traces, buffalo robes for warmth, pemmican (a mixture of dried buffalo meat, fat, and sometimes saskatoon berries) for sustenance—all had to be regularly transported over the Rocky Mountains. The original point of entry at Peace River Gap was too far to the north to efficiently serve McLeod's Lake, so another entry close to the headwaters of the Fraser River was established. The new entry was first called Leather Pass for the hides which passed through it, but today it is known as the Yellowhead Pass.

A superb surveyor and explorer for the North West Company, David Thompson, sought out alternative routes through the mountain ranges of the Rockies, discovering routes that had long been known to the native people. Thompson used both Howse Pass and Athabasca Pass, north of what is now Golden, to gain entry to the upper reaches of the Columbia River. Set loose upon the huge watershed, in four years from 1807 to 1811 he thoroughly explored it, and as he did so, being a true servant of his company, he set up outposts and trading centres to exploit this wonderful new fur-gathering area.

In 1821 the North West Company was absorbed by its fierce rival, the Hudson's Bay Company (HBC). Combining two departments of the Company, the Western and the Columbia, the territory of the HBC stretched from the Pacific Ocean to the Rocky Mountains, and from Alaska (where they met the Russians from Sitka) to Yerba Buena or the present day San Francisco (where the fur traders met the first colonial Spaniards).

The major centre of this realm in the period between 1821 and 1846 was the central interior of British Columbia, comprising the northern half of the Interior Plateau, which had proved to be an excellent place in which to find beaver, so coveted in Europe during that time. This "New Caledonia" region extended from the Bulkley River to Leather Pass, and from the Stikine River to the Chilcotin.[1] The establishment of Fort Vancouver near the mouth of the Columbia River—where now the city of Vancouver, Washington, stands—created an ocean terminus for a transportation route from New Caledonia to the Pacific using the Columbia River as its super highway. From there, ships carried the furs half way around the world to Britain.

In the year 1846, the United States boundary was set at the forty-ninth parallel west of the Rockies, requiring the HBC fur brigades from New Caledonia to find a new route and a new overseas shipping point within the region north of that line still under British control. The need to reroute came about quite suddenly, because although the Americans allowed the HBC access throughout 1846, they immediately charged duty on every fur bundle taken through. The largely Scottish field managers of the fur trade could not stand that for long!

A usable route was needed between Kamloops and Fort Langley. One obvious way was by the Fraser River, but its dreaded Canyon proved to be too difficult even for rivermen of the calibre of the voyageurs. The "Little Emperor," HBC Governor George Simpson, took some years before deciding that the walls of the Fraser Canyon above Hell's Gate were totally impassable for fur brigades.

In 1846, Alexander Caulfield Anderson, a surveyor in the employ of the Hudson's Bay Company, was appointed to search the Cascade Mountains for an alternate fur brigade route. The mountains, especially the northernmost prong, the Hozameen Range, were a formidable barrier. A wedge of ridge and summit forty miles wide, the Hozameen Range stretches from the U.S. border as far north as Lytton, and is haunched on either side by the Skagit Range and by the Okanagan Range. It definitely barred the direct route between Kamloops and Fort Hope. (See Landforms map in Chapter 7.)

Anderson was the first non-Indian to explore the seventy-five mile land and water route shaped like a reversed question mark through the Coast Range between Harrison Lake on the lower Fraser and Lillooet on the upper Fraser. When another forty miles to travel down to Lytton and the lower Thompson River was added, this route required travelling by water transportation for forty-five miles on four lakes separated by long and short overland portages. By any standards it could not be considered a good route for fur brigades. (See Lakes and Rivers map, Chapter 2.)

Ten years later Anderson was to supervise trail building on this route as a first measure by Governor Douglas to provide upstream access for the miners clamouring to get up the Fraser and Thompson to pan the rivers' gravel bars for gold. The route eventually had good wagon roads built between the lakes, and even a short stretch of rough railway, but it could never be considered a Coast Connection because it could not be sold as a transportation route even to the miners who first used it. Governor Douglas did, however, persuade them to work on the trails in exchange for board and transportation.

Northwest North America, 1811-1861:
The Routes of the Fur Brigades

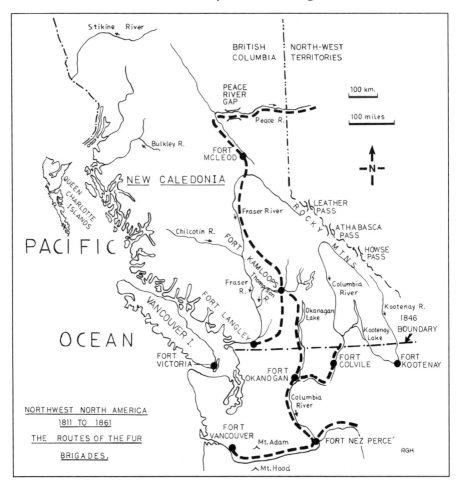

For immediate development, however, Anderson decided that the old trail from Kamloops to Nicola Lake was suitable for the fur brigades. Located east of what is now the route of the new freeway, this trail followed more or less the line of the present Highway #5. In those days the sixty miles took six to seven days to traverse with pack horses. Anderson then set out to find a suitable route for the trail's continuation down to Hope.

Led by his Indian guides, he no doubt travelled up the Coldwater River to its source. Until recent times the Coldwater Indian band never missed a year of savouring the generous crop of huckleberries and chokeberries to be had there, so they knew that valley well. It was an excellent start for Anderson's route to the south and west.

Anderson also explored the companion valley, that of the Coquihalla River, but it is not clear how well he looked at the difficult area between them. He certainly travelled the Coquihalla upstream from what was to become Fort Hope, and at one point he turned off up the tributary that joins just south of the upper canyon. This tributary became known as Boston Bar Creek, as it was the starting point for that destination. In its upper reaches, Boston Bar Creek parallels the Coquihalla River to a common headwater area with the Coldwater River. (See Trails map following.)

Whether or not Anderson went on over the top to the valley of the Coldwater River, crossing or climbing around the steep-walled Dry Gulch ravine, is not clear. In any event, at some time he crossed over into the broad valley of yet another river rising in that area. He left the Boston Bar Creek Valley at a point very close to Box Canyon and went up and over a steep ridge into the valley of what is now called the Anderson River. This stream flows west and north to join the Fraser River a few miles downstream from the present day village of Boston Bar.

From that point Anderson used yet another Indian trail following Uztlius Creek, Maka Creek, and the Coldwater River to Merritt.[2] Uztlius Creek soon became the more pronounceable Useless Creek. Anderson had reason to regret the discovery of this potential route, however, because when he combined this route with another from Boston Bar to Yale, his reputation was damaged, as will be recounted later.

Two considerations probably led Anderson away from the Coquihalla Pass as the route for the fur brigades through the Cascades. The first was the terrain around Dry Gulch and through the summit area. Steep and high sliding slopes of broken rock, sand, and silt made trail-building almost impossible. The second consideration was the difficulty of keeping a trail open in the casual "fix it as you go" way of the fur brigades, whose trips were usually months apart. These trails were described by a later traveller, Lieutenant Palmer of the Royal Engineers:

> It is difficult to find language to express in adequate terms the utter vileness of the trails ... dreaded alike by all classes of travellers ... slippery, precipitous ascents and descents, fallen logs, overhanging branches, roots, rocks, swamps, turbid pools, and miles of deep mud.[3]

There was no doubt that the upper Coquihalla was tough ground, both in human terms and in terms of the scarcity of feed

Early Trails

The map on the right shows the difficulties experienced first by the Hudson's Bay Company surveyor, A.C. Anderson, in trying to find a route for the fur brigades in 1849 between Boston Bar and Spuzzum, and then by the Royal Engineers when they sought a way for the wagon road in the same area ten years later. The brigades could not scale the cliffs at Hell's Gate, so Anderson tried taking them over the 3000 foot-high ridge between Anderson River and Spuzzum, a climb and descent of well over 2000 feet vertically in 12 miles. Willing as they were, this was too much for the pack horses and mules, and the trail was used only once.

The sappers tried a route up the Coquihalla and Boston Bar Creek Valleys, and over a 4300 foot summit to Anderson River, tracing it out in the winter of 1859-60, but they found the snowfalls and avalanche threat of Boston Bar Creek Valley too much. They finally followed Captain Lempriere's recommendation for a road up the Canyon, although they did not take his chosen route from the east bank from Hope to Boston Bar. They started at Yale and built a bridge across the Fraser at Spuzzum. The trail along Nicolum River eventually became the Dewdney Trail. That trail and the other eastbound brigade trail are continued on the map "Trails from the Skagit to the Tulameen," found later in this chapter.

Note: Locations of trails are indicative only. No attempt to accurately site them has been made.

for the animals. Another reason for dread of this route was the heavy annual snowfall coupled with the length of time that the high ground of the Coquihalla summit area remained deeply covered.

Anderson knew from his two years of exploration that people could travel the Coquihalla Pass at best for only five months in any one year, whereas the Fraser Canyon was free of heavy snow cover for most of a normal winter. It was no wonder that he tried to find a way down the Canyon from Boston Bar. It must also have been most frustrating to him to know that the land at the head of Uztlius Creek, along the Thompson Plateau, was usually very lightly covered in snow for most of the year and provided excellent pasturage.

He sought the help of the local Indians to try to find a way south close to the Fraser River. The temptation to use at least half of the Fraser Canyon, with its directness and lower altitude, was too great for him to resist. The route Anderson chose followed an old Indian trace directly south from Boston Bar by the Anderson River and then over the 2750 foot-high ridge down to the river's edge opposite Spuzzum. The Indians for centuries had speared salmon here at the river's edge, and the place was already the site of a small ferry and a trail, known as Douglas Portage or the Old Mountain Trail, leading up over the mountain on the opposite bank to Yale. But this route turned out to be a disaster.

During the first return journey, which combined two brigades, seventy of the four hundred animals died. The Hudson's Bay Company was probably more concerned by the fact that only fifty of the seventy precious 125-pound "pieces" of compressed fur pelts were recovered.[4] Chief Trader Manson swore that they would never use Anderson's trail again, and they never did. Anderson returned to Kamloops, his starring role as chief trail-blazer at an end. This was indeed unfortunate, as he had done extensive exploration throughout the area, and his advice would have been most valuable as future developments unfolded.

Susan Moir Allison, wife of John Fall Allison, recalls one day in 1860 when she was berry picking on the Hope-Similkameen trail and unexpectedly encountered a fur brigade nearing Hope from the east. She describes it in her memoirs:

> I shall never forget my first sight of a Hudson's Bay Company Brigade train coming in from Colville. I was getting a "feed" of berries when I heard bells tinkling and looking up saw a light cloud of dust from which emerged a solitary horseman, the most picturesque figure I have ever seen. He rode a superb chestnut horse satiny and well groomed, untired and full of life in spite of the dust, heat and long journey. He himself

wore a beautifully embroidered buckskin shirt with tags and fringes, buckskin pants, embroidered leggings and soft cowboy hat. He was as surprised to see me as I was to see him, for he abruptly reined in his horse and stared down at me, while I equally astonished stared at him. Then, as the Bell Boy and other horses rode up, he lifted his hat and passed on. I never met him again but was told he was a Hudson's Bay Company officer in charge of the Colville train and that he was never more surprised in his life than to see a white girl on the trail—he had lived so long without seeing anyone except Indians. [5]

Anderson's successor as pathfinder was another Hudson's Bay clerk named Henry Peers. He set to and found a route from the lower Coquihalla Valley across the Hozameen Range using a creek named after him. The route Peers chose turned out to be a poor one because the trail built on it climbed up over one steep ridge only to return to another tributary, Sowaqua Creek. From there the exhausted traveller had to scramble up over another steep ridge in order finally to reach the Interior Plateau. The pass over the ridge between Peers Creek and Sowaqua Creek became known as "Fool's Pass" when the weary trekkers realised its folly.

Had Peers gone downstream a little to Nicolum Creek (called N'Columne River at that time), he would have encountered a very low summit, which in turn would have led him into the Skagit watershed along the route of the present highway to Princeton. Then he would have turned north from the Skagit River Valley using Snass Creek for a short, steep climb up to the plateau, as Edgar Dewdney did later. About the only good thing that could be said about Peers's trail was that it did get up quickly into the high plateau where the ground was softer with areas of excellent pasturage. Here the Hudson's Bay maintained one of their brigade camps.[6]

In fact, the availability of good forage may have been the reason why the Hudson's Bay Company used a fur brigade trail in this area for so many years—from 1849 to the end of the fur brigade era. However, the company did modify operations throughout this period, and at times travelled the length of the N'Columne River instead. Both these routes converged on Otter Creek, and from that valley went on over to the Coldwater River at Brookmere, then known as Otter Summit, so the Hudson's Bay brigades were actually the first users of the Coquihalla/Coldwater route even if they did not go through the pass.

The spacing of the camps the HBC built and maintained for the fur brigades gives a good idea of the distance that could be covered at that time in one day's travel. Between Hope and Otter Lake, there were five camps in fifty miles! Starting from Hope, the first was called Manson Mountain Camp and was located at the head of Peers Creek. The second, *Chevreuil* Camp, which means "venison camp," was just below the second ridge crossed twenty miles out, and the next, Horseguards Camp on the high plateau, was thirty-one miles from Hope. Then there was Lodestone Camp nine miles farther on, and finally *L'Encampement des Femmes*, located at the junction of Otter Creek and the Tulameen River. There was also a summer tent camp at Cedar Flats near the junction of the Skaist and Skagit Rivers.

But the era of the brigades and the fur monopoly was almost at an end as Governor James Douglas sent out urgent cries for help to the Mother Country to save the fledgling colony of British Columbia from the arrival of the rambunctious Americans flooding in to seek gold on the Fraser River. On Christmas Day of 1858 help arrived in the form of Her Majesty Queen Victoria's Regiment of Royal Engineers. Under the able leadership of Colonel Richard Clements Moody, they were to be a major influence in the area's development for many years to come. Still basking in the glory of his restoration work for Edinburgh Castle, Moody was nonetheless well accustomed to working in remote areas: just before his British Columbia assignment he had returned to Britain from eight years as the Governor of the Falkland Islands.

Moody's assignment, issued by Colonial Secretary Sir Edward Bulwer Lytton, who was obviously intrigued by the problems of this fledgling colony, was to survey and set out townsites and rights-of-way for the already established roads. This was all part of an ongoing effort to fully define and legalise the British presence in the area, due to the threat of immediate absorption by the great overland migrations of settlers to Oregon and California from the eastern states of the American Union. Moody was in fact preceded by a survey party of the Royal Engineers who were at that time fully engaged in surveying the boundary on the mainland between British and American territory along the 49th parallel, as agreed to in 1846.

After Moody established New Westminster in its present location on the north bank of the Fraser, Governor Douglas put Moody right as to his top priority: that is, to build some sort of transportation route to the Interior. Reconnaissance parties went out in all directions.

The first of these was under young Lieutenant Henry Spencer Palmer, who turned out to be a first class pathfinder and mapmaker, as were many of the Royal Engineers. His accounts and maps of his trips are now in the Provincial Archives of British Columbia.

The Trail Blazers

Sir James Douglas

A career Hudson's Bay Company man, Douglas was promoted to Chief Factor in Oregon in 1840; two years later he visited the south end of Vancouver Island seeking a site for a new western headquarters for the HBC. This became necessary with the secession of the Oregon territory to the United States. In 1843 he founded Fort Victoria where the city of that name now stands. Douglas became British Governor of Vancouver Island and then of the colonies of Vancouver Island and British Columbia. He situated Yale at the head of navigation on the Fraser River and blazed the trail to Spuzzum, the native crossing place. His greatest achievements were in the transportation field.

Alexander Caulfield Anderson

The spark plug in the Hudson's Bay Company, Anderson was chosen in 1848 to find a route for the fur brigades from Kamloops southwest to Fort Langley. Unfortunately, both his discovery of the Harrison River route to Lillooet and his efforts to use the lower Fraser Canyon were to no avail: the final route was over the Cascades and by Otter Creek to Nicola Lake. Fort Alexandria (of which he was in charge), Anderson Lake, and Anderson River were named after him. He also served at Fort Nisqually (Tacoma, Washington) as Chief Factor, and at Fort Vancouver and Fort Colville. Anderson ended up as the first customs collector in B.C. and as Postmaster at Victoria.

John Fall Allison

Travelling from England to British Columbia via the California goldfields, Allison arrived in Hope in 1858. He found favour with Governor Douglas, who hired him to explore the Similkameen River area to the east. There he found "diggings," but they never made him rich. His trail-blazing included the discovery of Allison Pass, and a route from Princeton to what is now Westbank opposite Kelowna in the Okanagan. Allison pioneered a cattle ranch there until a succession of severe winters and an untrustworthy partner brought him back to Princeton. He also built the first good trail from Princeton to Osoyoos. He and Edgar Dewdney were brothers-in-law, having married the Moir sisters, Susan and Jane.

Palmer travelled due east from Hope along the boundary to explore a route to Rock Creek, where gold had been found, some forty miles east of the Okanagan Valley. He went as far as the Columbia River and returned via Kamloops, passing the site of Lillooet as well as Seton Lake and Harrison Lake. Later he made a notable trip—which he also wrote about—between Bella Coola and Williams Lake. (See Lakes and Rivers map, Chapter 2.)

The next man out was Lieutenant Arthur Reid Lempriere (later Captain). He submitted an excellent report of his expedition east and north from Hope which remains in the Colonial correspondence files. Included with this report was the first assessment of the Fraser Canyon as a route for a wagon road, dated January 2, 1860.

Lempriere made his trip in August of 1859, probably treading an Indian trace from where it left the brigade trail five miles east of the Fraser. He was followed by a party of sappers building trail, and assisted by a contingent of settlers from Fort Hope who were bent on making that place the transfer point from river boat to packhorse. The final destination was Spuzzum, the same point of crossing the Fraser River A.C. Anderson had considered fourteen years before.

Lempriere's report, reprinted in total at the end of the chapter, reflects the important role these engineering investigations played in planning for future communications to the Interior. It contains an excellent assessment of the Fraser Canyon as the best route from Hope to Lytton. The Royal Engineers in course of time followed Lempriere's recommendation and produced their masterpiece, the Cariboo Road.

But just then the Governor of the Colony had some other decisions to make, and the first was related to access east from Hope rather than north. James Douglas had been appointed Governor of the two colonies of British Columbia and Vancouver Island in November of 1858, and he had a great deal on his mind concerning transportation in the spring of 1860. The colonists were vehemently demanding roads to the Interior, and particularly to the American-oriented Kootenays.

Governor Douglas had already set Colonel Moody's sappers to work on building wagon trails to join up the various lakes and rivers from Harrison Lake to Lillooet, but he had serious reservations about the route because of its inconvenience and indirectness. The strongest pressure was from the hundreds of miners anxious to reach the gravel bars farther up the gold-bearing Fraser River, and that interest had now spread to the Thompson River, for a good strike had just been made at the mouth of Nicoamen Creek.

The Engineers' recommendation of the Fraser Canyon as the best route for a wagon road was too much at that point for the harassed Governor. However, Douglas knew he had to do something, and his decision was to build a good mule road from Hope to the Simil-kameen Valley, from which the traveller could swing north and reach the Thompson River as well as travel eastward to Okanagan Lake and beyond.

The year before, Douglas had welcomed two very promising young entrants to the Colony, both experienced surveyors of roads and railways, and both bearing recommendations from the Hudson's Bay Company. Edgar Dewdney came from England with a letter from headquarters in London, and Walter Moberly from Upper Canada with one from HBC Governor George Simpson of Lachine, Quebec. Douglas decided to give both men a chance and called for tenders to build his mule road. Dewdney won out with a bid of $380 per mile, a few dollars less than Moberly's offer. The Governor signed a contract with Dewdney, and Moberly joined Dewdney as a partner, and as his agent in New Westminster.

Dewdney started off up Nicolum Creek, following that stream and the Sumallo River right through to the Skagit. He then took a route up Canyon Creek, later called Snass Creek, intending to join the fur brigade trail from Peers Creek at the point where that trail left the Tulameen River and struck out across country for Lodestone Mountain. This was close to Horseguards camp, and it was probably as far as Dewdney intended to go. At that time the Tulameen River was identified as the North Fork of the Similkameen, and often simply as the Similkameen.

But before Dewdney reached that point, and when he was working near what was known as the "Punch Bowl Pass," the Governor had a sudden change of mind. He had originally intended the trail to follow the brigade's route from Horseguard's Camp to Otter Creek and then northwards, but now he redirected the trail builders towards a new settlement, at the forks of the Similkameen, which he had just named "Prince's Town," (later shortened to Princeton). This route had the added attraction of keeping the new colonists away from the Hudson's Bay operation, a way of thinking which was a legacy from his days as Chief Factor. (See map overleaf.)

At the outset there was a very serious accusation against Dewdney that he had used a part of the existing Whatcom trail, and dishonestly charged his per mile rate while doing nothing on it. However, Sergeant William McColl of the Royal Engineers, who was supervising Dewdney's contract, put this rumour to rest by confirming that he had not authorised payment for any trail-building that was not necessary.

Edgar Dewdney never did finish his full contract to build a mule road to Princeton, which was unfortunate as he had excellent specifications for the work, drawn up by the Royal Engineers. It is possible that this altercation, which Dewdney handled very respectfully, was one reason why Dewdney later took no direct part in the Fraser Canyon Wagon Road construction, although he did work in partnership with Joseph Trutch.

Dewdney and Moberly also got into a restrained and polite argument with the Commissioner of Lands and Works, the one and same Colonel of the Royal Engineers, Richard Moody, over the matter of the Governor changing contract destinations in midstream. This may have been the first but it was certainly not the last instance of political interference in a road contract resulting in a difference of opinion between the road authority and a contractor in British Columbia.

Dewdney and Moberly were eventually well compensated, following the intervention of the Governor, but the bottom line was that the mule road never got finished. The citizens of Hope and Princeton had to wait eighty-seven years before they had between their towns a good road fit for all types of vehicles: that is, the Hope-Princeton Highway, which was opened in 1949.

The first moves in the Canyon were made in 1860 when Governor Douglas, encouraged by Lempriere's report of January 2, signed two contracts with Franklin Way of Spuzzum and Joseph Beedy of Fort Yale. Both were for four-foot-wide mule trail construction. The first at $22,000 was signed early in the year for thirteen miles from Yale to Spuzzum, along the water's edge; the second was signed in August, with the same parties, for a similar trail from Chapman's Bar, at water's edge, through the infamous Hell's Gate. This one was for 14.5 miles at $47,185. The payment was in B.C. Bonds, one third immediately, the balance in installments.

These totals work out to $1692 and $3254 per mile respectively, very costly work for those days. One can only wonder what Dewdney thought of them in light of his Skagit-area contract at $380 per mile for a similar or better standard of trail. The first Way and Beedy contract was finished in the late fall of 1861, the second by mid-1862, by which time a wagon road contract had been called for the same stretch of mountainside but higher up. From reports, the Way and Beedy trails were little more than scars on the cliff face.

In the fall of 1861 Governor Douglas made an inspection and decided to go ahead with a wagon road with a minimum width of eighteen feet, his advisors wisely insisting such a width would be enough to let two wagon trains pass, or faster traffic overtake.

Trails—from the Skagit to the Tulameen

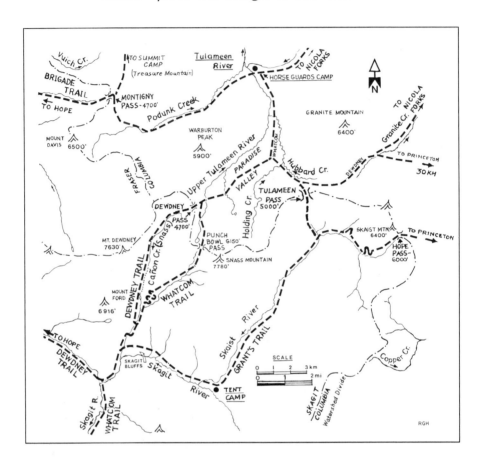

The area north of the Hope-Princeton Highway between Hope and Skagit Bluffs was a maze of trails in the 1860s. This map is an extension eastward of the trails shown on the map earlier in this chapter, "Trails North and East of Hope." Captain Grant's revision to Edgar Dewdney's trail is shown above; Grant started building a wagon roadway on it in 1861. If the decision had not been made to go via the Fraser Canyon, he might well have turned north by way of Hubbard Creek and the Tulameen River to Otter Creek, over to the Coldwater Valley and on to Kamloops, in the footsteps of the fur brigades.

To outfit American miners and get them into Canada while avoiding the Fraser River and the Fort Hope customs and mining fee collectors, the merchants of Whatcom County in Washington Territory hired U.S. Army Captain W.W. DeLacey to blaze a trail. Entering Canada at Sumas, he followed the Chilliwack River to Chilliwack Lake, then crossed the mountains to the Skagit.

Walter Moberly in his memoirs insists that he persuaded Douglas away from last-minute second thoughts about the Harrison/Lillooet route, and that he was assisted in this by Colonel Moody.[6] Moody had been against the awards to Way and Beedy, and it seems his judgment was sound.

A letter from James B. Leighton dated August 27, 1923, identifies him as a settler who came to B.C. in September of 1863 and went on to Barkerville in June 1865. Remarkably, he was still living in the area at the time he wrote to the Minister of Public Works, recalling from memory the contracts let for the wagon roads along the route. In one passage he says,

> I have spent 24 years on the old road between Yale and Barkerville. Have gone over it times without number at all seasons of the year. It is the only safe and sound route. No mud between Yale and Spence's Bridge. Nothing to make mud. All rock and gravel. It was a lovely road in its day, from 18 to 22 feet wide, all turns were 40 feet wide. Not a serious accident in all these years.[7]

In the account, Leighton specified contracts, contractors, and costs for road sections and bridges in great detail, although he did not include the footnotes to history of the occasional contractor going bankrupt or fleeing creditors and the cholera outbreak among the Chinese labourers working on some sections. The Royal Engineers themselves put the links all together: locating and surveying, constructing the worst sections themselves, choosing the sites of the river crossings, and instructing one and all in how to build cribbings, mine rock, and construct bridges.

Mr. Leighton wrote again to the Hon. Dr. Sutherland on December 31, 1925.[8] The subject was the decision at that time to reimpose tolls on the Cariboo Road, a decision Leighton supported in his correspondence. He pointed out that a toll of one cent per pound of freight was applied at Clinton in 1862, and another toll of the same amount in 1864 at Lytton. Both were kept on until 1872, although road tolls were reimposed in the Canyon around 1881 when railway building started and removed in 1886 when it ceased. He added the following comment:

> The tolls on the Alexandra Bridge and Spence's Bridge went to the builders of same. They had a charter to build them and collect tolls until paid for or for a term of years. They got renewals and made a fortune. . . . These tolls were lifted in 1876 or about that time.

In this rather innocently expressed statement, Leighton was saying that Joseph Trutch, while serving as the Province's Lieutenant-

Governor, had the toll privileges on his bridge extended for his full term of office, resulting in considerable personal enrichment.[9] It would be interesting to see what today's Conflict of Interest Commissioner would have to say about this!

Colonel Moody left British Columbia on November 11, 1863, and all his officers bar one went with him. Douglas had floated loans of $500,000 to pay for the road; he had wanted another $250,000, but London vetoed that. It was due to his cleverness in payment method and toll collections that the Colony did not go bankrupt. The road was completed from Yale to Barkerville, four hundred miles, in 1865 at a total cost of $1,325,000.

The Imperial Government had done well for the Colony in sending their sappers and miners, but they undermined their generosity and foresight by haggling for years over payment for the Royal Engineers' services. Considering the means and resources available to them, the work the sappers did was magnificent, and the road was truly of inestimable value to the Colony.

The detachment virtually disbanded in 1863, with almost all of the other ranks, 143 out of 158, deciding to stay on in British Columbia, as their contract included payment in pre-empted land. Unfortunately, the same was not the case with the officers,[10] as only Lieutenant Robert Burnaby, the military assistant to Colonel Moody, stayed to set up his home for a time in Victoria, finally returning to Britain ten years later. Two officers acquired wives in the Colony and took them off with them.[11]

With the completion of the wagon road through the Fraser Canyon, interest in the Coquihalla ranges to the east and the Anderson River and Boston Bar Creek valleys as primitive transportation routes through the mountains temporarily dried up. However, it was inevitable that all areas of the Interior would be settled by colonists, and attention soon turned to the development of alternate routes.

The Royal Engineers

Richard Clement Moody, R.E.

Colonel Moody arrived in British Columbia on Christmas Day 1858. Within a remarkably short time, he presented the colony with a wonderful present—the Cariboo Road. As the first colonial Commissioner of Lands & Works, he spent much time arguing with Governor Douglas while organizing and directing a reconnaissance, survey, and road construction programme unique for its day and age. Together with the capable assistance of his adjutant, Captain Henry Luard, and his chief of construction, Captain Jim Grant, he created within five years a wealth of townships, ports, and government buildings. In fact, Moody's own residence became Government House in New Westminster. He supported one of his officer's recommendations against the Coquihalla Pass and persuaded Governor Douglas to build through the Fraser Canyon.

Lieutenant Henry Spencer Palmer, R.E.

The glamour boy of the Royal Engineers, Palmer led the first reconnaissance of the Royal Engineers into the southern interior of B.C. in company with HBC Chief Trader Angus MacDonald of Fort Colville in 1859. He also made a notable journey from Bella Coola to Williams Lake in 1862, writing excellent accounts of both trips. Being ignorant of the sacredness of the salmon among the natives, he offended them on one of his trips by cutting through the fish's backbone, a blunder which nearly resulted in his summary execution. While in British Columbia, Palmer married a clergyman's daughter and took her back to England when the Engineers left the colony in 1863.

Sergeant William McColl, R.E.

Colonel Moody put much faith in his non-commissioned officers. McColl was the one who traced for Dewdney the line ahead on the mule road to Similkameen and who approved his invoices. He also reported direct to Moody on allegations against Dewdney. In addition, the sergeant accompanied the young Lieutenant Palmer to find a suitable site for the Alexandra Bridge. McColl set up business as a land surveyor after discharge from the military, but unlike many of the NCOs who stayed on in B.C. and left their mark, he did not prosper. He died as a tollkeeper on the bridge he located.

Report by Captain A.R. Lempriere, R.E.

2nd. January 1860

REPORT upon the Fort Hope and Boston Bar Trail by the Coquihalla and Anderson River Route; the Mountain Trail from Yale to Boston Bar, and the Proposed Road from Yale through the Passes (commonly called Canyons) of Frazer River to Spuzzum, Boston Bar, and Lytton.

Fort Hope to Boston Bar Trail

The mule trail lately constructed between Fort Hope and Boston Bar by a Detachment of the Royal Engineers and a party of Civilians, traverses the Hudson's Bay Company trail for the first five miles crossing the Coquihalla at the ferry about 3/4 of a mile from the town of Hope, and passing close to Lake Dallas, it again strikes the river at the foot of a steep hill: the H.B.Co's Trail recrosses the Coquihalla beyond this and goes over Manson's Mountain to Fort Kamloops, Alexander etc. The new Trail leaves the other at this crossing, and keeping along the right bank of the River passes over Belle Mount and two other rocky spurs, after which it goes through level country for about eighteen miles, it then leaves the main stream of the Coquihalla and, ascending a hill, strikes the source of the Anderson River at its fork, which it follows until it cuts into the Mountain Trail (from Yale to Boston Bar), about ten miles from the latter place. The country through which the Hope and Boston Bar Trail passes is generally speaking heavily timbered, with thick underbrush. There are some few hundred acres of tolerably good land in the vicinity of Lake Dallas, as also on the flats along the Coquihalla. I do not consider it desirable that this trail should at present be formed into a carriageway. The greatest altitude is probably about 1500 feet above the level of the sea, and the ascents and descents may be made of easy grades.

Yale and Boston Bar Trail

The old trail from Yale passes over two steep mountains and then strikes the Fraser River at Spuzzum, where a ferry is in use, for conveying Passengers and Mules across; from there it keeps the left bank of the river, on tolerably level ground for about 5 miles, until it reaches Chapman's Bar, where the trail leaves the river and with as long steep ascent reaches the Lake House, on the mountains separating the Fraser and Anderson Rivers: from here it descends until it strikes the last mentioned river, and shortly afterwards cuts into the new trail from Fort Hope: crossing the Anderson and four pretty steep mountains it reaches Boston Bar.

Proposed Road from Yale to Lytton through the Passes or Canyons of the Fraser River.

The proposed road from Yale through the Passes or Canyons of the Fraser river, I explored along its right bank as far as Spuzzum, at the request of H.E. Governor Douglas, and am of the opinion that, although the construction of a road would be attended with considerable outlay, it would be likely to turn out one of very great importance, as one of the main communications with the upper country as well as for supplies, and for convenient communication to the Bars along the river banks. Before, however, any Road through the passes or Canyons is commenced, I would suggest that both banks of the river from Yale to Lytton be carefully examined, and that the crossing of the river by ferries or bridges, if possible, be avoided, as far as regards the main route. I am of the opinion that the town of Yale should have been placed on the left side of the river, a far better site than the present one, and that a good road should be constructed from Hope to Lytton keeping the left bank of the river all the way if possible. The material for the formation of a good road along this route I am of the opinion would always be found close at hand as well as timber for bridging etc. A good deal of blasting would be required, and probably form the main expense in the construction of the road. The accompanying sketch will show the several routes described in this report, with the probable altitudes over which they pass.

Sig'd. A.R.Lempriere
Capt. R.E.
2nd. Jan'ry. 1860.

(a true copy H.R.Luard Capt. R.E.)

The Search for a Wagon Route

These are the "signs of fear-some snow falls" which Lieutenant Arthur Lempriere of the Royal Engineers saw when he blazed a trail up the Coquihalla River valley in 1859 in search of a route from Hope to Boston Bar without going through the lower Fraser Canyon. In other words, avalanche tracks. The constant movement of snow prevents the growth of trees, and the tracks show white in the snow. The sappers wisely looked elsewhere and finally built the wagon road through the Canyon. The view is of the lower Boston Bar Creek valley, western slope.

A Bridge Across the Mighty River

When the decision was made to build a wagon road through the Fraser Canyon, a site near Chapman's Bar was chosen for a 250-foot span suspension bridge, and a contract was let to Joseph W. Trutch to build it. The building on the left hand side of the picture is the tollhouse. The bridge was completed in 1863 and remained in service until the 1894 flood caused damage, which mattered little because the road by then had been destroyed by the CPR. The cables were finally cut in 1910. The bridge was replaced in 1926 at the same site. The deck width was 13 feet.

CHAPTER TWO

1865–1899

Edgar Dewdney's trail and Sir Joseph Trutch's vision of a trans-provincial wagon road system are both outshone by a railway and a fleet of sternwheelers, as British Columbia's transportation comes of age.

*T*HE ROYAL Engineers' Fraser Canyon wagon road served British Columbia well throughout its twenty-two years of life, from 1864 to 1886—the year when travellers and freight shippers abandoned it for the Canadian Pacific Railway. In 1871 about mid-way through this period, the Colony entered Confederation to become a full-fledged province of Canada. The traffic gradually changed from the frantic rush of the gold miners and prospectors to a more modest and steady flow of settlers and suppliers who put down roots to become a much-needed source of revenue to the newborn Province, particularly in the area between Barkerville and the settled south coast.

The last years of the 1860s and the early 1870s were a period of recession in British Columbia. After the gold rush to the Cariboo died down, the non-native population in 1870 dropped to 9000 (an estimated thirty thousand miners had entered B.C. in 1858)[1] which even the finding of gold in the Omineca River area did little to increase. However, by 1873 the surveys to find a route for the transcontinental railway gave hope of better years ahead.

Settlement in the Interior was slow, and despite the onerous and numerous tolls levied,[2] the maintenance costs of the Cariboo Road proved to be quite a burden. There was also an urgent need for roads elsewhere. Almost 45 percent of the provincial revenues went to roads in these years, and in the case of the Cariboo Road the tolls only paid 27 percent of the costs.

It is to the lasting credit of Nick Black, the first Road Superintendent at Yale, that he so efficiently looked after the sturdy roadbed and the many bridges throughout the Fraser Canyon wagon road's life as B.C's first trunk road. The relief in tolls achieved in 1886 when the railway was completed was only in effect until the roadway was rebuilt in 1926, when tolls went on again, remaining in effect until 1947. The excessive increase during the railway construction period sparked a reaction by contractor Andrew Onderdonk, who set up the renowned ferry the S.S. *Skuzzy*, which hauled itself through the worst of the Fraser River's turbulence using cable and winch.

The Cariboo wagon road was eighteen feet wide, and it widened to twenty-two feet or even forty feet where possible to allow the unwieldy oxen trains to ease around the sharper curves. The roadbed was compressed a little in width for the seven miles between Yale and Spuzzum. This was the most difficult section and was built by the Royal Engineers themselves, without the help of contractors. Here the road clung to the cliff side, and in many places the outer half of its narrow width was composed of a timber trestle. These trestles were nicknamed grasshopper bridges, because the wooden legs or pilings were so much longer on the outer side than on the inner side due to the steepness of the side slope. There were also many full-width trestles across gullies, and numerous timber cribbings and rock walls. Many of these were of necessity higher and raked more nearly vertical than such structures would normally be built.

B.C.'s first major bridge across the Fraser near Chapman's Bar was the Alexandra, completed in 1863 by contractor Joseph William Trutch under the supervision of the sappers who also built the approaches. It was originally intended to be eighteen feet in deck width, with sidewalks extending beyond that, but somehow in the building it lost the latter, and came down to twelve feet ten inches between curbs. The story goes that in the process of clamping together the bunched wire cables in the field, each over five hundred feet long, they could not quite attain the five and a half inches of diameter necessary. They also discovered that the iron rod hangers, delivered to the site from San Francisco, were one-eighth inch short in diameter. To solve this problem the width of the bridge was reduced—a successful and practical decision, but not one that could be used today, as there would certainly be an inquiry![3]

But Joseph Trutch had so impressed the citizens of British Columbia with his road- and bridge-building achievements that instead of being investigated, in 1864 he was appointed British Columbia's second Commissioner of Lands and Works, following Colonel

Moody. In 1867 Trutch was appointed Chief Commissioner of Works and Surveyor-General, a position he held until 1871 when he became the province's first Lieutenant-Governor.

The colony, and later the province, is indebted to Trutch for a submission to the Legislative Assembly in February of 1868 entitled "An Overland Coach Road between the Pacific Coast and Canada," which shows that at least one person was thinking of the future Trans-Canada Highway before B.C. was even in Confederation. Trutch surely could claim to be the father of the present Ministry of Highways. After his appointment, he immediately set about demilitarizing and improving the Department of Lands and Works, which was the first of several names given to the roads department. (See Listing of Name Changes in appendix.)

Trutch also describes the Cariboo Wagon Road in the same submission, and he goes on to estimate the cost of building a good wagon road from Savona to the Yellowhead Pass, which he puts at $1,050,000. In his account of the existing roads, he lumps together the Cariboo Road with its extension to Kamloops Lake, the Cache Creek-Savona Road:

> Of character very superior to that of roads in most young countries, they are eighteen feet wide, the surface being covered in broken stone, where (as in most parts of the Fraser and Thompson Rivers) such material is at hand, or with gravel well cambered up in the centre, with ditches on one or both sides as required.
>
> With the exception of some short pitches as steep as one in ten, the sharpest inclines are one in twelve, the curves being easy, and the bridges and culverts are substantially built of timber.
>
> Loads of seven or eight tons are handled along them by mules or oxen at an average draught load of 1200 to 1300 lbs. to each animal; and the Mail Coach, drawn by six horses, travels between Yale and Cariboo at the rate of nine miles per hour.[4]

Anthony Musgrave, the colony's governor until B.C. entered Confederation in 1871, declared himself most satisfied with the Cariboo Road after he made an inaugural trip to Barkerville on the Barnard Express Stage. The road in his opinion was safely and soundly built. The coach horses, he reported, were driven at a gallop, even when passing over the cribbings holding the roadway from sliding down the steep slopes. The stage held priority over the mule and oxen teams, which plodded slowly northwards, with up to eight pairs hauling and with spare animals behind. One mule train often stretched out over a hundred feet in length. Margaret Ormsby describes Musgraves' report in her history of British Columbia:

The Express had the right-of-way on the Cariboo Road; at its approach mule-teams dragged wagons laden with three tons of goods to the exact verge of precipices and stood immobile as it went thundering by. Not for a moment was its speed slackened.[5]

With changes of horses at way stations eighteen miles apart, conducted like pit stops at motor races a hundred years hence, it was no wonder that, running all the daylight hours, and often many moonlight hours as well, the 378-mile trip from Yale to Barkerville was made in four days (the record run was Yale to Soda Creek, 270 miles, in thirty hours).[6]

A significant challenge remained in connecting the East Kootenays to the Colonial Headquarters in New Westminster, a similar situation to that which had plagued Governor Douglas in 1859, before he had turned his attention to the building of the Fraser Canyon road. The earlier problem had been the result of gold being found at Rock Creek near Midway; this one, too, resulted from the discovery of the precious commodity, at Wild Horse Creek, a few miles from present-day Cranbrook.

In neither area did the gold last for more than a few months, but that did not stop great efforts being made to build trails to appease the vociferous merchants of New Westminster who wanted to be the suppliers of everything to everywhere in the mainland colony.

Before Douglas encountered the Rock Creek supply problem in 1859, he had sent parties out in various directions to seek and create overland routes that would bypass the difficulties of the Fraser Canyon, primarily to reach the various gold strikes farther upstream. One of these trail-building operations had set off from Hope eastbound, following the general direction of the old Brigade Trail. Douglas had placed the project under the control of the Royal Engineers, and he let a contract for the work under their supervision to a partnership of Edgar Dewdney and Walter Moberly. As a result, a trail was built in 1859 from Hope east to Princeton, totalling about seventy-five miles.

This construction, characterized by the description "A Good Mule Road from Hope to Semilkameen"[sic],[7] was in fact the start of the famous Dewdney Trail. Shelved in 1859, the Trail was taken up again in 1865, starting from Rock Creek, a point much farther east.

There was already a good trail from Princeton as far as Osoyoos, generally following the Similkameen River. This trail had been connected to Dewdney's previous work by John Allison, the leader of the local Princeton settlers, and a constant petitioner of Governor Douglas and his successors for better trails and roads. The trail previously had been established by the Indians and improved from time to time by the Hudson's Bay Company.

From Osoyoos eastbound, in order to stay within Canada, it is necessary to go over Anarchist Mountain, a very steep climb and descent over a difficult part of the Okanagan Highlands. To avoid Mother Nature's Canadian obstacles, the old trail ran south of the 49th parallel into American territory. Dewdney decided to leave this part of the route for the time being and start his trail-building from Rock Creek eastward.[8]

In later years, with the same reasoning, the Department of Public Works discussed with the American authorities a similar southern detour for a highway location, but the idea was quickly abandoned when the sovereignty problems became fully evident.

The route Dewdney chose in 1865 was through Midway, Grand Forks, Rossland, and Trail—all towns that came into existence later—and down the Columbia River. From there his location line went on through Salmo, over the mountains to Creston, across the Creston flats of the Kootenay River to a point near the present day hamlet of Kingsgate in the East Kootenays close to the American border, where it joined an existing trail from the United States called the Walla Walla Trail.

Two hundred and eleven miles from Rock Creek to Kingsgate were built in one summer. As was to become so strikingly evident 120 years later, with trail-, road-, or highway-building, haste may not inevitably make waste, but it does often make the original estimate somewhat incorrect! Dewdney's original estimate was $54,000, and the final figure was $20,000 more, a 37 percent overrun.

With the section from Hope to Princeton at $31,000, the whole improvement, from Hope to the East Kootenays, cost $105,000—a very large sum in those days. The 1865 work was contracted without open bidding, but with very extensive instructions and requirements, not only in the specification of the finished product, but also as regards notes, maps, and explorations to be undertaken along with the trail-building.

Dewdney left Rock Creek in April and in June hired William Fernie, the discoverer of the Crowsnest coalfields, as a foreman on the east end. At the same time Dewdney started various other parties from Rock Creek, in either direction from Fort Sheppard, and from other points. The section across the Creston Flats of the Kootenay River was reported to be the most difficult to build, and required extensive "corduroy," but despite this a four-foot-wide grade with the centre eighteen inches "firm," was finished by Sep-

Royal Engineers' Specifications for a Good Mule Road

Taken from an Agreement signed between Richard Clement Moody, Colonel Royal Engineers, Chief Commissioner Lands and Works, British Columbia, and Edgar Dewdney.

17th. August 1860.

The road to be not less than four feet wide, clear of trees and boulders and made firm throughout and one foot and a half along the centreline to be covered with gravel, hard earth, clay or small stones, and finished smooth and hard. All wet places either to be made solid and firm or to be corduroyed and in such places the road shall be ten feet in width.

In addition to the above width of road a clear space at the sides must be made sufficient in width for passage of widest packs. At all points of danger such as passing around bluffs, slides, slipping banks or precipices or crossing streams, ample space in width and careful arrangements in construction to be provided for the safety of the public and animals passing over the road.

The surface of the road throughout the line to slope inwards towards the bank or rock and a ditch or drain to be provided, when necessary, of sufficient capacity to cut off and carry away side and surface waters. The nearest edge of the ditch or drain to be not less than five feet from the centre of the road. The drain or ditches to be carried across the road at convenient intervals by proper culverts of such capacity and formed in such workmanlike manner that the discharge of water shall not endanger the future stability of the road.

Bridges to be formed where necessary of width in the clear not less than twelve feet. The bridges to be framed correctly in principle, strongly as to dimension of scantling; planking, tree nails, iron bolts; straps and spikes, and firmly as to execution. The roadway over bridges to be of hewn timbers, or stout planking, firmly spiked down.

Grades not to exceed one in twelve in steepness and that only for distances not longer than ten chains in continuance of rise or of fall.

For any short pitches up and down or to rise to level benches so that a generally good line throughout may be maintained with a view to future improvements, and yet in the meantime the necessity of deep cutting or high embankments may be obviated, the Chief Commissioner or his agent may sanction exceptional cases of still steeper grades. In passing around bluffs, precipices, or dangerous places, the grades not to be steeper than one in fourteen.

On approaching or leaving bridges the road for a short length to be level or slightly ascending to bridge.

Trees on each side of the road at distances not exceeding twenty yards apart to be conspicuously blazed at a height of not less than six feet above level of said road.

(**Author's Note**: These basic specifications differ very little from those used to build the much admired Cariboo Wagon Road except of course for roadway width, and in fact are remarkably compatible with sensible road building practices even today.)

tember. However, its construction was sufficiently unsatisfactory that it had to be reworked in 1867.

Overall, this trail was a poor investment. It was never maintained properly, and regular use for mail delivery along its entire length never became the reality it was intended to be. If the fault lies with anyone, it lies with Moberly, who did not realise that the maintenance of so many miles across so many mountains in that period was beyond the means of the small colony.

As well as organising the various crews—each of which took on between ten and twenty miles—Dewdney located the entire route that summer. British Columbia's earliest fully professional engineer really earned the lasting recognition his energy brought him—a recognition that led to his later appointment as Lieutenant-Governor.

As to the question whether Dewdney's location surveys were suitable for the roads that followed, this could best be answered, "close, but not quite," despite Moberly's instructions:

> You will also carefully note the different lines examined in order that you may be enabled to give approximate estimates of the cost of constructing wagon roads either 18 or 12 feet in width over them, and what the maximum grades will be.
> You will make accurate sketches of the different lines examined, with full notes of the nature of the soil and timber, the course and size of the streams and rivers, the quantity and probable extent of the prairie and grazing lands, the nature of the different rock and where found, the height of as many points above the level of the sea as can be obtained, and if possible the latitudes and longitudes of all important points, and such general information as may be useful in preparing a map of the country through which you pass.[9]

These early engineers—Trutch, Dewdney, and Moberly—were indeed remarkable men. Moberly, for his part, went down in history for his discovery of Eagle Pass between Sicamous and Revelstoke, supposedly from watching an eagle fly through it. This was in 1865, when, as Assistant Commissioner of Lands and Works, he explored from Kamloops to within thirty miles of Howse Pass, possibly in search of a Trans-Canada wagon road route.

In the years 1865 and 1866, Moberly built a trail from Shuswap Lake to the Big Eddy in the Columbia River (near Revelstoke). In the fall of 1866 he walked back to the coast, climbing the various ranges en route. Despite such efforts, the editor of the *British Colonist* was merciless with him:

> The creation of this office was as unnecessary and inutile as would be the addition of a fifth wheel to an ordinary coach. The Assistant was a

The Gentlemen Adventurers— and Civil Engineers

Sir Joseph William Trutch

Trutch came to B.C. in 1849. Having been a civil engineering apprentice with a U.S. railroad and married to the daughter of Oregon's Surveyor-General, Trutch expected to be offered a high office in B.C. When this did not immediately come about, he became a civil engineering contractor, building both the Alexandra Bridge over the Fraser and a section of the Cariboo Road. With these successes to his credit, Trutch became a spokesman for the colony's commercial and transportation community. In due course, he served as Chief Commissioner of Lands & Works, Surveyor-General, and finally as the new province's first Lieutenant-Governor. Having made a fortune from his bridge tolls, Trutch spent time in England before returning to become Dominion Government Agent for the Canadian Pacific Railway construction, a position for which he was knighted.

Edgar Dewdney

A civil engineer trained in England, Dewdney was in many ways the father of road building in British Columbia. He contracted the good mule road to Similkameen in 1859, in fact the start of his famous Dewdney Trail, and went on in 1865 to build from Rock Creek near Osoyoos right through to Kingsgate near present day Cranbrook. Given the geography of the route, this was an amazing accomplishment. He was a Member of the Legislature for Kootenay, taking part in the Confederation debate, and later a Member of Parliament, a railway surveyor, Lieutenant-Governor of the North-West Territories and Lieutenant-Governor of British Columbia. He finished his varied and brilliant career as a mining broker in Victoria.

Walter Moberly

A Toronto-trained civil engineer, Moberly arrived in B.C. in 1858 and worked with Dewdney on the contract for the mule road to the Similkameen. In 1864 he surveyed roads in the Cariboo, including the first route to Barkerville, on which he built a sleigh road. Having served as an elected member in the legislature for that area, Moberly resigned his seat to become Assistant Commissioner of Lands & Works and Assistant Surveyor-General under Joseph Trutch. In that position he assigned Edgar Dewdney the task of building the Dewdney Trail. After a time in the United States, Walter Moberly returned to B.C. in 1871 to survey the CPR line from Shuswap Lake to the Rockies.

gentleman chiefly remarkable for his habits of lazy luxuriance . . . and he supplied material for many a good story among the miners and traders of that part and period. The Assistant's forte consisted of exploring the country whilst stretched out on his comfortable bearskin couch in his tent indulging in Havana cigars and Hudson Bay rum. After thus spending the season right pleasantly, he repaired to his headquarters at the Capital where a glowing and wordy official report was cooked up and published in the Government Gazette.[10]

With the completion of the Dewdney Trail, it could be thought that the era of trail-building in British Columbia was over, but that was not quite the case. Stage coaches and wagons served the mining economy well, but British Columbia was slowly diversifying. The first indication was the growing number of cattle ranches, both in the Cariboo and in the grassland area south of Kamloops, which the fur brigades had found so convenient to reach by the Nicola River.

One key occurrence in this agricultural development was the decision in the fall of 1872 by John Douglas (no relation to James) to settle down and raise cattle around a small lake later named after him. Douglas Lake is located near Nicola Forks, the settlement where the Coldwater flows into the Nicola, now the townsite of Merritt. Douglas Lake Ranch, which continues to occupy this area, is now one of the largest cattle ranches in North America.

Settlement was slow because there were so few routes out. In those days beef only moved on the hoof. Because the Cariboo Road was forbidden to them, the only way the early ranchers could get their produce to market was south to Princeton by the old brigade trails, then west to Hope by the Dewdney Trail. There was a trail from Nicola Lake to Spences Bridge, but that was not much used because it re-entered the forbidden route at that point.

There were several reasons why the ranchers could not use the Canyon road. The first was the number of animals that the ranchers wanted to drive at one time—up to seventy-five with five to ten cowboys riding herd; then there was the narrowness of the roadway and of the bridges, the obvious penalty for straying over the edge being instant death below; and finally, of course, there was the impossibility of combining all these with the already hectic mix of mule and oxen trains and galloping stage-coach horses that made life interesting enough at that time between Yale and Spences Bridge. Another reason could well have been the added expense of the tolls they would have had to pay both to use the road and to cross the Alexandra Bridge.

The early trails between Merritt and Hope were maintained as well as they could be throughout the 1860s and the 1870s, but there

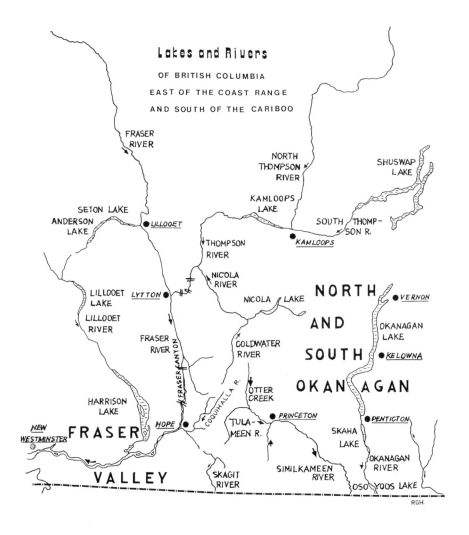

Lakes and Rivers

OF BRITISH COLUMBIA

EAST OF THE COAST RANGE

AND SOUTH OF THE CARIBOO

There are two main river systems draining southern B.C.: the Fraser-Thompson and the Columbia-Kootenay. The first, shown above, is throttled off from the south coast by its rivers' lower canyons. Its lakes were only used tentatively for water transportation: the multi-portage and inconvenient Lillooet to Harrison route, and the Kamloops Lake to Shuswap connection made obsolete early on by easy road-building alongside. The magnificent Okanagan, the Arrow Lakes, Slocan and Kootenay, shown to the right, reflect more hospitable routes with the Kootenay River even looping south to afford access for southern neighbours to mineral wealth lying north of the U.S. border.

Leaving Utah in 1891, William Roger Huscroft led two families, his own and the Arrowsmiths, by wagon train from the U.S. into the Creston area where they became the first settlers to arrive south of Creston on the Kootenay flats. They reached Libby, Montana, on the Kootenay River in late September. The main

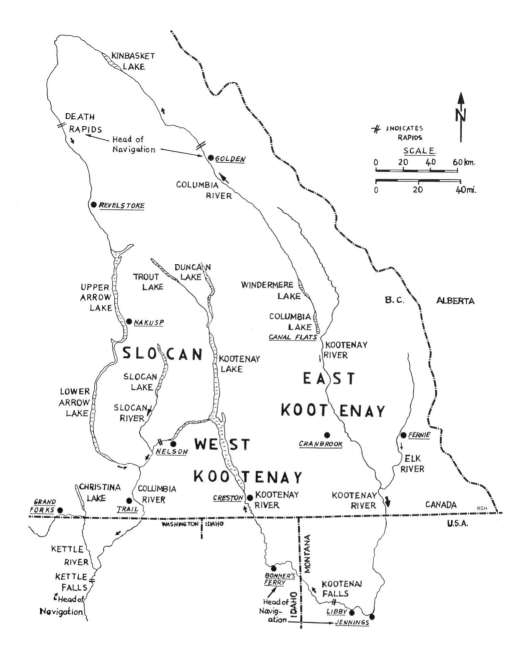

KINBASKET LAKE

DEATH RAPIDS

Head of Navigation

GOLDEN

COLUMBIA RIVER

REVELSTOKE

⊣⊢ INDICATES RAPIDS

N

SCALE
0   20   40   60 km.
0   20   40 mi.

DUNCAN LAKE

TROUT LAKE

WINDERMERE LAKE

UPPER ARROW LAKE

NAKUSP

COLUMBIA LAKE
CANAL FLATS

B.C.   ALBERTA

S L O C A N

SLOCAN LAKE

KOOTENAY LAKE

KOOTENAY RIVER

E A S T

LOWER ARROW LAKE

SLOCAN RIVER

K O O T E N A Y

W E S T

NELSON

CRANBROOK

FERNIE

ELK RIVER

K O O T E N A Y

CHRISTINA LAKE

COLUMBIA RIVER

CRESTON

KOOTENAY RIVER

KOOTENAY RIVER

CANADA   RGH

GRAND FORKS

TRAIL

WASHINGTON | IDAHO

U.S.A.

KETTLE RIVER

KETTLE FALLS
Head of Navigation

BONNER'S FERRY

Head of Navigation

MONTANA

KOOTENAI FALLS

IDAHO

LIBBY

JENNINGS

party went on horseback westward using the unbuilt but cleared right-of-way of the Great Northern Railway transcontinental line, eventually opened in 1893. Huscroft and his sons, Charles and John, built a log raft on which they floated the wagons downstream to Bonner's Ferry where they were rejoined by the others to build more rafts and continue by quieter waters into Canada. This account comes first hand from the author's wife who was the daughter of Charles Huscroft.

were frequent periods of fiscal restraint during these years. The trails soon became a problem to the early cattle ranchers due to a lack of both width and maintenance. The difficulties of driving large herds of cattle over them can well be imagined: mostly they were only a few feet wide, clearing out to as little as four feet between the trees.

After the gold rush miners left and their mining fees and road tolls were no longer available, the road expenditure quickly fell from a high of $135,000 a year to $45,000, the latter sum mostly being spent on the Cariboo Road. Confederation brought temporary relief in the Interior by means of the construction of a wagon road seven to ten feet wide, from Kamloops to present day Kelowna, and of a similar type road from Kamloops to Spences Bridge.

Kelowna in those days was simply called "the Roman Catholic Mission." The road went through Falkland, then called Grand Prairie, and Vernon, then known as Priest's Valley; and Spences Bridge was still often called Cook's Ferry. After 1876 and through to 1882, funds continued to be very short, and practically nothing was done on roads beyond minimum maintenance.

In 1874, ten years after the opening of the Cariboo Wagon Road, the settlers of the Douglas Lake area petitioned the Lieutenant-Governor of the province for "the construction of a road from the south end of Nicola Forks (Merritt) up the Coldwater River to the summit of the Coquahalla (sic), thence down the Coquahalla to Fort Hope."

Robert Beaven, Chief Commissioner of Lands and Works as well as the sitting member of the Provincial Assembly representing Victoria, wrote back, saying that "the Coquahalla Pass includes a very bad rocky slide composed of immense fragments of granite," and that other ways through included "either a mile of precipices" (presumably Skagit Bluffs), or "were much longer," (presumably the route via Uztlius Creek).[11]

Beaven was in office from 1872 to 1876, and during this period he re-organised the Department of Lands and Works on the mainland following the passage of an Act setting up Road Districts throughout the province. Prior to this, such districts only existed on Vancouver Island. He appointed Road Superintendents, and he was the first Commissioner since Trutch to advocate a systematic approach to road building and maintenance in the province. His vocation in private life was selling real estate.

Despite Beaven's doubts, and probably over the objections of the civil servants in Victoria, work went ahead in 1872 to build a trail up the Coldwater River Valley and through the Coquihalla Pass. A further and last objection put forward by the Commissioner's staff was that it "would involve the building of sixty-four bridges," but these carping critics were ignored, and the trail was built—including the bridges! The mileage ended up twelve miles longer than they had expected.

That they ever reached Hope was probably due to a rancher by the name of Forbes George Vernon, who became Chief Commissioner of Lands and Works in 1876. Vernon was a pioneer cattleman and the owner of a large ranch located where the city that bears his name lies today. The trail was quickly finished and remained in existence until 1913 when it was destroyed by the construction of the Kettle Valley Railway through the Coquihalla Pass.

George Landvoigt, who was the Road Superintendent at Hope in 1876, regularly corresponded with his superior, Commissioner Vernon. Fated always to be in the shadow of his colleague at nearby Yale, Nick Black, who had the much more important Canyon road to maintain, Landvoigt was an associate of Thomas Spence in the building of the Yale to Cariboo Road, and in the construction of the original Spences Bridge.

Originally from Hanover, Germany, Landvoigt was merchant, postmaster and Justice of the Peace, as well as pack train organizer, sawyer, and road superintendent. His wife was Belgian and very kind to newly arrived English "wilderness brides" such as Susan and Jane Moir, the sisters who married John Allison and Edgar Dewdney. Apparently, Landvoigt died from the effects of a fall in February 1878. It would be interesting to know more about him, as his letters were well composed and written, and from them a clear picture of the condition of the trails of that period and of the maintenance done on them can be drawn. Landvoigt was more outspoken in addressing authority than an ordinary civil servant would have been. Road Superintendents were elected in those days, and elected officials have always said more than unelected ones.

In August of 1876 his subject was the trails in the Hope area. In this correspondence he was most critical of the trail to Princeton, and his comment was: "This trail should be re-built into a good six foot trail, similar to the Hope-Nicola mule trail."[12] This indirect praise of the Hope-Nicola route seems to be the only comment available at that time on the first transportation route to pass right over the Coquihalla and Coldwater summits, the trail that Vernon and his predecessor built for the Douglas Lake ranchers. After two years of construction, it was in full use that summer. An informal journal Landvoigt kept of a sixteen-day Hope to Keremeos round trip in February 1877 is on file in the Provincial Archives.

On June 10, 1877 Landvoigt again wrote to his Commissioner.[13]

51

Describing the restraint of that period, he reported that due to lack of funds he had cut his crew on the Hope-Nicola Trail to "one white man and two Indians." He requested special funds for a bridge over the Coquihalla River at 48 mile. This is probably at the site of a bridge on the oil pipeline access road near Hidden Creek. The trail moved from one side of the river to the other, as does the oil pipeline road today; it is probable that their locations coincide in many places.

Letter from George Landvoigt to the Hon. Forbes George Vernon, Chief Commissioner of Lands and Works of British Columbia.

Hope, B.C. 10th. June 1877.

Sir,

I have the honour to enclose returns of work done under my superintendence up to May 31st. My superintendence extends over 236 miles. Not yet having received your instructions as to the amount of work to be expended on the roads I have reduced the working parties to a minimum of one white man and two indians on the Hope Nicola Trail and on the Similkameen Trail, and it is my intention, unless you should order otherwise, to still further reduce these parties, as soon as the more essential work has been finished. It is of course out of the question to undertake any of the much needed permanent improvements with the small force at present employed.

The 48 mile bridge over the Coquihalla on the Hope Nicola Trail, as well as the piece of trail between the 5th. mile post and the ford of the Coquihalla, should if possible be constructed this summer as both these works are much needed for the fast increasing traffic over this trail. Already five bands of cattle, about 250 head, have passed over this trail this spring, one band of 75 head having been driven from Sumas to Nicola, the rest having come here from Kamloops and Cache creek for shipment below. The cattle arrive here very tender footed as I have not been able to clear the trail of loose stones.

The Hope Similkameen Trail as far as Princeton is in fair order, inclusive of that portion known as the Grant Trail, providing a trail not averaging more than 18 inches in width can be called in good order! The season has been unusually favourable & the few people passing over the trail have made no complaint. I presume that unless some accident should happen by some of the rotten cribbing giving way—which is quite probable—the people using this trail will have no reason to complain. I believe however that it will be necessary to open up the Canyon Trail unless you should authorise the construction of that portion of a new trail, lying between the 34th. and 48th. mile, as suggested in my report of 27th. May.

The work at present being done by the small party engaged on the trail—Bristol and two indians—consists of grading the bad hillsides below Princeton. The trail is not graded to the desirable width of six feet, but it is made only from three to four feet wide, in order to make it safe for horses and pack trains as soon as possible.

It is now very apparent that a cattle trail should be at least six feet wide. The graded portions of the Hope Nicola Trail being fully six feet wide remain comparatively undamaged by the passage of bands of cattle, where the narrower grades of the Hope Similkameen Trail are in many places almost destroyed by every band of cattle passing over them. The cause of this is that cattle can pass by each other on a six foot trail, while on a narrower trail, when crowded they will either destroy the outer edge of it, or in climbing up the hillside, will fill the angle of the trail with stones and gravel.

I regret to state that the trail around the Bluff, about nine miles below Keremeos which had been repaired at a cost of 30$ has again been destroyed by a band of frightened cattle passing along the hillside above it. I have requested Mr. Haynes, the owner of the cattle to repair the trail at his own expense but doubt very much if he will accede to this request. It is certainly very discouraging to find the work on a trail destroyed by the first band of cattle passing over it, when such accidents might surely be avoided by a little care. Only one band of cattle (65 head) has passed over the trail this season (arrived at Hope today) it is however thought that the number of cattle to be driven over it this season will exceed that of last year.

On the Hope Popkum section of the wagon road almost nothing has been done this season. I regret to have to report that one of the damaged bridges about 11 miles below Hope, has lately broken down. The accident was caused by a band of cattle being driven over it many of which were injured, fortunately none of them killed. There are now two bridges destroyed on this section of the waggon road, and it has become impassable in consequence.

I have the honour to be,
Your obedient s'v't.
S'g'd. Geo. Landvoigt.

The hardships of driving large bands of cattle over these steep, winding wilderness trails in such mountainous country can hardly be imagined, and it took a special breed of men to do it. That trail and the one to Princeton were maintained regularly until the Canadian Pacific Railway went into service, following which the cattle were taken to Spences Bridge for shipment by rail.

From 1872 to 1875 attempts were made to build a fully serviceable road from New Westminster to Hope in order to drive stock all the way to salt water; however, the floods of 1875 and 1876 kept sections impassable. These events were followed by a chronic lack of funds: a usable road for four-hooved or wheeled traffic was not attained until much later.

A notable traveller through the Cascades at that time was the American General William Tecumseh Sherman, who passed through the area in August of 1883. His trip resulted in there being deposited in the U.S. National Archives, "A Map of the Country between Old Fort Colville, W.T. and the Fraser River, B.C. showing the Trail followed by the General of the Army." He also visited with John and Susan Allison at their ranch at Princeton on his way through.[14]

Other visitors were the surveyors of the first Canadian trans-continental railway, who trod the trails on several occasions, but, as did the Royal Engineers before them, the railwaymen finally chose the Fraser Canyon as their route.

From the very start, politics turned the wheels in the Department of Lands and Works. In the provision of roads in British Columbia, a process of political expediency resulted in short-term solutions to long-term problems. When applied to the planning and building of a road system such a process seldom leads to good results. But despite this fact, from the very beginning, many good men tried to organize a coherent road system in the Interior of the province in the first half century of its existence. They also hoped to connect the province with the rest of Canada.

One major event that profoundly influenced the early development of a road system in British Columbia was the arrival of the national railway. The impact of the railway on the province was rivaled in the 20th century only by the impact of the two World Wars and the Great Depression.

From Confederation to the end of the century, the B.C. provincial political system could only be described as a Premier's personal albatross. The elected Member with the largest number of supporters from among his elected colleagues became Premier, and the Member with the next largest number of friends became the leader of the opposition; all supervised, after a fashion, by the Lieutenant-Governor. There were no political parties, and practically no political platforms. The primary political motivation was patronage, and there was no lack of that.

The problem in all of this was the instability that developed from lack of tenure. A Premier could lose his supporters overnight, and when enough dissidents had joined the opposition, they could call on the Lieutenant-Governor to recognize them as the governing group, or to call an election. One or the other could be guaranteed to happen every two or three years.

Patronage was primarily centred on the Chief Commissioner of Lands and Works, who was the man in charge of road and trail building and of land allocation. This position was so powerful that the Premier often appointed himself, especially if he had no colleague he could fully trust.

In any event, the Premier watched the incumbent carefully and often replaced him. In one five-year period there were four commissioners, and a similar number in another six-year period. Such did not bode well for stability in the Department of Lands and Works, nor in the government as a whole. In the thirty-three years between 1871 and 1903, five Premiers were also Chief

Commissioners of Lands and Works, and there were fifteen different Premiers.[15]

A document drawn up by a project engineer in the Department of Public Works in 1953, subtitled "From an Old File," by H.L. Cairns, serves well to describe how the system for the allocation of funds to roads worked.

> The methods of these years militated against the systematic development of roads. As settlers reached beyond existing roads they demanded extensions, and district allocations were made, administered by an elected road foreman, by employing the settlers to work with pick and shovel, or supplying their own wagons. The appropriations were generally considered more in the nature of a dole to furnish employment to the local people rather than to procure part of a systematic road system. In places settlers looked to the annual road appropriation as their chief means of livelihood, and the term "wagon road pre-emptor" came into use.[16]

The term "pre-emptor" comes from the process of free land transfer to settlers on the understanding that improvements would be made, including roads. However, since most settlers could not afford the luxury of working without pay, the government often hired pre-emptor settlers to build roads in their own areas and paid them to do so.

The "elected road foremen" were chosen by a primitive ballot among the settlers, and these were supervised by Road Superintendents, who were more formally elected and who came into being from an Act passed in 1873 to set up Road Districts throughout the province. The road district boundaries were similar to those of the electoral ridings, although some contained a number of ridings, especially in the Interior. This was unfortunate as the Road Superintendents who were in charge of each, or several, Road Districts—(George Landvoigt was one)—were thereby destined to become an important and influential part of the political machinery. However, their influence was late in coming, as the province was such a poor sister of Confederation in its first thirty years that there was not much money to spend. There were few civil servants, as known in present times, especially outside of Victoria. Road construction and maintenance was performed by a mixture of contract and day workers—predominantly pre-emptors, except for the Cariboo Road—and the funds in payment for such were distributed by the superintendents.

The closure from Yale to Spences Bridge in 1891 due to railway construction left a network with no way out to the west. The citizens of the area had to wait until 1927 for the road to be replaced.

Timetable of Wagon Road Construction in British Columbia, 1860–1902

1860–1866   Yale-Cariboo Road; Cache Creek to Savona.

1872–1876   Savona-R.C. Mission Road (7 to 10 feet).

1873–1877   Ladner-Hope Road; Kamloops-Nicola Road; Hope-Yale Road.

1883–1884   Mara Lake-Sicamous-Revelstoke Road (Impassable within a few years).

1886–1891   Spences Bridge-Princeton-Osoyoos-Okanagan Falls-Penticton Road. (Rushed through after opening of the CPR).

1887–1891   Vernon-Kamloops Road; Vernon-R.C. Mission Road, both widened to 18 feet.

1890   Mission-Hatzic Road; Squamish-Cheakamus Road; North Thompson Road extended to Louis Creek.

1891   Ladner-Hope Road is deemed permanent; Yale-Lytton and Lytton-Spences Bridge Roads are closed; Kamloops-Salmon Arm Road; Merritt-Mamette Lake Road.

1893–1897   Penticton-Cascade Road (via section over Anarchist Mtn.); Okanagan Falls to Bridesville (via Camp McKinney).

1895   Sicamous-Craigellachie Road rebuilt (Original destroyed by CPR).

1897   Port Douglas-Lillooet rebuilt; Golden-Donald and Moyie-Cranbrook-Fort Steele Road; Salmon Arm-Shuswap Road.

1898   Cranbrook-Jaffray-Elko Road.

1900   Keremeos-Hedley Road rebuilt; Peachland-17 mi. South Road; Peachland North Road begun; Penticton-Hedley Road (Commenced by owner of Nickle Plate Mine).

1901   Vernon-R.C. Mission Road (Relocated slightly to newly named Kelowna); Penticton-Keremeos Road.

1902   The gap remained between Peachland and Summerland. Trunk roads in the Interior became feeder roads to the CPR; the possibility of a main arterial road system in the southern Interior faded into the past like the stagecoach.

NOTE: The above is a sampling rather than an exhaustive list of construction.

Attempts to complete the Lakeshore Road from Kelowna to Penticton were defeated by flooding and slides. There was not even a reliable ferry service until 1917. East of Cascade, there was only the Dewdney Trail and a few miles of road around Cranbrook and Golden.

Control of these quasi civil servants was as important to a Premier as was his power over his supporting Members. The primary means by which the Chief Commissioner retained authority over the Road Superintendents was the allocation of funds to their Districts, and each District received a separate fiscal vote in the Legislature. There were also separate votes for trunk roads and for special projects.

As was evident when George Landvoigt reduced his crew to one white man and two Indians on each of the two trails and one wagon road he maintained out of Hope, the 1870s were not a great decade for road-building in British Columbia. All expenditures whether for new or maintained routes reflected the cheapest possible solution to meet the demands.

One early failure was the road from Ladner's Landing at the mouth of the Fraser to Hope, a road that succumbed almost immediately to Mother Nature's wrath and the poor economy. Five contracts were let for the construction of this one hundred miles of road early in 1874.[17] Two deep ditches were built on the first section east of Ladner, twenty-one feet apart, the spoil was heaped up between as a dyke, and the road was built on top of that. Beyond, the new road included part of a trail already built from Semiahmoo Bay to Brown's Landing, opposite New Westminster, and bringing the traveller within a river's crossing of the former Colonial capital. The route then swung south of Sumas Lake and close to the U.S. boundary. The land was said to be so fertile that settlers were bidding on it from as far away as the Willamette Valley in Oregon.

The twenty-mile section from Popcum (or Popkum) Bar to Hope required quite a bit of rock work, especially that part past Murderer's Bar. This section had twenty-six bridges and numerous timber cribbings. The road was never kept fully usable for through traffic for at least thirty years after it was built due firstly to several bad flood years on the lower Fraser, and then to numerous years of weak economy. The main reason for building this road—to facilitate the movement of cattle to salt water for shipment south—was never realised, but the road itself served a more vital long-term function in speeding the settlement of the Fraser Valley.

The floods in both 1875 and 1876 brought desolation and destruction throughout the valley, especially at the upper end. That steadfast correspondent, George Landvoigt, reported yet again to his Chief Commissioner with his detailed account of June 30, 1876, making for rather depressing reading as he advises that five of the principal bridges as well as many other road structures had been seriously damaged.[18]

Equal havoc was wrought on the Cariboo Road in the Fraser Canyon even farther upstream. As reported by the Government Agent at Yale, that roadway was inundated up to twenty-five feet in depth, and the bridges at Anderson River, four-mile and eight-mile, had simply floated away. The Alexandra Bridge, in the official's opinion, would have done the same if the water had been four feet higher.

The Government Agent, William Teague, wrote for Nick Black to the Chief Commissioner in the same month:

> During the past week the high stage of water in the Fraser is unprecedented . . .the highest point was reached on the 24th and was six feet higher than any previous year . . . the current runs wild and furious, and there are eleven points between Yale and Boston Bar where the road is overflowed . . . the most terrible proof of the forces and the rapidity of the water is the destruction of buildings, bridges and property. On Friday last a house was washed from its bearings at Yale, and when reaching the vortex was drawn down and sunk like a sponge. Slips have occurred at (various) places . . . the Indians have been picking up floating fragments of sawn timber, belonging to some newly constructed bridge, and from the description of the bolts, are supposed to be portions of the Quesnelle Bridge.[19]

The damage to the Cariboo Road was repaired. The Province, however, could not find the funds to restore the twenty-mile Hope to Popkum section of their first lower Fraser Valley trunk road, and the cheaper river transport from Ladner to Yale was by necessity restored. It remained in effect until the CPR opened up rail service from Port Moody about eight years later; then, of course, cattle were driven by road to Spences Bridge or to Ashcroft and shipped out by rail.

Another consequence of the destruction of the road farther down the valley was that the fifteen miles of road from Hope to Yale, finished in 1877, was rarely used thereafter except for local traffic. It had been built efficiently by L.F. Bonson—an ex-sapper and Road Superintendent for a while—at a cost of $19,970. The Ladner to Yale Road, later known as the Old Yale Road, did not become permanently passable until 1908, and was not fully finished until ten years after that. Ferry service was sporadic at Hope until a combined rail and road bridge was built by the CPR in 1914.

One outcome of this fiasco was the appointment of the province's first Chief Engineer of Public Works, Joseph A. Mahood. His early recommendation of the appointment of District Engineers is of historical note, but it was not put into effect for a further forty years, due to the power of the Road Superintendents.

From 1875 onwards some hard years passed. The outstanding feature of the provincial government's actions in the matter of roads was the lack of any comprehensive planning. The Ladner to Hope road had been a good idea, but it was typical of what was to follow: the ambition to build always exceeded the ability to maintain. That the authorities still remained unaware of this, and would continue to be overly optimistic about their abilities in building and maintaining roads over huge distances, was evident in the statement of Robert Beaven, Chief Commissioner of Lands & Works. He said in his 1874 report to the Assembly (referring to the Ladner-Hope Road, then called the Ladner Trunk Road):

> Should the connecting link of wagon road be subsequently constructed by way of the Coquihalla from Hope to the head of Nicola Lake, 80 miles, there would then be a road from Ladner's Landing on the lower Fraser River, connecting at Yale and Spence's Bridge, with the Yale and Cariboo Road, opening up and running through the best lands in the Province for agricultural and pastoral purposes.[20]

The following years under Andrew Charles Elliot as Premier and Forbes George Vernon as Chief Commissioner saw a road built from Nicola to Kamloops, and a narrow seven- to ten-foot wide wagon road pushed through from Savona to Kamloops and on to Kelowna. However, the effects of another recession and the expense of the repairs made necessary by the Fraser River floods blighted Mr. Beaven's hopes for another Interior road connection from the Lower Mainland (although, of course, the cattle trail through the Coquihalla was built in this period). Beaven returned as Premier and Chief Commissioner in 1882, but only for one year. Any further action was offset by his departure and the 1883 appointment of William Smithe, a Cowichan Valley settler, as Premier.

Smithe's four-year tenure as Premier and Chief Commissioner was a long one for anyone living beyond the coast mountains. He shut down nearly all Interior road work, and in so doing underlined another weakness of the political process. He predictably spent all the money available to him on Vancouver Island, his own backyard.

There was one development that saw some road work take place east of the Cascades, but typically it did not cost the government any money. In 1883 a special Act of the Legislature was passed to enable Gustavus Blin Wright, the road-building genius of the earliest road construction in the Cariboo, to build a wagon road from Shuswap Lake to Revelstoke.[21]

For this work, Wright obtained the right to charge tolls for five years, and a land grant of sixty thousand acres. He had the road completed by the end of 1884, but by 1891 much of it was impassable. Once again the ambition to extend the road system overcame the ability to maintain it. While Wright's wagon road echoed Trutch's vision of a route to the rest of Canada, it was premature, and it was not what the province needed at that time. It was soon surpassed and rendered uneconomic by the building of the Canadian Pacific Railway along roughly the same route.

That railway, and the boom it brought to the lower mainland, spurred on the next administration to resume road construction in the southern Interior, not from any great master plan, but mostly from a desire to connect the Interior settlers to the wonderful new iron road along its B.C. route.

Before that happened, however, in 1886, as a last gasp of William Smithe's term as Premier and Chief Commissioner, a seven- to ten-foot-wide wagon road was rushed through from Spences Bridge to Princeton, and on to Osoyoos and Penticton, but almost all of it had to be rebuilt within the next ten to twenty years; it was primarily just a widening of existing trails. (See map, Wagon Roads up to 1902.)

When Alexander Edmund Batson Davie became Premier in 1887, and Forbes George Vernon went into his second term as Chief Commissioner of Lands and Works, work started again on Interior roads, primarily in the Okanagan area. Vernon's term saw the Kamloops to Vernon wagon road rebuilt, and the Vernon to Kelowna road widened to eighteen feet. The quality of the construction certainly made it the equal of the Cariboo Road, which was the leader in design and maintenance up to that time.

Also in this period, a connection in Canada between Osoyoos and Rock Creek was built in response to demands in 1891 from the settlers in the Anarchist Mountain area. By 1897 a tri-weekly stagecoach service was in operation between Penticton and Grand Forks, and the road was extended to Cascade. The old Dewdney Trail was actively maintained that year between Cascade and Rossland. (Kruger's tavern on the Osoyoos Lake spit prospered in these years!)

The maintenance of the Cariboo Road, which had been privatised by handing it over to contractors in 1882, was returned to Departmental personnel and day workers in 1887. This first effort at complete privatisation of road maintenance was an utter failure, a spin-off of Premier G.A. Walkem's budget-balancing act in 1881, which also saw the road appropriation reduced from $122,000 per year to $86,000.

The newly-restored civil servant workload was soon reduced, however, because the CPR had finally rendered the Cariboo Road between Yale and Spences Bridge virtually impassable by 1888, and thereafter all maintenance ceased. As a result, the Barkerville stage-coach southern terminal was moved north to Ashcroft from Hope. The road was officially closed in 1891.

The section between Lytton and Spences Bridge was not wiped out initially by the building of the CPR. It happened progressively, first by slide material being dumped over onto it, and then by the replacement of railway trestles with fills that spilled over onto the road. The roadway thereby became unusable for most of its length, even for the hardy vehicles of those times.

Almost from the day the railway started operating through the Canyon, the province seemed to lose interest in the roadway still hanging there alongside the new transportation wonder. There was a pretense that all this roadbed was still in existence up until 1910, but the fact was that only up to 1888 could wheeled vehicles pass from Yale to Lytton. After the 1894 flood seriously damaged the Alexandra Bridge—and in fact partially dislodged the cable anchor-ages—the bridge was usable only by persons on foot or horseback, and it was not really safe for them, either. Eighteen years later, the Road Superintendent finally cut the partially collapsed cables, as the bridge was a potential hazard to navigation downstream.

The last quarter of the century saw the province sink into eco-nomic stagnation and political dissension. In fact, without the con-struction of the CPR and the discovery of minerals, the Interior of the province might well have returned to the Indians. A letter sent to Victoria from a settler in 1879 begs for work and states that since the last gold rush (the Big Bend Rush of 1867 on the Columbia River), the non-native population of the Kootenays had dropped to below thirty.

In the mid-1890s, large amounts of mineable and refinable lead, silver, and other precious ores were found quite close to the surface within the mountains of the Kootenays, just as the world price of these metals took a huge upturn. Right on cue, the CPR suddenly became aware of the superior quality of the southern Interior of British Columbia, both the Kootenay and the Okanagan area.

This was the same year that a newly-elected Premier, John Herbert Turner, made his traditional trip to London, which was about the only substantial perquisite of the job. On this occasion he was also to wear the additional hat of immigration promoter.

Greatly concerned to obtain more returns from its very large investment in the province, the CPR encouraged the government to join with it in launching what was destined to be a hugely successful publicity campaign to lure immigrants from Britain.[22] The main point of the first advertising campaign was how blue the lakes were! In the early 1900s the promotional peak was reached, with immigrant fares from England being offered at forty dollars—less than the cost of a wagon trip across Trutch's bridge in 1866!—and glowing descriptions of fruit ranching in the Okanagan bringing on an epidemic of land speculation. In 1907 one million fruit trees were planted, and prime waterfront land went up from one dollar to one thousand dollars per acre.

The influx into the Kootenays was not composed solely of land-seeking immigrants; it included grizzled and aggressive American mining and railway promoters. While they challenged the government and the CPR in their own way, they were not nearly as difficult in terms of demands for roads as were their fellow newcomers to the west, particularly those from Britain intent on becoming fruit farmers.

The Canadian railway met the American challenge by also building numerous rail lines in such a grandly competitive manner that it is worth digressing for a moment from roads to railways and river- and lake-boat service in order to gain an understanding of the transformation of transportation in southern B.C. that took place during the last decades of the 1800s and early 1900s.

First, a line was built from Sicamous to Okanagan Landing at the north end of Okanagan Lake, and leased by the CPR in 1893 (see map of Railroads and Sternwheelers following). Two years later, the CPR established the Nakusp and Slocan Line, which never got as far as Slocan, having been diverted by a mining boom elsewhere. Nakusp was then joined by lake-boat service to Arrowhead, which, in turn, was joined by a rail line to Revelstoke. Other lines were planned and started in the region, but before they managed to connect the system together, the boom period was over.

Boom or not, the sternwheelers sailed forth on the usually placid lake waters. Where water levels and other conditions permitted, there was also service on the rivers along the Columbia to the town of Trail and from Windermere to Golden. Why blast rock and dig dirt when God had created a wonderful waterway free for the using? Lake-boat service continued, although not on all routes, until the 1950s, with the S.S. *Moyie* sailing until 1957. Finally, quantity prevailed over quality and speed over grace to mark the end of the sternwheeler era.

A total of thirty boats went into service on the Columbia and

Wagon Roads up to 1902

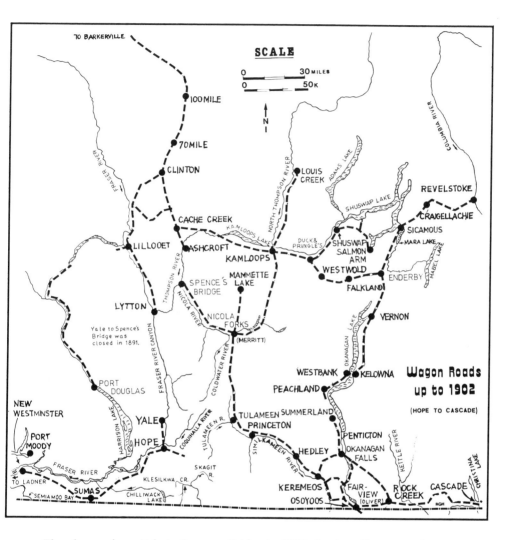

The closure from Yale to Spences Bridge in 1891 due to railway construction left a network with no way out to the west. The citizens of the area had to wait until 1927 for the road to be replaced. Attempts to complete the Lakeshore Road from Kelowna to Penticton were defeated by flooding and slides. There was not even a reliable ferry service until 1917. East of Cascade, there was only the Dewdney Trail and a few miles of road around Cranbrook and Golden.

Railroads & Sternwheelers: Railway and

An early steamboat service in British Columbia operated in the 1860s from Savona at the west end of Kamloops Lake to Seymour on Shuswap Lake via the Thompson and South Thompson Rivers.

Spur lines spread south after the Canadian Pacific main line was opened in 1886. The map also shows the British Columbia Southern Line of the CPR from Crowsnest Pass to Midway, which opened in 1900. From 1910 to 1915 the Kettle Valley Railroad (CPR) was built from Midway to Princeton.

The American Great Northern Railroad (GN) skipped its way in and out of B.C. along the border, first to Rossland and then from Cascade to Princeton and up to Brookmere, where it met the CPR from Merritt in 1914. GN gave up the race to the coast and leased the Princeton-Brookmere line to the CPR, which built through the Coquihalla Pass to Portia and on to Hope.

Many of these lines were first built as separate companies. For example, the Kalso and Slocan Railway was originally of narrow gauge before it was purchased by the CPR and brought to standard.

A total of eleven railway companies were incorporated in southern B.C. between 1886 and 1902 in hectic competition to serve the new mines. A note of elegance was provided by the graceful sternwheelers

SCALE

0   40km.

0   30 mi.

−N−

CP MAIN LINE

ASHCROFT

SPENCES BRIDGE

SAVONA

Kamloops Lake

NORTH THOMPSON R.

Adams Lake

Shuswap Lake

SOUTH THOMPSON RIVER

KAMLOOPS

RAILWAYS
CP - CANADIAN PACIFIC.
GN - GREAT NORTHERN.
KV - KETTLE VALLEY.

SICAMOUS

CP

VERNO

OKANAGAN LANDING

TO HOPE

CP

MERRITT

Okanagan Lake

BOAT SERVICE
OKANAGAN LAKE
SHUSWAP LAKE
SKAHA LAKE
N & S THOMPSON RIVERS

CP

BROOKMERE

KELOWNA

HYDRAULI CREE

PEACHLAND

KV

KV

KV

KV

PORTIA

TO HOPE

GN

PRINCETON

PENTICTON

KETTLE RIVER (West Fork)

Skaha Lake

KV

KV

SIMILKAMEEN R.

GN

KEREMEOS

OKANAGAN R.

ROCK CREEK

OSOYOOS

INTERNATIONAL BOUNDARY

NIGHTHAWK

GN

GN

┿┿┿ – RAIL LINE

┄┄┄ – RAIL BARGE SERVICE

Steamboat Service in Southern B.C.

that appeared in these waters in great numbers at the start of the century. They blended perfectly with the scenic backdrop.

The rail lines were connected by railcar barge service as shown. The sternwheelers either pushed barges or simply carried passengers and freight. Steam tugs were also used to handle barges. Sternwheeler racing got under way on Kootenay Lake at high speed when competition blossomed between the CPR and the GN. The GN rail line at Creston ran to the lake, and the GN sternwheelers ran as far as Kaslo until they bowed out in 1911.

The peak of lake service was reached with the launching of the S.S. *Bonnington* on Arrow Lakes in 1911 soon followed by similar vessels (the *Nasookin* and *Sicamous*) on Okanagan and Kootenay Lakes. These sternwheelers were 200 feet long with 40-foot beam; they accommodated passengers overnight and served five-course dinners.

With such attractive alternatives available in rail and boat transport, it is little wonder that wagon road construction lagged both in the Kootenays and on the west shore of Okanagan Lake. Sternwheeler service began to decline in the 1920s and reached a low point in the 1930s, although some notable exceptions were still afloat in the 1940s and 50s.

Chief Commissioners of Lands & Works

Robert Beaven

Beaven was both Premier and Chief Commissioner of Lands & Works from 1872 to 1876, and again in 1882. Although a weak Premier because he had little political support, he proved to be a good administrator, especially reorganising the Department of Lands & Works to create Road Districts and Road Superintendents. By 1874 Beaven had let five contracts for the completion of a road from Ladner to Hope, but in the following two years the flood waters of the Fraser River washed out much of this effort. His dream of extending the road from Hope to Nicola over the Coquihalla Pass, which he unveiled in a speech to the Legislative Assembly in 1874, in fact took 112 years to come true. When not serving in the government, Beaven was a real estate agent in Victoria.

Forbes George Vernon

Co-founder with his brother of the Coldstream Ranch near the city that bears his name, Forbes George Vernon owned in his lifetime 13,000 acres in the Okanagan which he sold in 1894 to Lord Aberdeen. As Chief Commissioner of Lands & Works from 1876 to 1878 and from 1887 to 1895, he completed the Hope-Nicola cattle trail through the Coquihalla Pass and built many roads (mostly in the Okanagan) during his second term. Acting in his Lands capacity, Vernon cancelled the townsite of Princeton, which enabled his friend and far-off neighbour, John Allison, to pre-empt it and move his entire ranching operation to this fine grazing area.

Robert Francis Green

Green was a member of the Legislative Assembly from 1898 to 1906 and Chief Commissioner of Lands & Works from 1903 to 1906. Before that he was Mayor of Kaslo in the riding he represented. As Railway Minister, he got in trouble with land deals at Kaien Island, the future site of Prince Rupert, where he and Premier McBride were accused of dealing with "a band of adventurers," otherwise identified as a group of American railroad promoters. Green lost his office over this affair even though neither he nor the Premier were ever proven to have gained from it. In 1912 he became a Member of Parliament in the Dominion Government and a Canadian Senator in 1921.

Kootenay Rivers and on the Okanagan, Arrow, Slocan, and Kootenay Lakes, between 1888 and 1914. The first was a wooden vessel, the S.S. *Despatch*, with twin catamaran hulls fifty-four feet in length. The last was the S.S. *Sicamous*, 201 feet long, with berths for sixty passengers and a dining cabin seating travellers for five-course dinners served with the best of linen and silver. Such grand travel tended to discourage road improvement in the area: a rattling, dusty stagecoach seemed an unattractive alternative to the luxury of boat travel. All ferries were built on-site, some by expert craftsmen from the United States. The last ones, such as the S.S. *Moyie*, had prefabricated steel hulls hauled by rail from Eastern Canada in sections.

As shown on the maps, the real competition to transport the bounty of the Kootenay and Boundary area unfolded when the CPR built their southern line from Lethbridge, Alberta through the Crowsnest Pass all the way west by their connecting Kettle Valley Railway to Princeton. The head-to-head struggle for routes between the CPR and the Great Northern Railway ultimately subsided when both parties realised that the challenge the Coquihalla Pass presented to railway construction could be met only by cooperation.

The century ended with Gus Wright's road partially rebuilt and extended to Mara Lake; the old Douglas-Lillooet road rebuilt after thirty-six years of neglect despite the fact that its use was very limited; and a good road built throughout the east Kootenay region from Moyie Lake to Cranbrook, Elko, and Fort Steele.

The province had stumbled into the twentieth century still without any overall road planning, and still without a workable political system. However, there was one ray of hope that something would be done to straighten out the cumbersome road administrative system. In 1899 an Act of the Legislature was passed dividing the Department of Lands and Works into a Lands Branch and a Public Works Branch. This Act ruled that all public works, including roads, where public monies had been spent to build them, or to maintain them, were hereafter public property. This was a very important legal precedent for the future Department of Public Works and the Ministry of Highways.

The Act also gave Cabinet the power to appoint Road Inspectors. The first Chief Public Works Engineer appointed under this Act was F.C. Gamble, who was in office until 1911, and the first Road Inspector was W. Kileen.

However, the century did not end without the newly appointed Mr. Gamble receiving many letters from recently arrived American and English immigrants to the Okanagan. Two are quoted below, and were to be the forerunners of many more.

On June 23, 1899, George W. Hall, schoolmaster at Westbank, wrote to the Department of Public Works:

> We need a road from a point opposite to Kelowna to Peachland. An appropriation should be made for a road from Penticton to Vernon, with a branch from Peachland to Princeton. Some of the people have been here some years and begin to despair of making a living off the land as they have no roads and no wharf and consequently no encouragement to put in crops in any quantity.[23]

He goes on to write that $500 would do the work (presumably Westbank to Peachland), and he suspects CPR influence due to the fact that to date the settlers have received no answer to their petitions. He gives his address as "West Okanagan via Kelowna."

A letter of July 3, 1899 from farmer N.S. Marshall to the Hon. F.L. Carter-Cotton further drives home the point:

> The Indian Trail on the west side of Okanagan Lake is in bad shape. It is not fit to ride at night. I received a reply to my last letter from Gamble saying it would receive prompt attention and I have not heard further for three months. There is a fair population, but a ranch without a road is like a kite without a tail.
>
> We can stand on the hills above the lake and see the loaded wagons hauling hay and grain from Kelowna—see the beautiful teams and vehicles going at rapid speed on good roads, note the advancement and progress that the East side of the lake is making whilst the West side is at a standstill dragging a pack horse up and down the Indian trails by the head.[24]

In the last years of the century the system of "personal" government by Premiers instead of parties began to collapse, as did the practice whereby the Chief Commissioners of Land and Works directed roadwork patronage. Road-building on any large scale had virtually come to a halt due to the public's fascination with railways, a fascination shared by many in the government. However, there were forces at work that would soon change the attitude toward road-building in the province.

The Great Bluff on the Cariboo Road between Spuzzum and Lytton in the Fraser Canyon. *Above,* five pairs of mules pull a typical double-axle wagon. *Below,* double-yoked oxen teams haul freight through Boston Bar.

Above, The future overtakes the past on the Cariboo Road in the Cariboo. The early automobile has enough clearance for the ruts—as long as the weather stays favourable—but to pass the wagon train, this motorist was forced to leave the road.

Below, The first freight trucks in the Cariboo.

CHAPTER THREE

1900–1917

The railways continue to dominate, but the advent of automobiles, trucks, and immigrants brings a demand for better roads in the Interior, and an interest in a Canadian Highway, all of which were postponed by the First World War. A new Department is formed and eventually gets its District Engineers.

THE TURN of the century brought profound industrial change and labour unrest to British Columbia. The extremely bitter four-month strike at the Pullman Palace Car Company's plant outside Chicago in 1894 was the forerunner of a strong reaction to the exploitation of workers in the burgeoning industrial revolution throughout North America. The early 1900s in B.C. saw the first stirrings of socialist philosophy in workers' movements in the coal mines, the smelters, the logging camps, and the salmon canneries.

Premiers came and went within months. After Turner was defeated, Charles Augustus Semlin, Joseph Martin, James Dunsmuir, and Edward Gawler Prior all had their turn at the job. Finally, by the greatest good fortune, a young lawyer from B.C.'s northernmost settlement of Atlin, Richard McBride, found himself the leading member of the largest dissenting faction in the legislature. When, for the fifth time in five years, the Lieutenant-Governor dismissed a Premier and turned to the opposition to form a new government, he introduced a new breed of political leader to the provincial scene.

Born in New Westminster in 1870, Richard McBride was not only the youngest Premier ever appointed but also the first native son. He was a member of the Canada-wide Conservative Party, a carry-over from his days of studying mining law at Dalhousie University in Nova Scotia. A true populist politician, McBride was good-looking, charming, and possibly the first Premier that B.C. ever had who possessed what might be called "charisma." Some might also say he was the last! He soon came to be known as "glad-hand Dick" and "the people's Dick"—the latter a bit of wish fulfillment in view of the timely stirrings on the provincial labour scene.

McBride appointed, as his first Chief Commissioner of Lands and Works, another "personality politician," Robert Francis Green. Bob Green had also been elected for the first time in 1898, to represent the Kaslo-Slocan riding. Before that he had been elected three times as Mayor of Kaslo, so he was no stranger to the rough-and-tumble politics of the time. Green's period in provincial politics was not long but it was eventful. He quickly became known as "the Minister of Patronage," a rather unfortunate application of the new title "Minister," which was becoming popular for Cabinet positions at that time.

After only three years in Lands and Works, Green had to resign over irregularities in a land deal, but in 1904 he produced a report for the Public Works Branch that was something of a classic. One passage, in particular, for the first time addressed the problem of efficiency in building roads:

> It is the intention to introduce, wherever possible to do so, with advantage, the newest methods of construction of highways, modified to the different climatic and physical conditions existing throughout the Province.
>
> It is admitted that the introduction of approved methods and machinery will meet with no inconsiderable opposition but it is hoped that as time passes this opposition will be overcome by the recognition by the intelligent public of the permanent benefits and economy that will follow, and that every encouragement and assistance will be forthcoming in furtherance of a matter so vital to the progress and prosperity of the Province.
>
> In the carrying out of public works a strong effort will be made to raise the standard of work to a higher plane. This does not mean expenditure simply for the sake of outward appearances, but it does mean that the work will be done in the best manner suitable to the circumstances of each piece of work, and that a fair day's work will be expected for the wages paid in the Government Services, such as other employers insist on.[1]

Green must certainly have realised that the phrase concerning the introduction of new methods and equipment would be closely read by the Road Superintendents, at whom it was aimed, and who still enjoyed considerable power. At that time, with the slim majority that McBride commanded, such a declared new policy restricting patronage took great courage. To convince an experienced politician such as Bob Green that the old order had to change, a powerful force was needed. That force was, quite simply, the automobile.

As soon as vehicles were available in British Columbia, they had a potent effect on the disorganized road-building scene.[2] The first cars appeared in the province in 1900; some were steam-powered and others were driven by the newest fuel—gasoline. In 1894, when automobiles were few and far apart, the first Good Roads Association was set up in British Columbia, soon to be followed by the B.C. Automobile Association. The year 1900 also saw the Canadian Good Roads Association set up a branch in Vancouver, and they held their inaugural meeting that year in Kamloops.

Good roads associations demanded just what their name said, and British Columbia unfortunately did not have many good roads, especially in the Interior. This getting-together of enthusiastic motorists was to become one of the most successful special interest groups in British Columbia's history and to remain a part of the provincial scene for many years. The clincher, as far as politicians like Green were concerned, was that the movement caught and held the interest of the wealthiest and most influential citizens of the province, such as James Dunsmuir and Richard McBride. All with one voice chorused the immediate need for better road planning and construction.

The first area to be attacked was the essentially unplanned distribution of road allocations by the Road Superintendents to the politically faithful. The first public assault on this misdirection of public funds was at a meeting of the Canadian Good Roads Association in Kamloops. Representatives from all over the province gathered, with a strong contingent from the farming community, and on the opening day, September 27, the main speaker was Colonel Warren, the City Engineer of Vancouver. As this quotation from the *Victoria Daily Colonist* of December 19, 1900 shows, Colonel Warren had strong opinions concerning patronage and Road Superintendents, and their friends, the chosen Road Foremen:

> . . . a grant is made by the government of the day for a road or trail. The money is handed to John Brown, general merchant, Sleepy Hollow. A number of his customers, who owe him money, are employed at the highest possible rates, and one is appointed foreman. He is a good fellow but knows nothing about roads. These men have hay to make, consequently the work is done late in the fall, shovelling mud and snow onto the road whilst the traffic is going on, making it worse than before.
>
> The next year John Smith thinks he ought to have a show, employs men, and goes through the same performance, with the difference that his foreman thinks it is the chance of his life to immortalize himself as an engineer, and will change a mile or two without any reference to the general lay of the country, and expend most of the grant on his pet scheme. The government then goes out of power and the opposition

steps in. The same performance is gone through, with, perhaps, changing the road back to where it was before.

Warren then goes on to say that if a District Engineer were employed his desire to keep his position would affect his handling of the money and make him strive to have the best roads in the country. He concludes:

Politics would have nothing to do with him. The Ministers would have nothing to do with the expenditure, so that would relieve them.[3]

However, agreement was not unanimous. One farmer from Delta, a Mr. Ladner, stated his opinion that one practical man was worth six experts in the building of dykes. Whether or not Ladner was correct, the good Colonel was naive indeed in his belief that politicians would give up control of public funds when votes were at stake. He was also in a dream world if he thought that engineers involved in public roads could be divorced from politics in the conduct of their duties.

The next two years saw limited funds available for road work, with a financially strapped province borrowing money for the first time in its history just to stay solvent. A "Report to the Delegates to Ottawa" in the Sessional Papers of 1902 reported that the province, in its life to date, had constructed 6000 miles of road valued at $12 million, and that year had built fifty miles of main wagon road, with widths of nine feet in the East Kootenays and Slocan, and ten to fourteen feet elsewhere, with an average cost of $2300 per mile.

It was not a happy situation that greeted Richard McBride when he became Premier the next year, but at least he had before him the wants of the citizens, and he had no lack of good men to help him. After Green left in 1906, the position of Chief Commissioner of Lands and Works went to Robert Garnet Tatlow, a Vancouver businessman, a close associate of Green, and a man as introverted as Green was extroverted. Tatlow quietly and successfully reorganised the finances of the Department, which he handed over in good order in 1907 to Frederick John Fulton, a lawyer from Kamloops.

Fulton's major task, completed in 1908, was to help draft sweeping new legislation to reorganise the administration of roads in the province. Two new departments were created: a Department of Lands, and a Department of Public Works. The election of road superintendents disappeared, and thereafter they were appointed civil servants.

Fred Fulton became the province's first Commissioner of Lands at the end of December 1908, and the new office of Minister of Public Works went to the forty-three year old Member for Revelstoke,

74

Thomas Taylor. This was to be one of the most significant appointments that McBride ever made. For the next seven years the province's Minister of Public Works proved to be one of the most active and innovative British Columbia ever had.

Born in London, Ontario, Taylor was elected to the provincial Legislative Assembly in 1900, and as Interior members did in those days he promptly moved his home to Victoria. His elevation to Cabinet Minister in 1909 must have been a delight to the Good Roads supporters in that city, because he was definitely one of them. An enthusiastic automobile buff and an early member of the Victoria Automobile Club, he made the first car tour through the province ever undertaken by any provincial Minister in the summer of 1910. It was not long before he became known as "Good Roads" Taylor, a sobriquet that never left him.[4]

By the year 1911 the province's increase in road mileage was unprecedented, with a total of 14,633 miles, as against the last count of 6007 recorded in 1905. A similar increase appeared for trails: from 5008 miles to 8207. As a report in 1905 indicated a yearly building of sixty miles of main wagon road, the huge increase of 8626 miles in six years must have been predominantly composed of pre-emption roads. This is supported by the increase in population between 1901 to 1911, which was from 179,000 to 394,000: a gain of 120 percent paralleling the 136 percent increase in road mileage.

Within these years a rough wagon road was completed from Kelowna to Penticton, a new road was built from Nicola Lake to Princeton, and the North Thompson road was extended to Little Fort. The latter was the result of a rivalry that had sprung up between the government members for Kamloops, Revelstoke, and Golden, each competing for their town to be the centre of supply to the Grand Trunk Pacific Railway construction then centred in Tête Jaune Cache. With Kamloops the winner, a road up the North Thompson was rushed into place. This was an area not quickly settled, so the decision proved to be a millstone around the government's neck for the next fifty years.

Farther east, a wagon road was completed from Nelson to Balfour, and from Kuskanook, the southernmost Kootenay Lake landing for sternwheeler lake service to Nelson, to Creston, and from there on to the Crowsnest Pass. In 1911 a motor stage run was started from Merritt to Princeton, but three years later it was only usable as far as Coalmont.

The Province was building an Interior network of wagon roads, but the standards were so low and the resources so inadequate for the distances involved that many miles had to be rebuilt with minor and in some cases major relocations over the next thirty to forty years. By modern standards the condition of the majority of these roads was dreadful. They were a morass of mud in rainy weather, impassable in many places in the spring thaw, and a bone-rattling dust bath in summer. In winter the trips by snowplowing parties were six weeks apart. Little wonder that the Province had limited all automobiles to fifteen miles per hour in 1903!

Of much more lasting significance to the long-term development of a provincial highway system were two events that occurred in 1910. The most contentious happened late in the year, when Premier McBride, now hailed as "the colossus of roads," was reported in the *Manitoba Free Press* on November 30, 1910, as suggesting that his government was interested in reopening the old Cariboo Road between Yale and Spences Bridge. This was a matter of great interest to eastern Canadian automobile enthusiasts who were sporadically making pioneering trips across Canada, negotiating across B.C. with the greatest of difficulty.

In the resulting surge of interest, Minister of Public Works Taylor hurriedly clarified that the Premier was only talking about the section in the Thompson Canyon, not that in the Fraser Canyon; in other words the Premier was referring to the section from Lytton to Spences Bridge. The reason for this amendment, which no doubt came about after he had quickly checked with his boss, was related to actions that Taylor had taken earlier in the year.

McBride and Taylor were both split personalities when they were dealing with roads and railways, especially in the Fraser Canyon. On the one hand, the Premier and his Minister "of Good Roads" were fervent road boosters; on the other hand they were even more fervent when wooing anyone at all who was interested in building railways anywhere in British Columbia.

At this time the B.C. government was offering the Canadian Pacific Railway (through its subsidiary, the Kettle Valley Railway) an outright grant of $750,000 cash if it would build a line from Midway to Vernon, which it declined to do. This was a potential political minefield. A few years before, one of McBride's Ministers, R.F. Green, had been forced to resign because he had gone too far in arranging a lucrative land deal to induce the Grand Trunk Pacific Railway to build a rail line right into Prince Rupert.[5]

The Victoria politicians did everything possible to interest the Howe Sound and Northern Railway to go north from Squamish, which it did after the line was reorganised as the Pacific Great Eastern in 1912.[6] Earlier in 1910, Premier McBride electrified the province by announcing that another trans-continental railway would

76

be built through British Columbia, terminating in Vancouver. That railway, which started as the Canadian Northern Pacific Railway and ended up as the Canadian National, made application to the Board of Railway Commissioners in Ottawa on January 25, 1910, "to interfere with and wipe out the Cariboo Road where adjacent," in the very graphic wording of their Chief Engineer.

On this matter, Taylor requested a report from his Public Works Engineer, F. C. Gamble, who wrote:

> Since the opening of the C.P.R. the Government has abandoned the Yale-Cariboo Road between Yale and Spuzzum, and between the Suspension Bridge, which cannot be repaired, and Boston Bar, and consequently it has become impassable and practically non-existent. It is used only by Indians on foot or horseback, who have made trails around the slides, or cave(-in)s, etc. Unless the Government intends to replace the Suspension Bridge—which is altogether unprobable—there exists no objection to the C.N.R. from Mile 15 to 24.7 (their mileage).[7]

Gamble quite conveniently extends the situation between Yale and Spuzzum to a point approximately twenty-two miles farther north, which is unfair to the Royal Engineers as he included a section of the original road on the Fraser's left bank that was not tinkered with nor was it maintained. He quotes Road Superintendent Sutherland as saying that the old road, rebuilt between Yale and twenty-one miles below Lytton, was ". . . very poor, grasshopper trestles having been used to surmount rock bluffs." This description applied only from Yale to Spuzzum and was the section grudgingly replaced by Andrew Onderdonk.

On July 6, 1910, the Honourable Minister advised Gamble that the government did not intend to rebuild the old wagon road or the bridge at Spuzzum, and he in turn advised the C.N.R to proceed. By this letter the government effectively gave away the rights of the people of British Columbia to be compensated for the very severe damage done to Governor James Douglas's masterpiece of road-building during construction of the C.N. Railway.

As further evidence of split personality, the very next year the Deputy Minister of Public Works wrote to the Canadian Pacific Railway demanding that it compensate the Province for damage done to the old Cariboo Road between Lytton and Spences Bridge. Initially the government wanted compensation for the whole section from Emory's Bar to Spuzzum, but the CPR got out of responsibility for that by pointing out that the original contract between Port Moody and Savona was first of all issued by the Dominion Government, and it was only after construction from Port Moody to

Spuzzum that it was taken over by the CPR. The Province was referred to the senior government for compensation for the section south of Spuzzum, but they never pressed for it. The CPR did accept responsibility from Lytton to Spences Bridge. Several years later, by a weird, bureaucrat-inspired arrangement wherein the railway basically paid $1000 per railway crossing, the Province received $45,300 as full and complete compensation for the destruction of the Royal Engineers' wonderful road.[8]

It was 1911 when Road Superintendent D.G. Sutherland estimated that it would cost $87,000 to restore the road between Yale and Spences Bridge. In that estimate he did not include replacing the Alexandra Bridge, which he described as being "no good." The price seven years later had gone up to $604,000 for restoration, or $834,000 for a new road.

McBride and Taylor indulged their leaning towards railways, and, for the cost of repairs to a suspension bridge spanning 250 feet, denied the motorists of British Columbia the restoration of a road through the Fraser Canyon for another eighteen years. Although the road was clearly senior and should have been kept whole or restored to its previous condition, precedence was given to the CNR, which received permission to wipe the road out. The CPR got away with a minimum payment and also signed an agreement that gave them future precedence.

The Minister of Public Works first showed an interest in a road link eastward from Hope in 1910, perhaps revealing a few guilt pangs at having given away the Fraser and Thompson Canyons so freely to the railways. The issue was again a Trans-Canada highway, called in these years, by the Good Roads people, the Canadian Highway. To the dismay of his constituents, Taylor chose the southern route, which did not pass through his home riding of Revelstoke.

In the light of the times, it was a very logical choice. The Big Bend Highway from Revelstoke to Golden was not even a figment of anyone's imagination, and the public was both enthralled and intimidated by stories of huge snowdrifts in Rogers Pass. The province did not even have a fully usable road through Eagle Pass; on the other hand it did have a sturdy, if narrow, wagon road all the way from Princeton to Crowsnest Pass, except for the gap alongside Kootenay Lake. This provided a complete if somewhat tenuous southern route through to Alberta.

There had been rough surveys in 1902 and 1903 to address the difficulties between Hope and Princeton, so in 1910, in an attempt to settle the matter, an assignment was given to a Professional Engineer by the name of A.E. Cleveland, of the Vancouver firm of Cleveland and Cameron, to find a route through the Cascade Mountains eastward from Hope.

The best description of the chosen route comes from a mimeographed typed report, unsigned and widely distributed in the Department's files. Dated July 11, 1913, it bears the rubber stamp of the Victoria Engineering District and the title "The Pacific Highway." The section on Cleveland's survey goes:

> Every known pass between Coquahalla-Coldwater (sic) on the North to the Light(e)ning Creek Pass near the international boundary together with all the routes leading to them were personally examined, ultimately a location was made on which a road with grades not exceeding 8 per cent could be built at a reasonable cost and it came as a matter of surprise to those who had a close acquaintance with the features of the broken country.
>
> Beginning two miles to the West of Hope the chosen route lies by way of Silver Creek, Strajet River (sic), Cody Creek, Roche River, and Similkameen River. From the old Yale Road the road winds pleasantly through stretches of the finest merchantable timber with every here and there a glimpse of the rushing Silver Creek, well named for its many cataracts. Further on along Klesilkwa Creek and (Skagit) River the road passes through beautiful areas of meadow land and Alder Flats, while in the valleys of the Roche, and the Similkameen, stretches of grazing land are passed through. The maximum summit is 4485 ft. but this will be reached with no greater grade than 8½ per cent, the ruling grade being 8 per cent with only a short length of the maximum when this road is completed. The distance between Hope and Princeton will be about 95 miles.[9]

There seems little doubt that without the intervention of the First World War this connection would have been built; in fact, twenty miles out of Hope and fourteen out of Princeton were roughed out. Maintenance problems at the west end would probably have been much greater than with the later route of the present Hope-Princeton route by Allison Pass, because Silver Creek (or as it is known now, Silverhope Creek) runs along the foot of the slopes of Silvertip Mountain (glaciated) and Mount Rideout. These peaks of the Skagit Range are both in excess of 8000 feet high, and steeply sloped.Those maintaining the present logging road find out from time to time that they generate a considerable number of debris torrents, mudslides, and avalanches.

Once he had things moving between Hope and Princeton, Taylor immediately initiated work to improve his southern trans-provincial route farther east. He started by reconstructing the old road through Richter Pass between Keremeos and Osoyoos to avoid excessively heavy grades, and then he widened the road from Osoyoos to Cascade throughout to an average width of twenty feet. Farther east he completed a road along the West Arm of Kootenay Lake from Nelson to Balfour, at a cost of $11,178 for the twenty-three miles, and he built a road from the CPR landing at Kuskanook to Creston. (See map, "Wagons to Motor Trucks," following.)

The gap between Fraser Landing (near Balfour) and Kuskanook was left to the CPR lake service, which lasted until the Province leased the S.S. *Nasookin* as a car ferry on April 15, 1931, running it between Fraser Landing and Gray Creek. Until that date it had been referred to by the Department as a "steamboat connection" and had run from Nelson to Kuskanook, a long trip. The road from Kuskanook to Gray Creek was finished in 1931.

The CPR did not complete the rail line up the west side of Kootenay Lake between Kuskanook and Proctor until December 1930. Before that, the company moved rail cars by barge and passengers by sternwheeler. Adventurous motorists were taken along as well. The S.S. *Moyie* continued railway lake service for rail cars by barge from Proctor to Ainsworth, Riondel, Kaslo, and Lardo until 1957, all of which indicates the importance of the steamboat and sternwheeler paddling along well into the 20th century.

Taylor did not hesitate to bring what he was doing to the attention of other Public Works Ministers in the western provinces. With the blessing of the Canadian Good Roads Association, of which they were all members, he challenged the other Public Works Ministers to match his actions and start their own surveys and construction for the Canadian Highway. A publication put out by the provincial government in the 1930s called a "Manual of Provincial Information" traces some historical highlights:

> In 1909 consideration of trunk highways was followed by co-operative effort of the four Western Provinces in a project for a trunk highway from Winnipeg to the Pacific Coast. The Hope-Princeton Route was suggested and surveyed in 1911 through the Hope Mountains.
> Routes were discussed for many years and in 1924 the decision was made to build through the Fraser Canyon to Spence's Bridge. The section to Lytton was completed in 1926, followed by building that part between Lytton and Spence's Bridge, completed in 1928.[10]

It was tragic that a far-off war should have so broadly influenced and delayed this first all-Canadian building initiative. The Manual does not mention the fact that the decision to rebuild through the Fraser Canyon in 1924 was primarily that of the Dominion Government in the distribution of its postwar reconstruction funds. Without that war, it is quite possible that the first Trans-Canada Highway would have gone by the southern route.

The work on the Silverhope Creek location was never resumed after the war. Why Cleveland did not use the Nicolum-Sumallo route, where several miles of wagon road were already built, was never explained. Although he reportedly did look at Hope Pass, he apparently totally ignored Allison Pass. It must be assumed that he was deterred by Skagit Bluffs since his route enters and leaves the Skagit Valley downstream from them.

Just exactly where the Pacific Highway was headed the publication does not make clear. It ends up extolling the road from Ashcroft to Barkerville via Quesnel:

> With a view to avoiding much of the freight traffic and dust a great deal of the automobile traffic is conducted at night, and one has to make the journey from Ashcroft to Quesnel in the still quietness of a summer's night to fully realise the beauties of the wonderful Panorama which is constantly unfolding, indeed, one is torn between the desire to travel slowly and admire the scenery and the wish to open the throttle and take full advantage of the excellent surface with which this road is almost entirely provided.

This composition is in fact one of the provincial government's first literary tourist promotion efforts. Later ones, although more effusive, stop short of describing how the motorist can observe the scenery while travelling during the hours of darkness! The Manual further notes that with the increase of winter traffic on the Cariboo Road it was found possible, by a constant "rolling of the snow," to create a hard, smooth pavement capable of carrying automobiles.

In fact, the very first section of the Pacific Highway is all that has ever retained the name of this most ambitious of projects: today it is shown as an arterial route of 19.2 kilometres from the American border through the Vancouver suburban community of Surrey. The Pacific Highway appellation really came into existence south of the border, when in the fall of 1909 the Seattle Automobile Club summoned all Good Roads Association enthusiasts in British Columbia to discuss the proposal for the designation of such a highway from Vancouver to Los Angeles. Apart from the route from Vancouver to Blaine, Washington, the name never caught on in B.C.

Another milestone in the emergence of the automobile was the unique feat of a Mr. T.W. Wilby, who in 1912 drove his car from the Atlantic to the Pacific shores in fifty-one days.[11] As there was no completed road across the province, the reports that he drove many miles on railroad tracks may well be true.

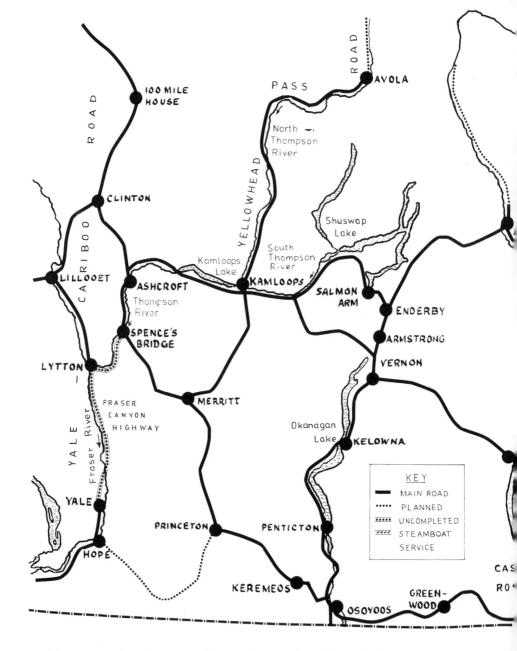

The uncompleted sections shown above and on the right-hand page were all finished within two or three years but the major gaps from Hope to Princeton and from Revelstoke to Golden took twenty-four and fifteen years respectively. During these years, driving across B.C. to or from Alberta was far from simple, resulting in most motorists, including those from B.C.'s southern interior, using highways south of the border. The road north from Avola to Tête Jaune Cache was not finished until 1971.

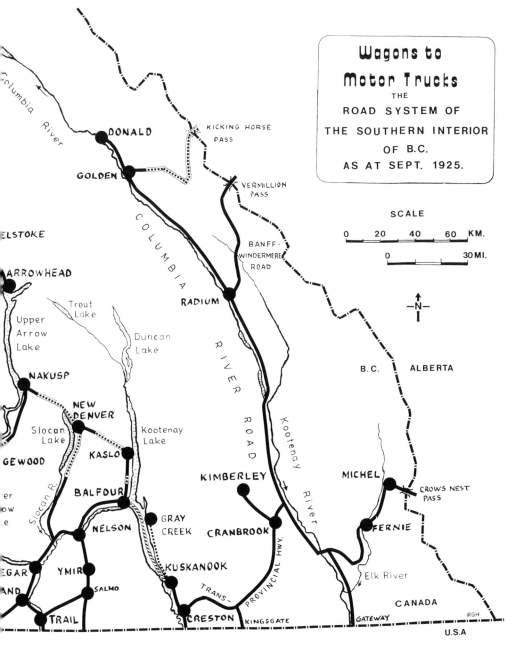

SCALE

0   20   40   60   KM.

0   30 MI.

—N—

KICKING HORSE
PASS

DONALD

GOLDEN

VERMILLION
PASS

ELSTOKE

BANFF-
WINDERMERE
ROAD

ARROWHEAD

Columbia River

Trout Lake

RADIUM

Upper
Arrow
Lake

Duncan
Lake

B.C.   ALBERTA

NAKUSP

NEW
DENVER

Slocan
Lake

Kootenay
Lake

GEWOOD

KASLO

KIMBERLEY

MICHEL

BALFOUR

er
ow
e

Slocan R.

CROWS NEST
PASS

NELSON

GRAY
CREEK

CRANBROOK

FERNIE

EGAR

YMIR

KUSKANOOK

Elk River

AND

SALMO

TRANS-   PROVINCIAL HWY.

CANADA

TRAIL

CRESTON

KINGSGATE

GATEWAY

RGH

U.S.A

COLUMBIA RIVER ROAD

Kootenay River

The steamboat service indicated above was provided by the S.S. *Nasookin*, which ran between Fraser Landing (near Balfour) and Kuskanook until 1931, the year that its trip was shortened by moving the eastern terminal to Gray Creek. It was the only east-west link until 1940 when the Big Bend Highway between Golden and Revelstoke was opened. Up to that year the heaviest cross-provincial traffic was on the "honeymoon route" from Seattle to Banff, Alberta, via Kingsgate and Vermilion Pass. The *Nasookin* was replaced by the M.V. *Anscomb* in 1947.

In 1913 there were financial problems in British Columbia due to a sudden withdrawal of British capital; the following year these problems deepened with the start of the war. A joint Dominion/Provincial project to build a road through Vermilion Pass between Banff and Windermere had to be abandoned by the Province due to lack of funds, after $202,000 had been spent. The Dominion Government took over and finished it, but at a considerable price. The Province had to agree to give up a strip of land five miles wide and sixty miles long on either side of the highway. However, in return, B.C. did obtain a further concession that Canada would maintain the road "for ever."[12]

The onset of hostilities in Europe saw the zest and vigour of B.C.'s young men who so energetically had settled the wilderness now turn to patriotism. In fact, British Columbia sent to war 55,000 of its best sons from a total population of 450,000, a level of recruitment unmatched anywhere else in Canada.[13]

To offset the lack of manpower that was experienced by 1916, the government decided to employ German prisoners of war on road work in B.C. Between two and three hundred were sent to work on the Monashee Pass Road (Vernon-Edgewood). At first work went well, with reports of 1700 feet of construction each month, but when summer turned to fall, the workers complained of the cold, which was natural enough considering they had no warm clothing and were living in tents. When nothing was done, they refused to work. The Road Superintendent in charge said: "No work, no food" and stopped sending in the supplies. A similar situation arose between Mara Lake and Sicamous, where German internees also refused to work for similar reasons.

Finally, the military authorities in Ottawa were persuaded to better outfit the prisoners and to replace some of the more abrasive officers in charge. R.W. Bruhn, then Assistant Road Superintendent at Sicamous, begged unsuccessfully for permission to hire regular day workers to get some more work done. In the end he went into politics and became Minister of Public Works himself.

In general, lack of manpower combined with lack of funds brought all of Thomas "Good Roads" Taylor's widespread plans to a halt. Even the completion of the Grand Trunk Pacific, the Canadian Northern (CNR), and the Kettle Valley Railways within a period of twelve months did not prevent Sir Richard McBride (who had been knighted in 1912) from seeing the writing on the wall. On March 7, 1915 he prorogued the Legislature with an indication that he intended to dissolve his government. McBride spent some months in London and finally resigned as Premier to become Agent

General. He worked so hard encouraging and supporting British Columbians in their fight against the Germans that he died of exhaustion in 1917 at forty-seven years of age.[14]

Taylor also resigned in 1915, bringing a sad end to a tenure that had established a potentially fine road administration.[15] Despite all the efforts of Thomas Taylor and Richard McBride, British Columbia still did not have even one road anywhere connecting the most densely populated area at the mouth of the Fraser River to the Interior of the province. To make road travel at least twice as fast, drivers of the new machine had to travel through the United States to go east of the Coast and Cascade Mountains.

Thomas Taylor's contribution to road-building in B.C. was substantial. Not only did he bring bountiful enthusiasm to his appointment, but he also was the first author of proper roads legislation to meet the challenge that the internal combustion engine had brought to the Department. During Taylor's administration in 1911 the first comprehensive edition of a workable Highway Act was passed; it was to prove to be one of the most successful pieces of legislation ever produced in B.C., although it never lacked for critics.

This Act covered the establishment and control of highways, and it conferred sweeping powers on the Minister. For example, Section 8 gave him the powers to enter onto any property to vary, alter, or create roads without the necessity of giving notice or receiving the consent of the owner or occupier of the land. Section 14 required the Minister to pay compensation only when the area taken was more than one-twentieth of the area of the original Crown grant, and only when there was a building or an orchard or garden, and his taking up to one-twentieth "was an extinguishment of every title and claim thereto." These powers—and the extension of them to the Land Act and to the Municipal Act to enable the Minister to dictate and regulate the creation of roads in the subdivision of land and in municipalities—were the cause of continuing problems to the Minister and to the Department.

An election did not take place until September 14, 1916. It then took several weeks to assemble the absentee ballots from the soldiers in Europe before it could be announced that the Conservatives were out and the Liberals were in. By this time the trickle of letters and petitions for better roads had become a torrent flowing between the Interior and Victoria. The new government had no choice but to establish the priorities the people demanded, even though the amount of money available for transportation routes in this constantly challenging provincial scene was small.

Ready to Start Constructing Missing Link

Tenders for Fraser Canyon Section of Trans-Provincial Highway to Be in Before Legislature Meets

(Journal of Commerce Special Service)

VICTORIA, Sept. 11.—Simultaneously with the arrival of the trans - provincial highwaymen, Capt. E. S. Evans and Mr. Austin F. Bement, from Winnipeg by Packard car, the provincial government authorized the statement that the public works department was about ready to proceed with the construction of the highway that will link up the coast, by a Canadian route, with the east.

The Legislature will have a say in the matter of the trans-provincial highway. Tenders for the highway work will be called very shortly by the department of public works and will be returned just before the legislature meets this fall. This will be done so that the members of the legislature can decide for themselves whether they want the highway completed or not.

Before making the decision, the government members will have all facts before them. In view of the incalculable benefits that will ensue following the completion of the trans-provincial highway, particularly to the interior sections of the province, it is improbable that any serious opposition will be offered to the scheme.

The contractor whose tender is finally accepted by the government on this highway project will be required to deposit with the government a bond equal to 20 per cent. of the estimated cost of the work. The bond is usually ten per cent on ordinary contracts, but the amount will be doubled in the case of the highway, because of possible damage to C. P. R. or C. N. R. main lines in the Fraser River canyon.

Construction of "The Missing Link"

The reproduction at left from the *B.C. Journal of Commerce* datelined September 11, 1924, is remarkable for several reasons. First, it infers that the provincial government decided to go ahead with the construction of the missing link— that is, the highway from Yale to Spences Bridge through the Fraser Canyon—because two trans-provincial highwaymen arrived from Winnipeg by Packard car. Second, it advises that the Legislature of British Columbia will decide if the bids received for the construction are suitable and acceptable, an innovation never repeated. And third, it states that the security bond of the contracts will be increased from 10 percent of the total of the contract to 20 percent to allow for possible damage to either the CPR or the CNR in the Canyon— perhaps an unprecedented example of wishful thinking.

On October 11, 1924, tenders were called for three contracts stretching from Yale to Spences Bridge , and that section was opened to traffic on May 24, 1927. Two of the contracts over-ran by more than 100 percent, largely because of the restoration or protection of the railways, and all was paid for by the B.C. taxpayer—except for a small return in tolls, which were in effect for twenty years following the opening.

CHAPTER FOUR

1918–1928

Canada helps with the road from Revelstoke to Alberta, including a start on the Big Bend Highway. British Columbia rebuilds from Yale to Spences Bridge on its own.

*H*ONEST JOHN Oliver, the self-styled Delta dirt farmer, with his native midland English accent still evident in his speech, became Premier for the Liberals when Harlan Carey Brewster died from pneumonia while returning from a trip to eastern Canada in March of 1918. It seemed that the health of B.C. Premiers would be safer if they stayed home!

Brewster had been discussing financing of postwar reconstruction with the Ottawa government, and a requirement of public works assistance under that program was that the administration of it be carried out by professional engineers—an admirable feature not always extended to present times. In fact, Brewster had already reorganised the civil service of British Columbia in 1917 at which time he replaced the Road Superintendents with Professional Engineers.

The first of "the doctors," James Horace King M.D., the M.L.A. for Cranbrook, was named Minister of Public Works, ushering in an era of professionalism previously unknown in Public Works. Ten District Engineers and ten assistants served the populated areas of the province under the watchful eye of a modest ministerial staff based in Victoria.

The first thing impressed upon the District Engineers was that they must not be influenced in any way by politics. Roads would be built only after careful examination of their need compared to other uses for the money. However, to this clinical approach the ruling politicians were careful to add a rider that the District Engineers must personally explain carefully to the public why they would not build their road, and why they were building elsewhere, and this explanation must be accompanied by a logical engineering reason for their action!

The engineers entered enthusiastically into the fray, widely criticising the Road Superintendents, some of whom had retired. While many observers waited for politics to reassert itself, political influence on roadbuilding did not return as quickly as many expected. John Oliver lived up to his nickname and was one of the most honest and straightforward political leaders B.C. had had for some time. He abhorred the prevailing political patronage, especially the incident involving the PGE Railway, where the Liberals claimed that Premier McBride had handed over $7 million to the company.[1] In his anger Premier Oliver declared a hold on all public works but soon had to relent on roads due to the pressure to settle veterans in the north.

One of the best at dealing in the new direct and logical style was District Engineer W.K. Gwyer. A letter dated July 23, 1919 from his Penticton headquarters to Public Works Engineer A.E. Foreman illustrates the point. The subject of the letter was a petition from ex-servicemen wishing to have an extension of the road from Princeton to their new homestead sites in the upper Similkameen valley. Gwyer gives an estimate based on the figures at hand, and adds:

> This appears to be one of the heaviest sections on the whole route. Might I offer the suggestion that it would be well to have the agricultural possibilities of this region carefully looked into before the expense is incurred—also bearing in mind that interested parties may at times try to influence the resolution of returned soldiers to serve their own ends.
>
> The point often occurs to me that when the Department is expected to spend large sums to open up Districts for Settlement, there appears to be no obligation on the part of the Settlers to settle. Do not encourage people to settle on land from which it is obviously impossible to ever obtain a living.[2]

Gwyer also wrote a gem of a letter to Foreman about the Vernon-Salmon Arm road. This letter was dated February 14, 1919:

> A great many scurrilous articles have appeared recently in the local papers re: the intolerable condition of the road in question, which are intended as a reflection on this Department. Of course, we do not actually take any notice of these articles—which emanate from the brains of feeble-minded persons who expect Engineers to build permanent roads on wind.[3]

The Vernon-Salmon Arm road was not the only one in trouble in

Gwyer's district: the Lakeshore Road from Penticton to Peachland had serious problems as well. Just the year before, in February of 1918, a survey showed that even at that date of low levels, eleven of the twenty-six miles of road were within six feet or less of the lake level.

That side of the lake was not known for tranquility among those who resided there. The transported English residents had not lost their skill with the pen, as a letter dated January 16, 1919 from N.S. Davidson, the owner of the Idylwylde Ranch at Trepanier, was to prove. Addressed to the Hon. J.H.King, it read:

> I would like to draw your attention to a piece of very bad road, in fact it is dangerous to drive on. Autos come along and drive the poor devils of farmers either into the Okanagan Lake or into the ditch, and if you were ever on the Red River Trail in Manitoba—well if not, I have been— and this single trail I speak of is far more dangerous than anything we have today in Canada to be used by automobiles.
>
> Some few years ago the old McBride Bowser Party undertook to give us a good road around the west side of the Okanagan from Penticton to Westbank ferry, and the present single track trail full of devilish holes is the result. I had a chat with Mr. MacAlpine your Road Superintendent recently and he told me that it was the object of the government to get the Municipality of Peachland to undertake the upkeep of half the distance through the said municipality.
>
> Now I wish to add for your information that I am pretty well acquainted with the Local Reichstag, and if a Grit government can get a Von Chancellor of the Reichstag to agree to any such a proposition, I will buy him a new silk hat. I would advise your Department to give up any such notion of ever getting a poverty stricken municipality such as we have here to even keep in repair a piece of road let alone build a new piece.
>
> Several autos have smashed up in collision around the sharp corners between Peachland and Penticton, the distance is about 20 miles, and the amount of turns and curves amounts to 162, and 21 of these are certainly dangerous. I purchased a Car this fall and now I find it a dangerous article to run, and rather wish someone else had it. I paid $20 for the right to run it on these hellish trails. I came here 15 years ago, and we had better roads than we have today.[4]

This creative epistle was sent on to Gwyer asking for a report so that the Minister could answer Davidson personally. Gwyer replied:

> I was at first distressed at this communication—as this is our show Road (as it were), being the main trunk road to Kamloops and Salmon Arm. I am however advised by Mr. MacAlpine that these parts which are under the jurisdiction of the Summerland and Peachland Municipalities are the portions most complained of.
>
> In this respect, I venture to suggest that as Mr. Davidson is just learning to drive a new car, he probably requires more room than the ordinary traveller.

The Minister was left to do the best he could with that. Some time later Gwyer sent his Assistant to attend a protest meeting of the residents of Summerland. The Assistant could not drive there as the road was impassable between the ferry and the hall, and he had to go by boat. He drew Gwyer a typical cross section of the road, benched in rock and nine feet wide. Davidson certainly needed more room, no matter what kind of a driver he was, and it was not much for a "show" road. They obviously had a long way to go in 1919 with the Okanagan Highway.

A few years later, when Gwyer was quite heavily under fire, he saw fit to advise the Deputy Minister:

> I do not think I would pay much attention to any adverse criticism either from newspapers or individuals. There is really so little for them to find fault with in my district that it is expected that certain factions would take every possible chance to criticise and blame the Department for any occurrence whether we are to blame or not.

Confidence in his own ability was one of Bill Gwyer's chief assets. District Engineers needed that in those days! Herbert Bourne, a District Engineer at Nanaimo during this same period, recalls that the phone rang so persistently some days that he would drive his car to a far part of the district and sit in it until quitting time (a respite now denied by cellular phones!).

In 1919 the Dominion Government passed the Canadian Highway Act for expenditures of $20 million countrywide, with $1.25 million allocated to British Columbia. This was the same year that Gwyer, in his dual duty of Department Location Engineer and District Engineer, was given the task of assessing the restoration possibilities of seventy-seven miles of road through the Fraser and Thompson Canyons, between Yale and Spences Bridge. He produced an excellent report, which criticised both railways for unnecessary destruction and complimented the Royal Engineers for "the care taken with its location and stability."[5] Of the seventy-seven miles of road examined, he declared that 44.5 had been destroyed— thirteen miles by the CNR, five by the 1894 flood, and the rest by the CPR, including nineteen out of the twenty-three miles between Lytton and Spences Bridge. He assessed the railways' joint liability at $375,000, but he added:

> This bears no relevance to the road we are presently surveying, the probable cost of which is Yale to Lytton, 54 miles, $604,000.00, and Lytton to Spence's Bridge, 23 miles, $230,000.00, (a total of $834,000.00).

Gwyer also examined the Coquihalla route for the government, but the severe snowfalls of those years ruled against it, as did the presence of a railway. As part of the study, an engineer of the Dominion Government was sent through on the Kettle Valley Railway one winter, and he made a special note of the extremely heavy snow cover alongside the Coquihalla Line as compared with the small amount of snow evident on his return trip through the Fraser Canyon by the main line.[6]

On October 6, 1919 in Vancouver, the Minister of Public Works, Dr. J.H. King, made a speech outlining the roads policy of his government to the Good Roads League of British Columbia (the province had both a league and an association at this time):

> The objective of the government is to make it possible to travel from the Coast through the whole central part of British Columbia. This will be possible when the Hope-Princeton, or the Hope-Kamloops link is built.

It was a typical politician's speech, so worded because at that time there was most active lobbying both for the southern route started by Taylor before the war, and for the restitution of the old Yale-Cariboo Road through the Fraser Canyon. The latter proved to be the stronger voice, and the one supported by the Dominion Government.

Nothing happened in the way of commitment or construction on either of these routes for the next four years, except surveying. During this time there was a short recession, and a provincial election. The government was beset by demands for better surfaces—preferably pavement—on the existing roads, possibly because of the advent of motor trucks, especially those with tandem rear axles for which the truck weight limit more than doubled, from between six and seven tons to between fourteen and twenty tons. The new District Engineers came to realise that, when used by heavier trucks, hard-surfaced roads did not last nearly as long as they had previously estimated.

With the return of the Liberals in 1922, Dr. William Henry Sutherland became Minister of Public Works. Later in that year, after a bad winter, work started on many roads: in the Kootenays and the Okanagan, in the north, where the Cariboo Road was extended from Quesnel to Prince George, and in central B.C. where various projects resulted in an acceptable road from Ashcroft right through to Revelstoke.

This road became particularly significant when the Dominion Government announced in 1923 that it would build a road from the Alberta border to the west boundary of Yoho National Park, only sixteen miles east of Golden, with the last section to Golden to be completed by B.C. in 1926 to meet the other completed in 1927. The year 1923 is also notable for the signing of a joint cost-sharing agreement between the Province and the Dominion Government to build a road between Revelstoke and Golden, around the biggest bend of the Columbia River. The only real problem with this project was distance, about 170 miles to Donald, with the result that the project was not finished until 1940.

For the opening of the road an unknown author composed a pamphlet which paid glowing tribute to the history and beauty of the area:

> Here only the highway is new. The Selkirks, the Gold Range, and the Rocky Mountains are incalculably old. The river chafes in the rocky bed where it has chafed throughout all the ages. Could David Thompson launch again from Boat Encampment, he would tread the same fearful channels, would steer by the same old landmarks. A country lost in dreams, silent where once it echoed to the chants of the voyageurs, to the ringing picks and shovels of the miners of Downie Creek. A country of languorous days and keen clear nights, where the velvet sky pulses with the streamers of the Northern Lights.[7]

The work between Golden and the Alberta border connected up that centre to the rest of Canada, which in turn had already been connected to the rest of British Columbia by a southerly route. By 1922 there was a good road built to Cranbrook, latterly through the good offices of Dr. King, the outgoing Minister of Public Works and M.L.A. for that area.

Dr. Sutherland, on the other hand, represented the Cariboo district, so in 1923 the buck landed solidly on his desk. Would the motorist entering B.C. by Kicking Horse Pass or Crowsnest Pass end up at Kamloops or at Princeton before he circumvented or crossed the Cascade Range to the coast? It is a fair guess that Sutherland leaned toward the Kamloops-Hope route, which was much more favourable to his constituents, but he did have before him a detailed survey prepared in 1919 by respected Assistant District Engineer, Fred Dawson, to compare the Kamloops-Hope route with a suitable Hope-Princeton route.[8] However, the survey was kept away from public scrutiny until the time for commitment to the first Coast to Interior highway link had to be made.

Dawson's excellent analysis is open to question more in hindsight than on the basis of known calculations at the time. However, Dawson obviously swung the costs as he wished by the charge to the railways for the damage done to the roadbeds. This was both reasonable and supported by the facts, and resulted in the Fraser Canyon route to Kamloops being chosen.

In his overall summary of the report, Dawson's boss, W.K. Gwyer, shows almost uncanny perception projected into the year 1948 when speaking of the Fraser Canyon route:

> I venture to say that even if this road is constructed on the lines recommended it can only be considered as a temporary work at the best and that 25 years from now the public will demand a 30 foot roadway on a water grade through this Canyon regardless of cost. There are no engineering difficulties in the way of this—it is merely a matter of expense.

However, his comments on the future of the Hope-Princeton route are not so perceptive:

> It would be open only six months of the year, and generally only four or five. The cost of opening up would be very considerable and it is impossible to give a figure. It is by no means the logical route to serve the larger portion of the Province. The initial cost would be about the same.

There is no doubt that the extreme difficulty experienced by the Kettle Valley Railway snow-clearing crews in the Coquihalla Pass during the railway's first ten years of operation also influenced this observation and the final recommendation.

It is interesting to note that after the construction was complete, the final cost of the Fraser Canyon section of the road as compiled in September 1926, after the road had been pronounced passable but not fully finished and opened, was almost twice Dawson's estimate.

The construction of the Yale to Ashcroft road, which started in 1924, was not included in the Canadian Highway Agreement and, as a result, Ottawa paid nothing towards it. Because the Province intended to apply tolls on this road, B.C. had to bear the full cost of construction.

Due to the recession from 1920 to 1922, provincial revenues were down and funding was restricted throughout the time of building the road, an unfortunate situation that led to reduced standards of construction and a legacy of continuous upgrading from the day the road was completed. In 1929, after the Lytton to Spences Bridge section was finished, the total traffic reported paying tolls for the year was 11,523 cars, and no trucks. In 1936 the total was 21,136 cars, 2861 trucks and 116 motorcycles.[9] At one dollar per car the government was definitely not making much money. Throughout these years, the road was open to traffic only between May 1 and November 15.

The costs, estimated and actual, for the new Alexandra Bridge are of interest. The estimate by Dawson came in at $45,143, almost the

Early Ministers of Public Works

Dr. James Horace King

King was the first of the two medical doctors who served as Minister under Premier "Honest John" Oliver. Representing Cranbrook in the Legislative Assembly, King held sway in Public Works from 1915 to 1921. It would be nice to think that King, as a professional himself, had instigated the introduction of professionals in the Department; however, Ottawa must be given the credit for making it a requirement of postwar funding that professional engineers be hired to supervise the spending. The Province thus had no alternative but to bring in District Engineers to displace the Road Superintendents in the larger districts.

Thomas Taylor

Appointed in 1908, Thomas "Good Roads" Taylor was the first to hold the title Minister of Public Works. Taylor came into office with a reputation as the most enthusiastic motorist in the province, and he accomplished much during his tenure, which ended in 1915. He was a mainstay and charter member of the Victoria Automobile Association (whose letterhead motto was "Good Laws and Obey Them—Good Roads and Plenty of Them") and a booster of the Good Roads Association of Canada. Although Taylor was from Revelstoke, he chose the southern route for the first attempt at a Trans-Canada Highway, a noble effort which was frustrated by World War I. During his seven years as Minister, "Good Roads" Taylor doubled the registered mileage of roads in British Columbia.

Dr. William Henry Sutherland

Sutherland became Minister of Public Works in 1922 and served in that office for six years. The Cariboo country doctor turned roadbuilder had his hands full in 1926, the most prosperous year in B.C.'s history and the most active in road construction up to that time. The re-opening of the Yale-Lytton section made 800 miles of continuous road available from Vancouver to Hazelton, a route through two major river canyons and three mountain ranges—quite a feat for a province only 55 years old! However, Sutherland had little time to celebrate because the next two years saw his beloved Premier dead and his Liberal Party defeated in a general election. Sutherland was one of many who have discovered that politics in B.C. has little mercy and a short memory.

same as the cost of the original bridge in 1863. The new span at 277 feet was fifteen feet less than the old; the deck was twelve feet higher and five feet wider. There was also a ninety-foot steel truss approach span. The final cost was $92,340.64.

Dawson's estimate was generally most impressive, as it contained over twenty separate items, with amounts compiled for each mile of the fifty-seven, and with all the trestles and bridges detailed. The structures included, besides the Alexandra Bridge, a 147-foot steel arch at Stoyama Creek, a 126-foot steel truss at Cisco Creek, a 60-foot steel span with approach spans at Nine Mile Creek, 139 feet of piled timber trestling at Anderson Creek, and a total of 200,000 square feet of timber cribbing and 24,000 cubic yards of stone retaining walls.

The section from Yale to Lytton was widely advertised as being scheduled to open on July 1, 1926, but it was barely passable for traffic by September of that year, and officially opened on May 24, 1927. This was a considerable embarrassment to the Department, especially as the Canadian and Vancouver Good Roads Associations had arranged a grand meeting in Kamloops for July with numerous automobile cavalcades coming from across Canada, all of which had to be cancelled.

One probable reason for the divergence between the estimates and the actual cost on all the contracts as bid is that there was no distinction for loose rock, as against solid rock, a differentiation which Dawson made in his estimating. At the time of construction, rock prices varied between $1.50 and $2.00 and dirt from 35 to 40 cents per cubic yard. Dawson showed the rock quantities evenly divided between solid and loose, and he estimated 75 cents for the latter. As was to be often repeated in years to come, road-building estimates foundered on classification.

The south bank of the Thompson River between the railway points of Gladwin and Thompson and separating Tank Creek and Nicoamen River consisted of very high terraced benches in sandy and gravelly material. Just east of the Nicoamen River there was a high unstable slippage in the shape of an inverted half cone. With its sides reaching up between eight hundred and nine hundred feet, it was about one hundred feet in diameter at the bottom and several hundred feet in diameter at the top.

The river had created and maintained the unstable anomaly by constantly eroding out the material between two rock outcrops. The original Cariboo Road had come along the river's edge and bridged over between the rock outcrops; the railway had later supplanted it and done the same. What remained of the old road for about two

Roads for Hardy Motorists

These pictures were proudly published in the D.P.W. Annual Reports of 1927 and 1928. They show why tourists from the rest of Canada at this time often shipped themselves and their vehicles by rail!

At right, the steep slopes of Slocan Lake at Cape Horn Bluffs—the water is about 1500 feet straight down.

Photographs Courtesy of the British Columbia Ministry of Transportation and Highways

The Okanagan Highway at Vaseaux Lake between Penticton and Osoyoos. Only necessity convinced local drivers to pass under the overhang.

miles west of this area after the railway had built over it was now washed away by the river, which in some places had cut an eighty-foot-high gouge where the old roadway had been. There was considerable anguish over this, with several alternative designs desperately being tried while the contractor looked on.

Finally, Deputy Minister Philip conceived the idea of going under the railway east of Tank Creek and along the edge of the river, a solution that required building thousands of feet of cedar log cribbing. (Much of the cribbing was replaced with metal bin wall as the road was widened in later years). After this was done the river was held in check and the slide was stabilised.

Some idea of the financial impact of such difficulties is given by the issuance of two extra work orders—one in 1926 and the other the next year—each in the amount of $100,000, and together exceeding the amount of the original contract. There were several relocations of the CPR line to admit the road between it and the river, and all of this was done by the railway, at cost to the Province, although the railway did contribute modestly to some of the river bank retention works from which it benefitted greatly.

The grand total for the 93.95 miles was $2,382,305.84, or $25,357 per mile, and with off-site improvements to the sections of the route from Hope to Yale, and Spences Bridge to Ashcroft, the total bill came close to $3 million.

It was extremely unfortunate that the final road width in the canyons was only sixteen feet, (on sidehill sections it was even reduced to fifteen feet), especially as the original Royal Engineers' road had been eighteen to twenty-two feet, and wider in many places. Right from the day it was opened, the Yale to Spences Bridge highway was to be continually widened, a process that went on indefinitely. The Department was none-the-less proud of it, and made note that on the day it was opened another mountainous section of road was also put into service, that from Golden eastwards to Yoho National Park boundary.

The second largest highway project in the short history of the province was over. It had encompassed the same section of roadway as the first, separated by a period of sixty years. The road was no wider, and in many places it was narrower, but the steepest pitches were gone and many of the bridges and some of the cribbings were much better. The railways had also been accommodated. The replacement for the Alexandra structure was twelve feet higher over the river than the original, but it was restricted to a 34,000-pound gross vehicle weight—later increased to 40,000 pounds when an open grid steel deck was installed. The weight limitation on the

Early Road Machinery

The two pictures shown here were published in the D.P.W. Annual Reports of 1927 and 1929. In that period the Department purchased twelve gas shovels (as they called them), for a total cost of $750,000. They reported a complement of 50 power graders, 100 tractors and 250 motor trucks. As may be seen from this picture, hand shovels were thereafter used for leaning on!

This Cat 60 tractor was purchased in 1929 for about $5600. The enclosed and heated cab, and the use of "non-freeze mixes," made possible snow plowing throughout the winter on main roads, something not done before.

These early gasoline-powered machines, especially the beloved Cat 60, lasted for many years and did wonderful service for the Province, although their capacity was very limited.

Photographs courtesy of the British Columbia Ministry of Transportation and Highways.

Alexandra Bridge and the narrowness of the road seriously restricted the road transport industry and created a windfall of extra revenue to the railways.

The old bridge remains today basically in good shape. Having reached retirement age, it still graces the historic crossing site, although it has not been used for the last twenty-seven years. The Ministry some years ago successfully resisted an application to make the old Alexandra bridge the support structure for a river-viewing restaurant.

The project established some rather significant precedents. First, in mountainous terrain, even with the most conscientious engineers and estimating, contract costs can, and usually do, exceed the estimates, and much more than 100 percent overruns at times must be contemplated. In addition, especially where time limits are applied to the work, large extra work orders may be necessary even though they do nullify the bidding process. A comment by the widely experienced Ted Webster, Director of Construction for many years, is worth considering: "The only time a highway project is on time, on budget, and unaltered is the day it commences!"

Patrick Philip, Deputy Minister and Public Works Engineer—the second after J.E. Griffith to carry both titles—was a very strong leader who made all the difficult decisions.[10] Throughout the building of the road, Philip made frequent visits to the site, always travelling by rail to either Yale, Boston Bar, or Lytton and sending telegrams in advance requesting that he be met at the appropriate station.[11]

On March 30, 1927, Philip wrote to the District Engineer at Kamloops about staff and camp conditions. This letter gives another view of Philip, and of the general outlook and attitude of the supervisors during these very different times:

> I have to advise that in view of the fact it is most desirable that Division Engineers should leave their camp as seldom as possible, it is only fair and proper that they should have their wives, where married, living with them. I have therefore arranged that wives of Division Engineers should be allowed to board free in Government camp. Wives of Resident Engineers will be allowed to board at the rate of $20.00 per month. Wives of other employees cannot be maintained in the Government camps. I do not think that the Fraser Canyon is a suitable place for children, especially when the work is going on, and while I do not wish to work any hardship on any of our employees, the presence of children in our camp would be better discouraged. They will be charged for at the same rate as an adult.[12] (Author's note: while Philip does not say so, children were normally boarded free).

He then adds something that is not mandatory today:

Please see that all Resident Engineers are Licensed Professional Civil Engineers of the Province.

While this connection from Kamloops to Hope was under way, a road linking it to the Slocan and Kootenay areas was nearing completion. This road crossed the Monashee Range between Vernon and Edgewood, a small settlement on the west shore of Lower Arrow Lake, and followed a trail first blazed by Captain Houghton, the founder of the Coldstream Ranch near Vernon. Houghton explored it as an alternative to the "vile" (his word) trail built by Walter Moberly between Seymour and the Columbia. German prisoners of war worked on the road in 1916 and 1917 but it remained incomplete after they left.

The last connecting twenty-five miles of this route were built under five contracts let between 1922 and 1925, all won by Rawlings and La Brash of Nakusp. La Brash was killed by lightning the year of the road's completion. Rawlings went on unpartnered to complete the road through to Nelson, contracting the last section at Cape Horn, a rock bluff high above Slocan Lake.[13]

This road was opened in 1930 as a shorter direct route from Nelson to Kamloops, and one not subject to delays by flooding or slides on the road between Penticton and Kelowna. However, it included several "hair-raising" sections, especially the cliff-hanger at Cape Horn and an intimidating twisting one-way tunnel by Slocan Lake south of Silverton. Never a very popular route, it was a particular nightmare for Prairie drivers heading for the Coast. Many of them gave up at Cape Horn and returned to Nelson to ship themselves and their cars by rail. The Monashee Pass section, rising to a height of 1200 metres above sea level, was not fully paved until 1965.

In the Ministry files there are several pages of a Bulletin of the Automobile Club of Southern California dated June 1, 1927 and detailing a trip through B.C. that was made shortly after the Fraser Canyon road was opened. The writer is very kind to the roads of that era, especially remembering that the road surfaces in those days benefitted from very little traffic on them compared to later periods. In one of the Annual Reports on file for those years it is stated that Cariboo Highway traffic seldom exceeded seventy-five vehicles a day, and the Kootenay-Columbia Highway, which many of the early motorists of the United States travelled from Spokane to the increasingly popular town of Banff, was reported as having seldom more than fifty vehicles per day.

Generally the Automobile Club Bulletin describes the roads near to centres as "good gravel and natural gravel road," and on occasions in the remoter areas it reads "dirt" or "poor if wet." The fact that tolls had been imposed on the Cariboo Road at Yale on May 20, 1927, was not noted: the tolls were one dollar for car and driver and twenty-five cents a passenger, ten cents per hundred pounds of freight, and a dollar for a semi-trailer. The tolls were collected at Spuzzum until 1938 when the toll house was moved to Yale. Tolls came off early in 1947.[14]

As the charge for shipping a car from Hope to Princeton was $38.50 (which would be the equivalent of $385 in today's prices), it is likely that only very wealthy motorists used the flatcar service on the Kettle Valley Railway. It was much cheaper to ship a car a similar distance of ninety miles from Revelstoke to Golden by the main line. This cost $17.50 for a large car and $3.75 per passenger.

Although the new Canyon/Cariboo Road was painfully narrow and incorporated curves such as one taking the vehicle around an arc of 220 degrees at a radius of fifty-five feet (at Mornylun Creek near Kanaka Bar), the connection was made. Now at least it was possible to drive from Vancouver to the Interior without leaving British Columbia.

The technical changes that would enable earth- and rock-moving at a scale to match the challenge of these mountains had not yet taken place. At least one contractor in the Canyon, Frank Leighton at Tilton Creek, was still basically a horse and wagon operator and recommended himself on the excellence of his stock. However, the young and strong province within ten years was quite prepared to take on building a highway from Hope to Princeton through Allison Pass and would have done so had World War II not intervened.

Their decision to use Allison Pass was based on the "discovery" of that route in 1922 by a Department surveyor by the name of H.E. Stevens (not to be confused with J.H.A.Steven a well known Locating Engineer of some years in the future). Allison Pass at 4380 feet was hailed as much superior to Hope Pass at 6000 feet, but Tulameen Pass, which was near Hope Pass and 1000 feet lower, certainly should have been considered.[15]

Allison Pass was known in Colonel Moody's day, as indicated when that farsighted individual wrote to Governor James Douglas about it on August 23, 1860:

I have a communication from a Mr. Allison who is at present on the Similkameen south branch, and he has been up that valley from the forks a distance of 25 miles, along an Indian trail in the direction of the Skagit, and the mule road now constructing from hence. This strengthens my recommendation that it should be explored.[16]

The exploration took sixty-two years. The good Colonel even suggested that one day Allison Pass could be used for a railway. A.E. Cleveland's Gibson Pass line at 4486 feet was not much higher, but it was five miles longer. Allison Pass was the chosen route.

Automobile Club of Southern California

ROAD BULLETIN
June 1, 1927

PACIFIC NORTHWEST
WASHINGTON STATE

Seattle to Vancouver, B.C., 161 miles.

Continuous pavement is traversed from Seattle by way of Bothel, Silver Lake, Everett, Marysville, Stanwood, Mount Vernon and the Chuckanut Drive (2 miles of which is gravel), Bellingham and Blaine, to Vancouver. A temporary permit, for which no charge is made, is granted for thirty days to motorists visiting Canada. Extensions not to exceed ninety days may be obtained in thirty-day periods from any Collector, Customs Officer or recognized Canadian motor club. This service is free of charge and granted upon request. The Custom Offices at the border are open from 7.00 A.M. to 1.00 A.M. Speed limits in British Columbia are thirty miles per hour on the highway, twenty miles in cities and towns, and ten miles in school areas on regular school days, from 8 A.M. to 5 P.M.

PACIFIC NORTHWEST
BRITISH COLUMBIA & ALBERTA

Vancouver to Cache Creek, 286 miles.

Leaving Vancouver via Main Street and Kingsway pavement prevails over the Pacific Highway to Frye's Corners from where good gravel is used to Hope, except for 2 miles of pavement at Langley, and 8 miles of pavement at Chilliwack. At Hope one may ship by train to Princeton, charge 77c per 100 pounds, with minimum 5000 pounds) or drive north over good gravel and natural gravel road through the scenic Fraser Canyon via Lytton and Lillooet to Cache Creek.

Cache Creek to Osoyoos
via Kamloops and Enderby, 296 miles
via Princeton, 216 miles

Via Kamloops, a fair to poor dirt road winding and hilly extends through the sage brush country to Savona, with good gravel road to the limits of Kamloops and pavement into town. Gravel road is then used for 7 miles with fair dirt, poor when wet, to within 9 miles of Salmon Arm, followed by good gravel road via Vernon to Kelowna. It is here necessary to ferry across Okanagan Lake (charges $1.00 per car and 10c per passenger). A good type of graveled road is then resumed via Penticton to Osoyoos. Via Princeton, good natural gravel road, poor if wet, parallels the Thompson River to Spence's Bridge with good gravel and short stretches of dirt via Merritt to Princeton, thence down the Similkameen Valley to Keremeos and Osoyoos.

Osoyoos to Cranbrook, 275 miles

Turning easterly, a fair sandy road climbs over Anarchist Mountain, (elevation 3,800 feet),thence fair to good natural gravel down through Kettle Valley to Midway. The same type of road then winds over easy grades through a mountainous country to Grand Forks and Cascade from where good two-way natural gravel road is used to Rossland and Trail, thence along the Kootenay River to Castlegar, where a free government ferry is used across the Columbia River. The same type of good natural gravel is then resumed to Nelson where it is necessary to ferry Kootenay Lake to Kuskanook Landing. The ferry leaves Nelson daily at 6:30 a.m. and leaves Kuskanook daily at 4:10 p.m. The charges are from $5.00 to $7.00 according to the size of the car and $2.20 per passenger. From Kuskanook Landing a fair natural gravel road is traversed via Creston to Yahk with good gravel to Cranbrook.

Cranbrook to Banff and Lake Louise, 186.5 miles

For details on this route see "Spokane to Lake Louise and Banff."

Spokane to Lake Louise and Banff, 379 miles

Pavement extends easterly to the Idaho State Line, followed by gravel surfaced highway via Rathdrum and Sandpoint to a point 5 miles beyond Bonner's Ferry. The next 5 miles is fair dirt, then good dirt via Addie to Eastport and Kingsgate. Fair dirt road then extends to Yakh, with good gravel to Cranbrook and Windermere, except for two miles of dirt at Canal Flats. A very good gravel highway is then traversed via Sinclair Canyon and over Vermilion Pass (elevation 5264 feet), and thence to Lake Louise and Banff.

M.O.T.H. File 5784-1

A Footnote to the 1920s—The Reaction Ferry

USK reaction ferry making its way across the Skeena River. (Photo courtesy of Frank A. Clapp)

The reaction ferry is one of the most environmentally acceptable and efficient means of transportation ever invented. No one knows who originally came up with the idea, or when the first one was put into use in British Columbia, but by the 1920s the province had thirty-five of them. They were ideal for the traffic of those days, and for saving the cost of bridging B.C.'s fast-flowing rivers. By 1989 the number of reaction ferries in operation in the province was down to six.

The principle involved in propelling the ferry is to drive it across the river by the force of the current. This is achieved by keeping the hull of the ferry at a constant angle to the direction of the current, an angle achieved by attaching cables from each side of the ferry to a wheeled traveller on an overhead cable, and by adjusting the lengths of these attaching guys with a winch. When the correct angle is attained, the reacting force to the current force starts the ferry moving at an angle to the current, that is, across the river. There is absolutely no noise and no atmospheric pollution.

B.C. had a long-lasting love affair with the reaction ferry. The pioneer residents adored them because they never broke down. Strong back eddies at the landings and the wind bothered them, as did low water and ice, but generally they gave sterling service. Sometimes this could not be said of the ferryman, who always lived right beside the townside landing. At Isle Pierre on the Nechako River near Prince George, the ferryman habitually slept in. One rough-and-ready commuter used to wake him up with a .303 bullet through the ferry house roof. However, the R.C.M.P. soon put a halt to that!

The very short rock tunnel shown in the 1928 photograph on the right is north of Slocan City at the edge of Slocan Lake on the road to Silverton. It is said that the District Engineer at time of construction hammered a wooden wedge into a crack above the opening and always checked that it was still firm and unmoved before he drove through. The tunnel was "day-lighted," and the rock above it was partially removed in 1940.

COURTESY OF MOTH

British Columbia needed some way to solve its problems with rock bluffs!

The section of road shown on the left is alongside one of B.C.'s Arrow Lakes. A certain Minister of Highways made a promise to widen it. When this promise was not kept, the residents renamed the rock promontory "Gaglardi's Bluff"!

R.G. HARVEY COLLECTION

Above, the Barriere Bridge over the North Thompson River was shown in the DPW Annual Report for 1934, the year it was built. The two Howe trusses—made from the finest Douglas fir—each span 150 feet. Similar bridges carried British Columbia's heaviest public-road-licensed logging trucks for decades. Built mostly in the 1920s and 1930s they were replaced in the 1970s on the main highways, and many still give good service on lesser roads.

Below, the Shames River Bridge between Terrace and Prince Rupert, March 1963, now replaced by a steel structure.

CHAPTER FIVE

1928-1952

The Great Depression and a World War do not stop the Province from beginning to step out of the mud. Some pavements go down, but the Hope-Princeton, Big Bend, and Hart Highways take many years both to start and to finish. The Okanagan Lakeshore Road has problems as a Coast Connection.

*O*N AUGUST 19, 1927, John Oliver died. For the road-builders of the Department, this was a particularly sad occasion which in fact started the decline of their "joie de vivre." It took a long time for this pathbreaking, adventurous spirit to return.

The Conservatives returned to office triumphantly in July of 1928 with thirty-five seats to the Liberals' twelve. Nelson Seymour Lougheed became the Minister of Public Works, under the leadership of a native son with the rather historic name of Simon Fraser Tolmie, a member of a prominent colonial family who was a veterinarian and part-time farmer from Saanich. Lougheed himself was a businessman representing the Dewdney riding.

Premier Tolmie came to the job with experience as Dominion Minister of Agriculture behind him. However, despite this political and administrative schooling, the Tolmie government was to be one of the most unfortunately inept that the people of British Columbia ever suffered through. The Premier almost immediately heaped coals of wrath on his own head by obviously favouring southwestern B.C. in all that he did. Such favouritism enraged everyone else in the province and was truly a dead-end road, as it remains for any politician of today.

When the effects of the October 1929 stock market crash hit with great force and speed (Vancouver unemployment increased by 300 percent in January of 1930), Tolmie's lack of reaction and resourcefulness became painfully obvious. Dissatisfaction with the economy soon expanded to include disgust with the provincial government and, like the economic conditions, it did nothing but get worse.

After great plans for Public Works in 1929, with intentions of increasing the use of the newly acquired machines of road-building, the situation changed almost overnight to become one of finding pick, shovel, and wheelbarrow work for the thousands on relief. Depressing, mind-deadening relief camps quickly proliferated.

The years of the Depression dragged on, and Tolmie and his colleagues became ever more afraid of calling an election. As the time approached where it could no longer be avoided, they repeatedly beseeched the Leader of the Opposition, Thomas Dufferin Patullo, the Member for Prince Rupert, to form a coalition with them. Duff Patullo, who was most effective in opposition even without the help that Tolmie afforded him, scornfully rejected such proposals.

The province's second Conservative government dragged out its full five-year term to mandatory dissolution, and in the ensuing provincial election in November 1933 went down to total and absolute defeat, with no members elected at all. There was a thirty-four seat Liberal majority, with seven seats to the previously unrepresented socialist Co-operative Commonwealth Federation (C.C.F.) party, and six to others. Tolmie later was elected back into the federal Parliament in Ottawa two years before his death in 1937.

In 1932 one notable adjunct to Tolmie's growing unpopularity was his over-reaction to a delegation of Vancouver businessmen at the height of the Depression. The delegation, led by forest magnate H.R. MacMillan, was motivated mostly by raw panic as the provincial economy got worse and worse and its members contemplated their collective corporate downfall.

When business leaders wish to save money under financially critical circumstances, their first proposal is predictably a reduction in taxes. The result in this case was the creation of a committee of tax reduction seekers known as the Kidd Committee after its Chairman. This committee was shortly enlarged and designated the Economy Commission. The Kidd Committee shot itself in the foot most effectively by issuing its first report recommending the reduction of the provincial budget from $25 million to $7 million, mostly by the shredding of the civil service which it bluntly described as incompetent. The Economy Commission recommended that social services—few as they were at that time—be grossly reduced. The Commission also proposed the abolition of the party system of government (a rather surprising reaction to a recession).

The government, although strongly business-oriented, had no alternative but to conceal this bomb: the report was never officially released, although enough of it got out to discredit Tolmie considerably. The budget wreckers did not achieve a two-thirds reduction on everything in the Public Works Department, but the road maintenance and construction funds for fiscal year 1933/34 were so tiny as to be almost nonexistent.

Considering that by the second winter of the Depression forty thousand people in Vancouver needed assistance (15 percent of the population), these leaders of commerce showed extreme insensitivity in lobbying to reduce social services. No wonder so many electors turned to the CCF, and some even to the Communists!

For those with money, the good life came cheap, and bargains in real estate were to be found on every side, but as the economic downturn dragged on, political leaders everywhere—except, finally, Franklin Delano Roosevelt—failed to recognize that only by somehow creating a purchasing power in the populace could business recover. The Economy Commission steadfastly depleted the civil service, and even more steadfastly reduced the salaries of the survivors. None rebelled, for they valued employment highly, but none went out and made purchases. It was a stalemate which lasted throughout the 1930s until World War II provided the turnaround impetus.

In the last summer of prosperity in 1929, before this situation came about, the new Minister of Public Works created a spectre that would later haunt him by announcing somewhat indiscreetly that his government would start the Hope-Princeton Highway connection in 1930 and finish it by 1932. Needless to say, this did not happen, and the Princeton and Penticton Boards of Trade never let him forget it for the rest of his term in office.

One reason the work could not be started in 1929 was that the B.C. Loan Act for the year, under which new road work was financed, had in fact twice as much dedicated to the Dewdney Trunk Road as it had for all of Yale and Similkameen districts combined.[1] William Smithe's precedent of looking after the backyard first was alive and well! Lougheed, as a bonus, gained immortality by having a highway named after him.

As a gesture toward the Hope-Princeton Coast Connection, a relief camp was established at the Sumallo summit. However, it was not long into the decade before these men without morale deserted from what is now called "sunshine valley" and crowded into Hope in sullen refusal to work for pin money. This rough road reached the Skagit Bluffs before grinding to a construction halt that lasted right through to 1938.

The affinity for businessmen demonstrated by Tolmie, together with the announcement in 1929 that the Hope-Princeton Highway would be built through Allison Pass, brought on an extraordinary campaign by the Coalmont Board of Trade. Spearheaded by a man named Robert Alexander Pope, the Board's objective was to have the highway routed from the Nicolum Valley by Eight Mile Creek to Vuich Creek, (a headwater creek of the Tulameen River), and down that creek and river past Coalmont to Princeton.

It was no coincidence that at the head of Vuich Creek lies Treasure Mountain, near the old fur brigade Summit Camp. (See map in Chapter One, "Trails from the Skagit to the Tulameen.") Many of the Coalmont citizens had invested in the mine and mining properties there, after the "finest steam coal in the West" had been worked out, primarily by Jim Hill and his Great Northern Railroad. It can logically be deduced that Pope was also interested in mining promotion, because only in that activity can exaggeration and imagination be found in the quantities that he showed in trying to have the main road brought to the mine as well as past the community.

Pope was an American, living in Seattle, and although he put no initials after his name, he claimed in one letter to be an engineer experienced in road location and design, and in another to be a leader in business. He also specialised in displaying various letterheads, using one from the Washington University Club, another from the Explorers Club, and one from the Seattle Arctic Club.

He started off by visiting Minister Lougheed and followed that with a letter dated September 9, 1929:

> Our committee of the Coalmont-Blakeburn Board of Trade have thought it best at this time to merely furnish you with the essential facts and conclusion rather than to delay until a formal and complete report with sketches and photographs could be prepared and submitted, in order that your surveying party might be got on the ground this season to complete the details of our preliminary location, and to furnish you with a proper estimate of cost.
>
> We traversed on foot the entire distance and are now satisfied that a road can be built out of Hope up the Nicolum River and Eight Mile creek valleys with a grade that ought not to average more than 6% in reaching the 5000 ft. pass.[2]

In fact, Eight Mile Creek has a severely sloped narrow valley climbing from 1000 feet above sea level at Nicolum River to a 5100-foot pass, which is simply a notch in a high ridge, in less than eight miles. From there an immediate descent is necessary to Sowaqua Creek at an elevation of 2500 feet, dropping down in a distance of four miles, then another climb to a 4700-foot summit, before the route would reach Vuich Creek on the plateau at 4000 feet elevation, seven miles farther on.

In this nineteen-mile roller coaster, grades in excess of 10 percent throughout would be a necessity. It is almost a carbon copy of the Peers Creek, Fool's Pass fur brigade route which it parallels one ridge over, and it demonstrates again how completely the topography of the southwest slope of the high plateau resists incursion by any roadway: be it by Peers Creek, Nine Mile Creek, or Snass Creek; they are all too steep and too confined.

Pat Philip declined to even contemplate putting out money for such a survey, not wanting to create his own Fool's Pass. When Pope learned of this, he exploded in a barrage of letters, ending with one in large agitated handwriting written on both Arctic Club and Explorers Club letterhead, and dated October 31, 1929 to Premier Tolmie:

> A mutual friend told me that you were not a politician and that you would get action regardless of political consequences once the welfare of B.C. was at stake. Yet the Coalmont Board of Trade has not yet been advised when a survey of our natural and easy cheap route will be made.
>
> Your engineer tells me that no parties for survey will be available for 18 months and it certainly seems imbecilic to say the least that the most important stretch of road to be built can get no action in six months of patient approach. Neither you nor I would exist long if we ran our business in such a dilatory way. I would of course expect this from politicians but not from a competent and successful businessman as yourself.
>
> If the present government dares to continue to praise, advocate or finance the southern route, advocated by a few politicians then it will be their certain demise. The complete condemnation of this route by the government's own engineer, Dawson, ought to be enough to determine its final disposition.
>
> However any officers of the government that are still willing to sponsor this route and its attendant extravagance will be suspected of ulterior motives of profit either personal or political.

Pope's mention of Dawson probably has some accuracy as it would come from Coalmont sources, and could be checked, but it is not clear if Dawson was against Allison Pass or Gibson Pass, or both. It is possible that Dawson echoed Gwyer's opinion that the southern route from Hope to Princeton was too long, passed through generally valueless country, and was not worth building. Pope disappeared with the Depression.

A work order for $50,000 was issued to the Similkameen District on May 27, 1930 for the Hope-Princeton Highway, Princeton to Roche River, its fifty-mile section; and at the same time a work order to the Yale District for its thirty-mile section for $30,000. Whether there was an intention to build it all for $1000 per mile is not known, but about four miles were built at the Hope end, and a tote road was built to Sunday Creek on the Princeton end twenty-four miles out, twelve miles on from the end of the 1917 work.

This minimum effort dragged on into 1932, with these work orders in fact the last regular allocations to the route, the continuing work all being charged from then on to Unemployment or Direct Relief to which the B.C. Loan Act was largely dedicated. All this followed an excellent comparative report on Allison Pass versus Gibson Pass by T.E. Clarke, an outstanding Department Resident Engineer prominent throughout the surveys and design of the route. He indicated that Allison Pass would be 20 percent to 30 percent cheaper.

In June of 1932 the Economy Commission asserted itself and asked how much had been spent on the route right back to 1911 (this question seemed political as well as economic).[3] The answer was $450,000. They also asked how much was required to finish the road and how much it would cost each year to maintain it. Answers were provided only for the Similkameen District fifty-mile stretch from Princeton to Allison Pass: $350,000 to build it, and $2500 per mile per year to maintain it, both very high amounts for that period. That seemed to be enough for the Commission, which asked no more questions and provided no extra funds, although it did leave the route on the relief program. The great procrastination seemed to match the Great Depression!

In 1933, H.C. Anderson, the Assistant District Engineer at Merritt, made the decision to use the high line in the upper Skagit Valley—that is, through the bluffs instead of by the valley bottom. This was also the year that the Department of National Defence took over the supervision and administration of all relief work on roads. The peak of the Depression had arrived: there were now 7,783 despairing men working on roads and other public works in B.C. Four relief camps were set up on the Hope-Princeton, seven on the Fraser Canyon and even more on the Big Bend Highway. There should have been a great deal achieved but there was not. As someone said, "What can you get for 20 cents a day?"

By 1936 the roll call was down to 5300, and on July 9th of that year a $1.5 million 50/50 program for highway work beyond relief work was signed with the Dominion Government. Things were starting to look up.

With T.D. Patullo now Premier, his famous namesake bridge at New Westminster was under way. Patullo was persuaded to borrow $4 million for roads. He decided to spend most of the money reconstructing and paving selected sections of roadway throughout the province, a politically motivated choice that was to be one factor in his eventual downfall. He was also accused of neglecting the Lower Mainland, a total about-face from Simon Tolmie's shortcoming of overlooking the Interior. Frank Mitchell MacPherson was Minister, in office from 1933 to 1939.

Also in 1936 the National Defence road camps were closed and the relief work came under provincial jurisdiction once again, with Dominion Government financial participation. The work on the Hope-Princeton virtually came to a standstill, and that situation, amazingly, continued right through to 1942. On November 30, 1938, H.C. Anderson reported on his 38.5-mile section, Hope to Allison Pass, as follows: 6.67 miles 100 percent complete, 18 feet wide, 20 feet on curves; 3.14 miles partially complete.

For the Princeton end, Mile 88.5 back to Mile 38.5, nineteen miles was described as "variously 18 feet wide," and for the remaining thirty-one miles the verdict was "12 to 14 feet wide, passable but expensive revisions are necessary at many points." Some of the old road of the sappers and miners was still in use as an access trail, and some clearing and tote road work was yet to be done, but the remaining twelve miles of the 28.5-mile gap, in Anderson's words, "had no road of any sort at all."

On June 9, 1942 the District Engineer at Kamloops prepared an estimate to build a standard gravel highway twenty-four feet wide throughout, totalling $1.54 million. From then on, the road was left to the reluctant attentions of the Japanese-Canadian internees, following in the footsteps of the down-and-out Canadians of ten years before.

It was not that the communities on either end of this unfulfilled promise were struck dumb. They were not. Rather, they were paralysed by the disastrous days of 1933 to 1936, ending their malaise only in 1938 with the formation of the Hope-Princeton Road Association. The letters and action committees really got rolling in 1939 with $60,000 raised to energetically harass the government on all sides, with newspaper advertisements, pamphlets, and public meetings. This reached an uncomfortable crescendo in late summer of that year, and when war broke out the relief in government circles must have been almost palpable.

During these years there was not very much going on elsewhere in the Interior, except the relief work and finally the contract work on the Big Bend Highway, which was to open in 1940. In 1930 R.W. Bruhn, the former Assistant Road Superintendent at Sicamous, had become Minister of Public Works. Before the coffers closed Bruhn did manage to build some large steel bridges, including replacements at Spences Bridge, Savona, and Ashcroft, and to complete the road up the east shore of Kootenay Lake from Kuskanook to Gray Creek, where a ferry dock was built. The S.S. *Nasookin* became a car ferry link; in so doing it lost one and a half decks and gained a new boiler, a reduction gear in its steering system, and an engine room telegraph.

Rolf Walgren Bruhn came out before the mast from Sweden. His fortunes in the logging industry at Salmon Arm ensured him a secure living until a boat explosion wiped him out financially. Deprived of his means of earning a livelihood, he joined Public Works, got his breath back, then plunged back into private industry to make a substantial fortune before becoming Minister of Public Works twice, first in the early 1930s and then in the early 1940s.

The Peculiar Powder Houses

There was a very peculiar structure created from time to time by the Department of Public Works—the "powder house" of the 1930s and even the 1940s. These were small log cabins built in very remote areas for the storage of powder, later TNT or dynamite, together with caps, fuses, and other detonation equipment.

Powder houses always received funding approval without question, but some of these structures, in a few cases built beside remote lakes, had nothing more to do with any sort of powder beyond that on the nose of the District Engineers' wives as they spent weekends there. This practice signified a subtle acceptance, first, that Public Works Engineers were not well paid during the Depression years and second, that life for them in the small introverted Interior communities could be unbearable if there were not a few unspoken "perks" within the Department to balance things up. One favoured diversion was the peculiar powder house.

Despite the ennui elsewhere, the Okanagan remained an eventful region, especially on the west side of the lake, mostly due to Bill Gwyer, that colourful District Engineer highlighted in Chapter 4. His first concern was the annual flooding of the Lakeshore Road between Penticton and Peachland, but there was an even more difficult problem in the offing which was to be a Departmental preoccupation for years to come.

With the opening of the Fraser Canyon road in 1926, the road between Westbank and Penticton was the Coast Connection for the South Okanagan, Boundary, and Kootenay Regions, especially after the government-operated ferry was instituted at Kelowna in 1927. It had been a chartered privately-run service of varying quality since 1905. For sixteen years after the ferry went in, the road was bedeviled with washouts and slides, as well as repeated quagmire conditions in

114

The S.S. *Nasookin*

Photograph courtesy of Frank A. Clapp

This photograph shows the S.S. *Nasookin* after it was refitted as a vehicle ferry at Nelson, B.C. Automobiles were loaded through the doors on the sides. Larger vehicles including the bus were stowed across the foredeck. When the rail line was completed along Kootenay Lake in 1930, the CPR had no further use for the *Nasookin*. The ferry had, however, been carrying a few automobiles as well as its railway passengers on its one round trip per day so that when the new landing at Gray Creek on the east side of the lake was opened in April 1931, the *Nasookin* became a government-operated vehicle ferry. Chartered by the Department in 1931 and purchased outright in 1933, it made three round trips per day in summer and two in winter.

Although listed as a 30-car ferry, the *Nasookin* consistently averaged no more than six vehicles per trip, based on annual accounts. This, of course, included the bus and the faithful Nelson-Creston freight truck. The only time the average load rose above that figure to ten vehicles was in 1946, the year before the *Nasookin* was replaced by the M.V. *Anscomb*.

the spring thaws. To properly understand the problems, it is first necessary to look at the nature of the terrain and its ice-age history.

The geology of the Okanagan Basin was greatly affected by a large glacier that completely blocked the valley close to Vaseaux Lake and formed a glacial lake many hundreds of feet in depth. The ancient shorelines are visible on the mountainsides today. Glacial action produced benches and terraces alongside Okanagan Lake in many places, and the soil is comprised of clay and silt from the lakewater deposition, interspersed with granular deposits in the haphazard geology that glaciers create. Between Penticton and Peachland, there are many high benches of deep silts and clays heavily eroded with sharply incised runoff channels and high bluffs near the lake edge.

In the 1920s these benches became the site of most of the fine orchards which were to give the area its reputation as a fruit-producing area. As they expanded their operations, the fruit farmers began irrigating heavily, with modern pumps drawing water from the lake. Nowhere was the benefit of thorough irrigation as a means towards increased fruit production more earnestly pursued than at the Dominion Government Experimental Farm located on one of these benches a few miles north of Penticton. This area has been named Sage Mesa by imaginative land developers in recent years.

Unfortunately, the lacustrine silts and gravel deposits placed there by glacial action, when subjected to excessive amounts of water, demonstrate a phenomenon known as "piping." Subsurface water conveyed in this manner often causes disastrous settlements or mudflow slides when it finds relief from underground pressure as it meets the face of an escarpment. In 1924 the irrigation water met the bluffs between Peachland and Penticton, the mud slides started, and it took many years to stop this nightmarish process.

Nowhere was the problem more pronounced than at the Experimental Farm itself, in a land movement that soon gained the name "the Experimental Farm slide." The road there, which ran along the lake edge, was so often subjected to running mud, and beleaguered motorists were so often in need of rescue, that the senior staff of the Farm wrote to Gwyer in 1927 suggesting forcefully that he relocate the road back from the lake, a course of action that was impossible due to the many gullies to be crossed. On September 3, 1927 Gwyer wrote to Assistant Farm Superintendent, R.C. Palmer:

> There is not the slightest hope of the Department abandoning the lower road. A bill will be submitted to you covering the total expense incurred this year in opening the road. I have decided to forget the expense incurred last year.

There can be no question of an argument between you and I, as our legal departments can very easily determine the responsibility as to who should pay. The Act is quite clear as to damage caused to Crown highways through irrigation operations, and I think that your Department is in the same position as a private individual in-so-far-as the rights of Crown highways.[4]

As time would tell, Gwyer was deluding himself if he expected a senior government to accept from a junior government the same treatment a private individual would receive.

Others besides the farm staff were concerned about the problem, as demonstrated by a fiery letter, dated September 9th, from the Similkameen M.L.A. J.W. Jones, who wrote to Deputy Minister Pat Philip:

I am forced to write to you in this matter as the Public are getting furious over the dilly-dallying methods in handling this piece of work. Your engineering department seems to be up a tree as to know what to do with it, and this is the third time a slide has occurred at this point, and the slide is now into its third or fourth week and is worse than ever.

A simple manner to get around the difficulty is to build a plank causeway or low bridge giving sufficient clearance for slush to pass into the lake. Two or three days and the work would be completed.

In fact, an eight-foot by six-foot timber culvert was installed, and for many months the mud was flushed through this in a flume, with none reaching the highway. Over the years there were to be many more such situations in which a suggestion from a politician provided a solution to a problem.

Jones's forthright manner did not save him from a certain ignominy of his own when he later became Minister of Finance under Tolmie, a thankless job that earned him the nickname "One percent Jimmy Jones" from the income tax he introduced while in that position. The unpopular tax applied to all single men earning more than fifteen dollars a month, and to married men bringing in twenty-five dollars or more.

By December 1928 Gwyer was shifted first to Prince Rupert, then on a rush assignment to survey and design the Big Bend Highway, one effort of the Liberals towards re-election. He worked very hard on it and gained Pat Philip's sincere praise, but when the Conservatives came into power, the new minister, Nelson Lougheed, refused to return him to Penticton. After a period of indecision which Philip described as the "interregnum," Gwyer disappeared into oblivion.

An interesting footnote to Gwyer's brief time as District Engineer at Prince Rupert was a task he undertook in locating a road east from the coast to the town of Terrace. Having decided it was impossible to use the north bank of the Skeena River because the railway was there first, he advertised across Canada for expertise to prepare B.C.'s first aerial photographic survey to seek another route. In fact, this innovative alternative to scrambling through the Coast Mountains turned out to be quite impractical as the aircraft of that day could not fly high enough, but it did demonstrate yet again his pathbreaking, fearless nature, quite uncharacteristic of the conventional civil servant. The road was eventually built alongside the railway.

Gwyer's departure was unfortunate for the Department, but good for the peace of the Okanagan mails, as yet another strong character came on the scene of the Experimental Farm contest. The new Farm superintendent, W.T. Hunter, had (fortunately for him) a much milder antagonist in the person of G.C. Mackay, Gwyer's successor. Hunter's letter of December 24, 1927 summarized his viewpoint:

> We have been only too willing to co-operate with you to the fullest extent to handle the difficult situation at the slide. However the responsibility for the slide is not ours. The slide has been caused by underground seepage and not by carelessness on the part of our Station in the handling of irrigation water.

Throughout the dispute Hunter maintained that as nobody could prove that the Farm actually poured water down the face of the bluff, the facility was not to blame. He also became abusive and threatening in the letter. Finally, Mackay wrote to his Deputy Minister:

> I am at a loss to understand the meaning of Mr. Hunter's letter, as I have always been on the best of terms with him. For my part I intend to remain on these terms.

However, he ended the letter with a recommendation that the Dominion Government be charged with the cost of all damage for the last five years. This was submitted to Ottawa and predictably rejected.

In this on-going dispute, Pat Philip then had the District Water Engineer measure the water metered to the Farm that year and determine the acreage irrigated. The results indicated that the Farm was irrigating at 3.7 acre feet (an acre foot is the amount of water covering an acre to one foot deep, roughly 270,000 imperial gallons), as against their permit for 3 feet. This despite the fact that all others in the area were restricted to 2.5 acre feet! Following this revelation, Philip persuaded the Hon. R.W. Bruhn to write to the federal Minister of Agriculture, who, in turn, referred the letter on to the Director of Experimental Farms for the government, whose comment was:

> Apparently there is a peculiar strata somewhere in the Summerland Station which allows the seepage of surface water, which finds its way to the banks, as is the case in other parts of the highway. I do feel however that this Department is not in any way negligent and we cannot be held in any way responsible for these slides.

Even a visit to the national capital by the B.C. Minister and his Deputy seemed to be of no avail, although Hunter resigned rather suddenly about this time. When his successor took over, he refused even to discuss the matter for six months. Meanwhile, the slides continued: between 1924 and 1943 there were twenty-five slides at this point, of which seventeen blocked the road for between three and six weeks. The Department used its first hydraulically operated, tractor-towed earth scraper on the job in 1929, and with a cable dragline working at the higher elevations moved dirt in large quantities. This is the reason why the lake is so shallow and full of reeds in some areas today. The road was eventually relocated out from the bank across some—by now—shallow bays. It was surveyed in 1935, but not built until 1939, as part of a Dominion Government fifty-fifty tourist highway building program.

Much later, in 1977, the Ministry of Highways conducted a study of the piping problem in the West Bench/Sage Mesa area,[5] and on special request made an assessment of the "potential evapotranspiration" at the Experimental Farm site. The study came up with the figure of 2.5 acre feet as the maximum irrigation possible without fear of slides, exactly the figure recommended by Gwyer in 1924.

This chronic struggle around Okanagan Lake did not prevent the progressive hard-surfacing of the Okanagan Highway, part of Premier Patullo's paving program between 1936 and 1940. Funding came from a Dominion/Provincial Works Agreement signed in July 1936, which finally saw the province come out from the grip of relief camp under-achievement, but even at that the government tried to do far too much with far too little. The idea was a good one but difficult to implement properly: offer numerous road contracts and let the contractors provide work for the unemployed. Late that summer forty-one road reconstruction projects were called to tender, and thirty-seven were let to contract, with four going to day labour.

The total price tag for all of these came to $1.4 million, an average of $35,000 per contract, and for this they reconstructed 138 miles of roadway, an average of 3.3 miles per job. Two Vancouver contractors, General Construction and Dawson Wade, received seven and six contracts respectively; two Alberta firms, W.C. Arnett and Fred Mannix and Co., won three apiece. This program, and the paving associated with it, petered out in the next year or so, and the drought in road contract work came back, but it did achieve one thing: it interested out-of-province contractors in B.C., and that was to be significant in the postwar years, when the door was opened to highway construction in British Columbia.

However, Duff Patullo did not fare well from this reconstruction largesse. It favoured the Interior too much over the Coast, and was too obviously politically selective in the choice of where the work was done, spotty and short-lived though the results were. British Columbia needed distance in its highway building, and to get that it had to spend money.

The Liberals went to an election in 1941, losing eleven seats. With various realignments of political groups into coalitions, Patullo had to step down in favour of Liberal leader John Hart, who put in a healthy six years as Premier. After nearly a year of the Public Works mantle being passed between elected members on a month by month basis, it finally settled on Herbert Anscomb, a Conservative from Victoria, who took over in September of 1942. Anscomb stayed in the position for almost four years and proved to be one of the best.

In 1940 the King George VI Highway, built to connect Patullo's bridge to the U.S.A., was opened with great fanfare, along with other four-lane connections. That same year the Big Bend Highway also became a reality. Arthur Dixon continued as Deputy Minister, soon to be assisted by A.L. Carruthers, who was promoted from Bridge Engineer to Chief Engineer in 1943.

Carruthers became a legend in the Department for the excellence of the bridges he constructed. He had a passion for bridges, a passion he never lost even as he moved up the ladder to Deputy Minister in later years. The story goes that he habitually fell asleep while being driven throughout the province, but always woke up when a bridge was approached. While working as a consultant after his retirement, Carruthers allegedly fell off the Peace River Bridge, but was rescued unharmed. He lived on well into his nineties.

Besides the new Minister and Chief Engineer, there was also a forceful new Assistant Chief Engineer in the person of H.C. (Harry)

Bridges Fit Strong and Handsome

When he was Bridge Engineer in 1942, A.L. Carruthers produced a remarkable booklet entitled *Bridges Fit Strong And Handsome*.[6] A copy of this beautifully bound and illustrated booklet is still treasured in the Bridge Branch of the Ministry. It is an eloquent plea to his colleagues for purity of line and form in the design of bridges and a rejection of redundancy and crudity which he abhorred. The booklet is signed December 25, so it was presumably a Christmas present.

The booklet contains pictures of twenty-four bridges, seven of which are in British Columbia, and describes their fine features and their relationship to their surroundings. B.C. bridges include the second Alexandra Bridge, the Hagwilget Suspension Bridge at Hazelton, several prewar concrete bridges that are rather "art deco" in appearance, and the Cottonwood River Bridge at Prince George.

Carruthers is quite lyrical in his prose and even quotes verse occasionally. Rejecting the word "beauty," he goes deeply into technical details of how to design "handsomeness" into bridges. These two quotations capture the direction of his thinking and illustrate that B.C.'s bridges were in good hands!

"Dead useless weight should be avoided even in piers. A deck structure with solid balustrade, a deep heavy floor system cantilevered far over open lattice trusses, supported by tall slim unbattered piers, which disappear into soft ground or water, gives one the same feeling as a tall, anaemic, thin-legged man standing ankle deep in a bog and supporting a big pack on his back.

"There must be no superfluous weight, no fuss about anything, proper proportions, manifest fitness and strength throughout. It should be handsome rather than beautiful. If, in addition, grace is achieved, the result is a triumph."

Anderson, appointed in 1943. The team of Anscomb, Carruthers, and Anderson was ready for the great things that began to unfold in 1944.

Early in the year three survey parties, later followed by two more, set out to locate and survey a highway from Prince George to Commotion Creek, near the present town of Chetwynd, through the Pine Pass of the Rocky Mountains' Misinchinka Ranges. This total of 181 miles linked up the Peace River Block, centred in Dawson Creek, to the rest of B.C. (See full map of British Columbia.)

The Pine Pass, at 2850 feet, lies between the headwaters of Misinchinka Creek, a tributary of the Parsnip River, and the Pine River, all in the Peace River watershed. The crossing of the continental divide is much lower and slightly farther west, at Summit Lake, a settlement about thirty miles out of Prince George at elevation 2315 feet. The Pine Pass is the lowest of all the passes through the Rocky Mountains in B.C. The survey work was completed that summer and fall, and the design was concluded the following winter. Only in hindsight was this speed to prove regrettable.

B.C.'s highway design and survey crews had a banner year in 1944. As well as the work they carried out in the north, the surveyors undertook to survey and design to modern standards the long-awaited section between Hope and Princeton, and to do the same on sections of the Southern Trans-Provincial Highway farther east.

Within the following two years, tenders were called to construct some of the most difficult mileage in the province: 210 miles in the north and 127 miles from Hope to Kaleden Junction, in the south, a grand total of 337 miles. British Columbia was now into the road-building business in a big way.

The Pine Pass Highway, which became the Hart Highway, was a companion project to the Hope-Princeton, all of which was part of the Coast Connection from the Prairies. The Hart Highway was the first started and the last finished.

Originally, it was proposed to build only between Summit Lake, 30 miles north of Prince George, and Commotion Creek, 13 miles west of Chetwynd, a total distance of 151 miles. This distance was split into Sections A and B, with the dividing point at Pine Pass summit near Azouzetta Lake. The contract for Section A, which was 94 miles in length, went to Campbell Construction Company Ltd. of New Westminster, a company that had recently arrived from Ontario and was a front runner in the construction boom. The 57-mile Section B contract went to Fred Mannix Co. Ltd. of Calgary, Alberta. Shortly after they started work in August of 1945, these two contracting companies combined into a joint venture, calling themselves Campbell-Mannix. Soon after that, they realized the whole contract was in big trouble.[7]

The access roads leading to the construction zone at either end were in a very poor state. Campbell-Mannix appealed to the government to rebuild these roads from Prince George to Summit Lake, and west from Progress, a small hamlet about 24 miles west of Dawson Creek. Between Progress and Commotion Creek lay 62 difficult miles, especially the 28-mile section from Progress to East Pine, the lower crossing of the Pine River where there was a 10-ton capacity reaction ferry. Commotion Creek, 13 miles west of Chetwynd, was the site of B.C.'s first effort at an oil well, a dry one, and the Department of Public Works had assisted the Department of Mines in 1939 by making it accessible from East Pine with an ungravelled 16-foot-wide road starting from the ferry.

Building in the Peace River gumbo without the benefit of gravel begged for desperate trouble when it rained. The rumour that to walk on it in the wet meant you progressively got taller as the gumbo built up under your shoes was quite true. It was also true that in the very worst of such conditions vehicles literally ground to a halt as the mud built up inside their fenders.

The government, when convinced of the "stickiness" of the problem, hurriedly called more contracts for reconstruction between Prince George and Summit Lake, and from East Pine to Progress, designated Sections C and D respectively. Campbell-Mannix was the successful tenderer in both cases, ending up with four contracts, 31, 94, 57, and 28 miles in length, for a total of 210 miles.

On the Hope-Princeton Highway, contracts were let early in 1946 to Emil Anderson Contracting Company Ltd., recently established in Hope from out of province, for the 28-mile section from Hope to Skaist River; to W.C. Arnett & Co. Ltd. of Grand Prairie, Alberta, previously brought in by the 1936 spate of contract work, for Skaist River to Princeton, 56 miles; to Campbell Construction Co. Ltd., for Princeton to Hedley, 23 miles; and finally to W.C. Arnett & Co. Ltd. for the Keremeos-Kaleden section, 20 miles, the last two contracts being called later.

It was the perception at the time that the Province seemed hung up on a small, select group of contractors whose estimators were expert at shaving their quotes closer to the edge than most. This evidently carried on up to W.A.C. Bennett in 1952 as indicated in an exchange between the new Premier on his first day in office and some unnamed official of the Department:

> I phoned down to the Department of Public Works, "Cancel all these preferred lists. Let everyone tender." "Everyone?" "Yes, everybody." "They might not be able to do the job!" "You get the deposit; you have the holdback. Give them a chance. Everybody!"[8]

Bennett thereby completely discouraged the process of pre-qualification of contractors on Public Works projects for at least the next thirty-five years, something that the Province has not missed during that time. P.A. Gaglardi, Bennett's first Minister of Public Works, echoed his boss in opposition to this protection of contractors against themselves by one of his more notable pronouncements: "Every man has the God-given right to go broke!"

The late Neil McCallum, Chief Engineer when Bennett became Premier, heatedly denied that there was a preferred list in Highways, but Bennett's words as quoted above do suggest that there might have been some sort of unwritten prequalification in effect. Be that as it may, the Province was highway-contractor-poor because so few contracts had been called during and immediately after the war, so it could be said that the few existing contractors were the result of no work rather than preferential treatment.

The decision to call very large contracts on both the Hart Highway and the Hope-Princeton attracted large out-of-province contractors, well funded and well experienced elsewhere in Canada. These out-of-province companies were generally successful in obtaining contracts immediately. Not completely understanding the construction problems related to B.C.'s mountainous terrain, they tended to bid low. They soon became fully aware of the problems!

At the time, many professionals thought that the second contract on the Pine Pass route, from Summit Lake to Azouzetta Lake, was too long at 94 miles. By the end of 1947 they turned out to be right. The contractor was in trouble, having only 26 percent of the job done while expending over 40 percent of the funds. Better progress was made in some of the other sections, with two of them even ahead of schedule.

By 1948 on the Hart Highway the Department was mired in litigation as well as mud. There were numerous claims based upon the specifications and the very poor condition of the government road between projects, particularly the section between East Pine and Commotion Creek, the last eight miles of which became totally impassable at one time. The government was forced to act when the contractor's financing collapsed, and on August 13 the Department finally closed down the Summit Lake to Azouzetta Lake job and seized all the equipment.

Soon after this, the situation became vastly complicated by the fact that all the road contractors throughout B.C. had gone to court as a group claiming extra costs because of the postwar enactment of the Hours of Work Act, which made them pay overtime past an eight-hour working day. Quite rightly, they said that this made it impossible for them to carry out their existing contracts, and a judge ruled in favour of an increase. On the Hart Highway it was 30 percent on Sections A and B, and 20 percent on sections C and D. Settlement was made by the John Hart Highway Act of 1949, which compensated Campbell $515,042.30 letting him off finishing his job altogether, and awarded Mannix $1,229,274.51.

The unbuilt roadway between Summit Lake and Azouzetta Lake was split into two new contracts for completion; totalling 70 miles, both were won on competitive tender by W.C. Arnett & Co. Ltd., for an additional cost of $1,824,000. The final bill for the 210 miles was $5,411,520, or $27,000 per mile, half as much again as first indicated. The most embarrassing thing of all for the Department— aside from the 35 percent overrun—was probably the Annual Report of 1946-47 wherein the Chief Engineer, A.L. Carruthers, wrote that both the Hart Highway and the Hope-Princeton Highway would be finished in 1947. In fact, the Hope-Princeton Highway was unveiled on November 2, 1949, and the Hart Highway was

124

opened on July 1, 1952 by short-term Minister of Public Works, E.T. Kenney, towards the end of his seven months in office.[9]

Aside from the delay in its completion, the penalty that the public paid for the mismanagement of the 94-mile contract from Summit Lake to Azouzetta Lake was the reduction in standards that took place. With the compromises made in roadway width and substitute contract negotiations, it was to be a good ten years after the opening before the whole highway was brought to a satisfactory standard sufficient for paving.

On the Hope-Princeton Highway, the overrun situation turned out to be much worse. Department rumour through the years has been that the job was estimated at three million dollars and cost twelve. This was not true, but all four original contracts were heavily overrun by a total of 166 percent. It must be remembered that bid prices are not the total charges properly made to these projects: materials purchase, engineering, and contingencies are legitimate additions.

There was another job thrown in: the Hedley to Keremeos section, which was done by day labour at $366,618. As well, a difficult section called the Waterman Hill was added to the Keremeos-Kaleden contract. A very steep and winding descent to Okanagan Falls on the Okanagan Highway just south of Kaleden, Waterman Hill became particularly notorious when prohibition of liquor licences in the Penticton area established Okanagan Falls as a watering hole. Fortunately, the drivers were sober on the way down but their weaving on the way back made the drive rather unpredictable for others!

Finally, the paving of the whole thing brought the entire cost of the project to $11,643,067 for a total of 126 miles. This was close to the rumoured $12 million figure ($92,000 per mile as against the bid price of $29,000 per mile). In retrospect, it is obvious that the $3 million estimate came only from the grading projects first called, and did not include the huge amount of paving and extra work that was done to produce the final package.

As a later inquiry into overruns on another highway project was to indicate, overruns of this magnitude totally offset the competitive bidding process. Chief Engineer Harry Anderson at times adhered more to the spirit than to the letter of the construction policy of the Department, but he did get the job done, at a time when the people of the province still put more store by that than they did in looking at the money spent. Harry Anderson had spent his whole career building highways with great enthusiasm, even while he had to compromise and cut corners on projects he would rather have seen completed with more inspiration and generosity. Anderson fully intended the Hope-Princeton Highway to be the finest achievement of his career, and he certainly did not want to pinch pennies when it came to fulfilling that dream.

As good fortune would have it, his friend and colleague from Public Works was now the Minister of Finance, a fact that undoubtedly loosened the purse strings a little more than might otherwise have been the case. Anderson delighted in telling anyone who would listen to him that by one stroke of a blue pencil he had cost the Province a million dollars by easing the curve at the end of the Whipsaw Creek Bridge.

The road, and the achievement that it represented, was Harry Anderson's alone, and no one at the summit opening that sunny November day could doubt it. When he drove back to Hope in his Cadillac, he scorned the procession and drove on the wrong side of the road all the way; those travelling with him were forced to the conclusion that had they met another car on the Skagit Bluff curves, he would have died in the collision a happy man. Anderson had, however, thoughtfully arranged in advance for Departmental personnel to stop all eastbound vehicles at Hope until the opening traffic had returned. There was a fatality later in the day when a westbound motorist left the new pavement in a light evening frost.

The pamphlet issued at the ceremony gave honour to an earlier Anderson, Alexander Caulfield Anderson, and contained this eloquent paragraph:

> It is the longest modern highway project ever to be undertaken by the Provincial Government. Its builders have been inspired with the same sort of ambition that took Anderson and his five companions on their quest for "a western passage." The skill of engineering, from location to the last yard of paving, gives British Columbia cause for pride and gratification. The highway is no less a monument to the present-day engineer, the steam-shovel and bulldozer and truck crews, than to the men who pioneered with axe and mule team.

The verdict on the Hope-Princeton Highway is that its opening in 1949 was a milestone in the development of British Columbia, especially the southern Interior. It was not built to an extravagant standard, but given the times and technology, it was fully adequate and did lend itself easily to the continual improvement and widening that has been going on ever since.

It is to the great credit of those who planned its construction that they did not stop the road at Princeton. The link was just part of a package extending right across the province to Alberta. In the years following, especially from 1949 to 1967, extensive reconstruction was a feature of the landscape easterly along the southern boundary of the province: over Anarchist Mountain, through Midway and Grand Forks, and on past Creston and Cranbrook.

Ernest Crawford Carson's six-year tenure as Minister of Public Works certainly provided a firm foundation for the expansion and consolidation of B.C.'s highway system up to 1952. This gentle, positive man from a pioneer British Columbia family inspired confidence that spread throughout the whole Department. The following anecdote spotlights the nature of this likeable man, who habitually drove around the province unaccompanied in a large DeSoto sedan. Always visiting the district offices without pomp or fanfare, he knew his territory like few other people in his or any other position of leadership.

A Divisional and a District Engineer found themselves early one Sunday morning at the site of flooding on an Interior highway. There they discovered a motorist bogged down in a washed-out section and got to work to help dig him out. In the midst of this, the Divisional Engineer's wife arrived to advise that Minister Carson had phoned their home. After being told of the flood situation, Carson was patient and encouraging. It was only later that the officials found out that the motorist's wife had earlier called Carson in Victoria and given him a thorough dressing down on the state of the road. The motorist eventually wrote to thank everyone for the service he got, probably assuming that these senior officials of the Department had been sent to his rescue in response to his wife's phone call.

Byron Ingemar Johnson—known always as "Boss" Johnson—replaced John Hart as Premier in 1947. Elected in a by-election in New Westminster, Johnson carried on the tradition of pro-roads leaders in British Columbia, started by McBride and Oliver, discouraged a little by Tolmie, then carried forward strongly by Patullo and Hart. Johnson knew how to tap the many good minds pondering the future of the highway system in order to carry out his limitless plans. He was the right man for the postwar period from 1947 to 1952, when it was of the utmost importance to foresee what kind of highways were needed in the bright new period of expansion currently dawning in British Columbia.

The problem with the Interior highway system in 1949 was not one of capacity: no route in those days needed more than a two-lane highway, and few would for another two decades, other than the various city approaches. Neither was the problem a need for new routes; the Hart and Hope-Princeton Highways filled the two major gaps, and it would be well over a decade before any ferry routes, such as the one on Kootenay Lake, would prove inadequate for the traffic. The problem that had to be addressed was the low standards to which the various Interior routes had been built prior to the war. In part, technological advances that had inevitably been accelerated by wartime led not only to an increase in the number of motor vehicles but also in the quality, speed, and weight, especially in trucks.

The Fraser Canyon roadway, built twenty years before to eighteen feet width or less, provided one graphic example: at the east approach to the Alexandra Bridge there were three 180-degree hairpin switchbacks, back to back, all with 75-foot radius curves. A jeep or a Model T Ford would have to slow below ten miles per hour to get around such curves, and the chances of a modern bus or truck negotiating such conditions at all were negligible.

This was not by any measure the only bad section—Nine Mile Canyon was just as crooked, and the situation with some of the smaller bridges was desperate. The problems of the early commercial truck drivers of the Canyon, (including Alex Fraser, later to become Minister of Highways), were legion. They were all, from time to time, hauled back onto the road by Cog Harrington's tow truck from Boston Bar, despite the fact that the road was only open from May 1 to November 16 each year. Alex Fraser reported that after November 16 they sometimes shipped the trucks by CPR flatcar between Hope and Ashcroft, and the drivers rode in the unheated cabs to save a fare. The truckers were a down-to-earth group never lacking for a sense of humour, even when that was almost all they had to support themselves at times.

For a colourful account of what was going on in the Fraser Canyon by 1949, who better to turn to than well known B.C. journalist, Paul St. Pierre. He describes the Canyon activities in a report to the *Vancouver Sun* dated September 30, 1949:

> They're changing the face of the old Fraser Canyon. For 90 years it's been famous for high mountains, short days, and winding treacherous roads. The mountains are as high as ever as any tourist can see, and they still keep the sides of the canyon in shadow most of the day. But men and machinery are changing the road. They are widening that long notch which Her Majesty's Royal Engineers scored along these cliffs between the years 1859 and '63.
>
> It's a massive piece of high level road construction.
>
> Construction men are riding their bulldozers today with death hundreds of feet below them, off-elbow as they mould the mountains into a modern highway. When the last of their series of jobs are done the old 16 foot wide road will have spread to 30 feet for its whole length from Yale to Lytton. Blacktop will be 24 feet wide, there will be a three foot gravel shoulder on each side, and on the bad corners high concrete retaining walls.[10]

This initial work was courageous, but the contracts were only in

Happy Funerals

In the summer of 1950, my parents visited from Scotland and we treated them to a drive from Kamloops to the coast. At one point we found ourselves parked on a grasshopper trestle near Hell's Gate waiting for some blasted rock to be cleared.

With every thrust of the bulldozers the flimsy structure shuddered and swayed, and my father, who had a fear of heights and was sitting in the front passenger seat on the "drop away" side, became understandably nervous. After we started off again, I noticed that he seldom looked out the side window, preferring instead to stare fixedly ahead.

We then picked up a hitchhiker with his right arm in a plaster cast. He turned out to be a most affable and talkative individual who insisted on telling us in great detail how he had sustained his injury when his car went over the bank. In fact, he showed us exactly where this had happened as we passed the spot, and he went on to point out the sites of other accidents, describing the injuries sustained and the fatalities registered.

By the time the hitchhiker left us at Yale, my father was slumped down in what appeared to be a terrified stupor. As farewells were being taken, though, he roused himself. Recognizing the humour of the situation, and with a twinkle in his eye, he wished our passenger, "Happy funerals!"

---

the hundreds of thousands of dollars, i.e. Alexandra Lodge East, one mile, Highway Construction Company, $364,574.60—the contract work witnessed by Paul St. Pierre. It took contracts in the millions and another six or seven years with the Trans-Canada Highway agreement in place before the Fraser Canyon Highway reconstruction really got under way.

Another inadequate section of this highway was from Cache Creek south, paved in 1949 to only eighteen feet wide and with no shoulders. The alignment in many places made 90-degree turns to follow land boundaries.

The bottom line was that by 1949 the Department was faced with the job of almost completely rebuilding its Interior highway system to suit the modern highway standards developed by its neighbour to the south for postwar highway vehicle needs. Neither the Hope-Princeton Highway nor the Hart Highway were included in this category, as their standards were more advanced.

The Hart Highway had been designated a "road to resources" under a program which had a proviso that the maximum grade would be 7 percent and the sharpest curve 10 degrees (574 feet radius). This radius curve had a maximum safe speed of slightly over forty miles per hour. Both the Hart and the Hope-Princeton Highways tried to achieve this standard and they generally did. There

The Slingshot Landing

British Columbia's interior lakes can be very stormy at times, and none more so than Kootenay Lake. In the early 1950s the last surviving sternwheeler, the S.S. *Moyie*, broke its sternwheel shaft while navigating near Kaslo and ended up on a beach— fortunately, not a rocky one. After tying the sternwheeler up to a tree and drawing the fires to avoid sparking a forest fire in the windy conditions, the crew awaited rescue. They hooked in to a nearby telephone line and sent out a "call for assistance,"— radios at that time being too modern a contraption for sternwheelers to carry.

By maritime custom, such a call must be heeded by any vessels within reasonable distance, so the Department of Public Works ferry, M.V. *Anscomb*, after unloading its passengers and vehicles, sailed north from Balfour.

The *Anscomb* arrived after dark, and because it drew too much water to get closer than 200 feet, put out a line to its sister in distress and pulled the *Moyie* off. No one thought to disconnect the mooring line with the result that both the tree and the telephone line broke! The *Anscomb* then set off south with the old sternwheeler wallowing along 200 feet behind. Lacking any suitable working winches, they could not shorten the tow, making it most difficult to deliver the old vessel to its dock at Procter.

Captain Don MacPherson decided to execute what is called in towboat vernacular a "slingshot landing." Stopping his vessel and using it as a fulcrum, he swung the *Moyie* on the end of its line like a bob on a pendulum, locating his ship with such precision that the arc of the towline intersected the dock on the shoreline. With darkness and strong currents, it is quite remarkable that he delivered the old girl to her dock so gently.

---

was a pitch on the west side of Azouzetta Lake which exceeded 7 percent for some years, and the Whipsaw descent from the west on the Hope-Princeton exceeded that limit and still does.

Both highways were paved with a 24-foot-wide, machine-laid pavement originating from the new paving plants and pavers, with three-foot-wide gravel shoulders. In retrospect, B.C.'s citizens might well have rejoiced that their highway administrators took so long to build these two highways, as prewar and postwar standards were light-years apart.

Contracts started coming out on the Trans-Canada Highway, both in the Canyon and east and west of Kamloops and Salmon Arm, and on the Southern Trans-Provincial Highway east of Osoyoos. The pace accelerated each year through to 1952, especially after the 1948 passage in Ottawa of the Trans-Canada Highway Act, even though the financing did not come to the provinces until later. In this period, according to Neil McCallum, Assistant Chief Engineer at the time, the basic blueprint for B.C.'s present highway system was laid down under the leadership of Ernie Carson and Boss Johnson.

Unfortunately, Premier Johnson extended the tradition of Premiers of British Columbia suffering accident or illness when out of the province. On September 24, 1950, while travelling by car from Quebec City to Ottawa, he was involved in a serious automobile accident. He remained in hospital in Quebec until mid-October when he was transferred to a B.C. hospital by the Royal Canadian Air Force.

Johnson was discharged finally in mid-December, but he never fully recovered and soon retired from the political scene. In his aging years, he suffered both physically and financially until in 1959 Premier W.A.C. Bennett arranged for him to receive a pension of $5000 a year. To arrange for the pension required a special Act of the Legislature, which greatly disturbed Mrs. Johnson, but she finally accepted it on her husband's behalf.[11]

With the ousting of Herbert Anscomb as Minister of Finance, the long period of coalition cooperation began to come unstuck once and for all. During the war, the political parties had quite correctly agreed to lay down their swords for the greater good, but after the war they were so comfortable with the coalition arrangement that they were very slow to return to the more adversarial and critical role political parties are expected to fill in a democracy. Neither the Liberal nor the Conservative parties read the public impatience in time to save their political credibility. It was a costly mistake that effectively removed them from influence for the next forty years.

William Andrew Cecil Bennett, M.L.A. for South Okanagan, was one politician who did demonstrate an astuteness that was to catapult him into power for more than twenty years. In 1951 he crossed the floor of the House, not only deserting the Conservative party but also laying the groundwork for establishing his own B.C. Social Credit Party. After a double election in 1952, Social Credit first became a minority government and then received a resounding majority. The province was headed down a critical path of dynamic change and leadership never experienced before; and swept along into this new era was the Department of Public Works and the highway system of British Columbia.

Postwar Planning Group

Left to right: H.C. Anderson, Assistant Chief Engineer; A.L. Carruthers, Chief Engineer; Hon. Herbert Anscomb, Minister of Public Works; Arthur Dixon, Deputy Minister of Public Works.

Published in the D.P.W. Annual Report for 1943, this picture shows the group that planned the postwar resurgence of highway construction in British Columbia. While they all started the major undertakings of the Hope-Princeton Highway and the Hart Highway, only Anderson remained in office long enough to witness the debut of the Hope-Princeton six years later. Both Dixon and Carruthers were among the first District Engineers appointed in the province.

The Canyon Road—
Some Light
in the Darkness

As the 1950s come to a close the highway through the Fraser Canyon starts to come into the sunshine

R.G. Harvey collection

Although the looming mountain slopes bring the shadows early, there were parts of the highway where the sun did shine for the motrists as can be seen on the photograph to the left. But the slopes were awfully steep! This section near to Hell's Gate was one where four lanes were impossible, with a railway below and an unstable hillside above. This led the Provincial Government in 1977 to the decision to build the Coquihalla Highway.

... And a Canyon within a Canyon

Nine Mile Canyon is about six miles north of Boston Bar. Until May 26th, 1958, it was a trial to anyone driving the Fraser Canyon Road. There the old road snaked steeply down the eroded and sliding slopes of the canyon within a canyon containing the creek of its name, and after negotiating the high horseshoe trestle bridge—shown in the photograph on below—the northbound driver faced an equally steep climb back up the northern slope, includ-

ing two switchbacks, to a point about one thousand feet from the point of descent. The day is notable because it saw the opening of a new 700-foot-long steel bridge, substituting this length for over two miles of hair-raising travel, especially in winter. It was well worth the one million dollars it cost.

Courtesy of the Transportion Collection

133

Philip Arthur Gaglardi

134

CHAPTER SIX

1953–1972

The Trans-Canada and the Southern Trans-Provincial Highways are rebuilt, with federal government help on the Trans-Canada. The Gaglardi regime yields to a gentler one. The bureaucracy builds problems for the future.

*T*HE REVEREND Philip Arthur Gaglardi, M.L.A. for Kamloops and first Minister of Public Works in the Social Credit government of Premier Bennett, blew in upon the Department, and particularly upon its engineers, with the force of a rare Northwest Pacific typhoon. Like the Douglas Firs of Vancouver's Stanley Park in such a storm, some stood against that force unbendingly and were uprooted and swept away, while other individuals with more resilience and less resistance gained strength and survived to grow steadily.

Gaglardi possessed many of the attributes necessary to become a great Cabinet Minister, but at first these were hard to see amid the sound and fury of his progress from evangelism to populist politics. In many respects, these were rather similar activities, which he presented to a bemused public in an outpouring of energy that confused some and delighted many.

Under the bombast that became his trademark lay a keen intellect and a remarkable astuteness, assisted by an uncanny sense for detecting dishonesty and prevarication. He also possessed a notable capacity to absorb information quickly, a valuable resource for a Minister of a large and active Department. Few Ministers of Highways since Gaglardi's time have had it; perhaps the one who came closest was Graham Lea in the shortlived N.D.P. government of Dave Barrett.

But most of all Gaglardi had one lethal weapon: his tongue. He could talk his opponents to a standstill, and often bring them

135

right over to his side as lasting supporters. An example of this was one occasion in the 1960s when he addressed the combined Chambers of Commerce of Northwestern B.C. The loggers had been waiting to cross-examine him on poor roads, but Gaglardi so swept them up in his oratory that when he left, to thunderous applause, no one had thought to bring up the matter. The editor of the local newspaper summed it up in his headline: "Gaglardi tells Chambers of Commerce to go to Hell and they give him a standing ovation."

Above all else, Gaglardi was an evangelist. He came into his new position with boundless fervour to move the Department over to his way of thinking, the same fervour he applied to bringing sinners to Christianity. All of the management of the Department who survived the transformation became "converts" to some degree, and some much more than others. However, the higher levels of the bureaucracy did take longer to become totally dedicated to his plans and ideas.[1]

The first major confrontation between the old way of doing things and the new was predictably Gaglardi's earliest relations with the Highway Board, that easy company of secure bureaucrats. However, in order to understand how his management strategy would affect the operation of the Department of Public Works, it is necessary to step back a decade and review the developments in the civil service structure leading up to his time as Minister.

From its earliest days the Department's line of authority was designed to quickly convey the desires of the Minister and the Cabinet to the civil servants for the necessary action to be taken. Because of its major significance in the province, Public Works had to be reactive to events—be they natural, economic, or political, especially the latter. The Minister's main contact was traditionally the Deputy Minister, who became the "political link"—the one who initiated or diverted departmental activities to suit the policies and urgencies of the politicians.

This process was normally carried out with the help of the Chief Engineer, the technical authority. There had to be give and take between these two officials, especially when it was not practical to enact the policies requested, either at all or in the time frame desired by the politicians. The crosscurrent of the political versus the practical was to be a major burden of the various Deputy Ministers throughout the years who, by necessity, had to combine diplomacy, persuasiveness, and mediation to keep everyone satisfied. Invariably their reputations as engineers were damaged as a result of the compromising involved.

The credibility and authority of the Deputy Minister were very important to the smooth running of the Department, especially during the coalition years when there were frequent changes of Minister. It was during Arthur Dixon's term (1934-47) that a major change took place in the chain of command, lasting from 1943 through to 1956. His Minister, Herbert Anscomb, was one of B.C.'s most effective Ministers of Public Works, a Conservative under a Liberal Premier, John Hart. If Anscomb chose to build a road in a Conservative riding, he was accused of bias, or if he did not build a road in a Liberal riding (for whatever valid reason), he was accused of political partisanship. His answer to this no-win situation was to create the Highway Board in 1943.

The Highway Board initially consisted of a Chairman who was the Chief Engineer and two members who were the Assistant Chief Engineer and one of the District Engineers. The Minister then had a wonderful answer to his critics when roads were built in locations not to their liking: "It's a Highway Board decision." Who could question that, especially when the leading technical authorities of the Department had made the ruling? It is notable that the Deputy Minister, who might be considered too close to the politicians to have totally objective judgment, was not appointed to the Board.

Anscomb had a statute passed in the Legislature to pay the Chairman of the Highway Board an additional remuneration that amounted to a 25 percent increase over his regular civil service salary. This placed the Chief Engineer at a higher salary than any other civil servant in the Department and established him quite solidly in the ascendancy over the Deputy Minister.

The Highway Board arrangement worked well for Anscomb and for his successor, Ernest Carson, another Conservative. In 1947 A.L. Carruthers became Deputy Minister, and Harry Anderson, a man with a very strong personality, moved up to serve under him as Chief Engineer. Carruthers was a technical authority in his own right from long service as a Bridge Engineer, a factor that tended to make him a less effective political link, even though the Ministers respected him. More of the political liaison function fell on Anderson, along with all his other duties and his role as builder of the Hope-Princeton and Hart Highways at that time.

Things went along quite well until 1948, when Carruthers retired and Anderson refused the job of Deputy Minister, which would have resulted in a loss of both pay and prestige for him. After a short tenure by a retired Deputy Minister of Public Works from Alberta, Evan Jones got the job, moving over from his role as District Engineer at New Westminster. Jones became an excellent political link for many years, while still remaining in the shadow of the Chief Engineer, who reigned supreme.

When the coalition collapsed with the elections of 1952, the Highway Board in its initial form should have gone with it. There was now a single party majority government with a strong Minister and Premier to guide the ship, but with the departure of Anderson to private industry, the chairmanship of the Highway Board was in the hands of Chief Engineer Neil McCallum, a man whose character was as strong and uncompromising as Phil Gaglardi's. Right from the start, it was inevitable that sparks would fly.

The story goes—(and Neil McCallum has confirmed it)—that when the new Minister of the Crown was first presented with a recommendation of the Board that went against his own wishes, he enquired as to why he was not the Chairman. When McCallum informed him that the Chief Engineer was "ex officio" Chairman, Gaglardi adjourned the meeting to consult the dictionary with McCallum. When he found out that the term meant "by reason of the position," he moved quickly to have the statutes amended.

Gaglardi lost no time in removing most of the decision-making authority of the Board as well as its extra remuneration, but he left it in place at the much reduced level of an executive committee that made recommendations to the Minister. Unlike some of his predecessors, Gaglardi had no intention of using the Board as an excuse for difficult decisions. However, he did leave McCallum's total salary untouched, so in effect he left the Chief Engineer as the most senior civil servant.

Unfortunately, not many months went by before he came to view his Chief Engineer as the "leader of the opposition" to his rather different theories, and with the top two links in the chain reversed, there was no one between the Minister and the technical authority who could successfully bridge the gap between them. After a few years, McCallum resigned.

For those who remained, this was sad indeed, for Neil McCallum was an excellent Chief Engineer and well liked. But as often happens in such circumstances a common adversity has a unifying and strengthening effect. In fact, the management group that evolved became one of the finest in the history of the Department. This was a good thing for the province and for Gaglardi in light of the huge highway-building program unfolding in British Columbia.

For a revealing look at Gaglardi's view of engineers, one need go no further than his recent biography, *Friend o' Mine*, published in 1991. It is obvious that he considered engineers to be the last people who should decide where highways were to be built:

An engineer is a very staid, solid individual who deals with facts but without imagination. . . . An engineer is not required to have vision. Why does an engineer need vision? All an engineer needs to know is what is the strength of a piece of steel or what type of material do I use in this type of soil after the soil has been tested and so on. An engineer is a man who comes up with the figures that he gets out of a book, and that he's been trained to follow just exactly the same as a train is told to follow on a track. That's what all professionals are taught to do. If you can find a professional that has vision plus the ability of what his profession requires, then you've found a genius, and they're very very scarce. An engineer can't have too much flexibility, so there's no use looking for those things in an engineer.[2]

Gaglardi brought the position of Chief Engineer down to one step below that of the Deputy Minister, where it remained thereafter, and he eventually appointed to the position an engineer from outside the Department, (which became the Ministry of Highways in 1955). That appointee, Fred Brown, successfully kept his name from public attention until 1963, probably at Gaglardi's insistence.

A spin-off from the change of function of the Highway Board was its concentration on settling claims for extra payment for highway contracts, an important contribution to the prevention of litigation throughout the years to come. In addition, the Board was an excellent and regular meeting ground for the Deputy Minister, who became the Chairman at no extra salary, and the technical staff, including the Chief Engineer.

Speculation that in the years to come a fully empowered Highway Board would have prevented major programming problems from arising in the Ministry is pointless: both in 1956 and in the years that followed, provincial politicians in power proved repeatedly that they were not ready to make nonpolitical the decisions of route and timing on major highway construction. This had not been the case under Anscomb—even then, the Board did not have decision-making powers: its function was advisory to the Minister, giving only the appearance of having more influence.

After McCallum left, Evan Jones took prominence as Deputy Minister and continued his quiet and skillful practice of political containment until his retirement in 1958. He oversaw in 1956 the reorganisation of the Ministry into four regions from the ten Engineering Districts that had remained from prewar days. The Engineering Districts were divided into thirty-one operational districts each covering one or more Electoral Districts. The operational districts were then split among the four regions. A new position of Assistant Deputy Minister was created in 1958.

Shortly after he came into power Phil Gaglardi fell into a practice

Introduction to the Chief

Not long after I became Regional Highway Engineer at Prince George in 1959, Highways Minister Gaglardi called a meeting of the four Regional Highway Engineers at Kamloops. I well remember his opening remarks on the first day—"Good morning, gentlemen. You are all doing a good job, except one or two." Despite his apparent desire to keep us on our toes, Gaglardi could not have been a more considerate patriarch when it came to personal misfortune or family ill health.

that was followed by Ministers after him (except for Wesley Black) without the benefit of Gaglardi's experience to control it closely. This practice was the appointment of his own men to report directly to him on the Department's activities. Originally, such appointments were made with the greatest of difficulty due to the power of the Civil Service Commission. At that time there were no such people as Ministerial Assistants or Executive Assistants for Ministers; W.A.C. Bennett would not stand for them, which was arguably one of the best things he ever did for B.C.

One of the first of these appointees, a construction supervisor by the name of P.A. Tondevold, appeared in 1956. He came from the U.S. Corp of Engineers in Alaska, and remained throughout his service an American citizen. Pat Tondevold was nicknamed "thunderbolt" from his early impact on the established bureaucracy of Highways, particularly those engaged in right-of-way acquisition. Told by Gaglardi to take over and expedite the rebuilding of the Hastings-Barnett street connection in Burnaby, Tondevold soon realised that one reason little was being done was that compensation settlements with the home owners were not complete.

These residents awoke one morning in amazed horror to find that the nice green front lawns and shrubbery separating their residences from the old roadway had disappeared almost overnight. They had been replaced by roughly excavated clay slopes, on the face of which Tondevold's men were erecting long wooden stairways so that they could reach their homes, while the power shovels and trucks continued widening the highway. It took a few days for residents to reach the Minister, and Pat Tondevold had been there first. They received little but assurances that they would eventually find it all for the best. Later Tondevold became the District Superintendent at Fort St. John. He was an unusual choice for the job, but he was a person who loved the north and left his mark.

The necessity to get your story in early was one essential principle of dealing with Gaglardi. If this were done before others reached him, it was rare indeed for him to reverse his decisions. The seeking of his attention in fact reached a peak later in his term of office when he had tired of being in Victoria (except during legislative sessions) and had set himself up in a penthouse suite at the Vancouver Hotel. This *modus operandi* that Gaglardi had acquired, which predated the creation of Cabinet offices in Vancouver, and which he combined with extensive use of his Lear jet, meant that the Minister was away from Victoria much of the time. When he did come to Victoria, he was constantly followed around by officials, including those at the very top, all carrying stacks of letters and files seeking decisions or signatures. Considering that his attendance at Cabinet meetings was reported to be about 50 percent, it was amazing that his Department functioned so well.

The relationship between Bennett and Gaglardi was a fascinating one. On Bennett's part there was an uncharacteristic reluctance to hold firm rein on Gaglardi, at least for the first half of his premiership. Gaglardi was always a loose cannon on the political deck (much as was Bill Vander Zalm under the younger Bennett's leadership). W.A.C. showed remarkable insight in realising early on that Gaglardi was the self-confident achiever he needed to offset his own shortcomings in politics and to add colour to the new party's image. While Bennett could be suave and charming in a one-on-one meeting, he was always rough and staccato on the speaker's podium. Gaglardi, on the other hand, was very impressive on the podium, but often rough and staccato face to face. Bennett always billed his Minister of Highways as "the greatest road builder since the Romans" until late in their relationship when he began to bypass his Minister of Highways to seek other opinions on highway costs and priorities. Even by his political opponents, the Premier was recognized as one of the most parsimonious and conscientious administrators of public funds the province ever had.

There was no doubt that Flying Phil would get things done. His energetic vision, however, introduced potential problems as the system was hardly capable of processing the work he envisaged. Particularly in contract administration, it proved somewhat difficult to maintain the basic Social Credit concept of carefully managed money. The new Premier was determined to do better than his predecessors, of whom he had been harshly critical when it came to control of both the method and the amount of public funds expenditure.[3]

Bennett resolved to be his own Minister of Finance, and he was, from late in 1953 until his retirement. Being a man of simple resolutions, he firmly held the purse strings and thereby effectively controlled his Cabinet and his Ministries. He brought in numerous rules for Treasury, and pledged himself to abolish secret Orders-in-Council, which he loathed. He is quoted as saying, "Before I am through every dime paid out by Government will appear in the Public Accounts, listed against the person who received it." This was a laudable goal for a man in public office, and Bennett was determined to carry it out.

In regard to public works Bennett's tactic was simplicity itself. He directed the introduction of an amendment to the Department of Public Works Act (to become Section 49), requiring all work to be let to tender, publicly advertised, and all bids to be opened in public. Awarding of contracts was always to the low bidder, with exceptions only by Cabinet approval. As a result, Bennett's control of Public Works expenditure, especially in its propriety, was completely successful.

The rule was simple and to the point: bid the job with everything out in the open, and take the lowest bid or explain to your colleagues in Cabinet why there should be more cost to the people of British Columbia than if you had accepted the low bid. There is nothing that Ministers dislike more than such a process, and the result was that, even with a fully legitimate reason for not accepting the low bid, Ministers have ever since almost always given instructions to their Deputy Ministers that the project should be retendered, rather than go to Cabinet for an Order-in-Council.

Gaglardi complied with the edicts, and among the hundreds of contracts that were tendered and awarded during his term in office, the number that did not go to the low bidder could be counted on the fingers of one hand. No awards were ever questioned on the legitimacy of the tendering process. However, the clauses giving flexibility to proceed in pressing emergency, or to do the work using employees of the Department, were bent frequently as the temptation to avoid the delay involved in the tendering process was too strong at times.

The method of operation known as "day labour," where equipment is hired by the hour and directed by civil servants, is one that continues to be used by the Ministry. At one time Premier Bennett proposed that all day labour hourly rental work be advertised for tender, but this was found to be too cumbersome to be practical. The Department became the leader of what was called the rental rate committee, which included the Department of Agriculture and B.C. Hydro and published lists of reasonable rates for hired equipment. There was also a practice at one time of posting the names of equipment owners and the rotation roster of their hire at all district offices and yards.

The restrictive nature of contracts led Gaglardi to undertake a considerable number of projects by day labour. Some of these were quite large, particularly in the early 1960s, when he experienced several failures by contractors to complete the work, or at least to do it on time. He also set up several Ministry road construction units well equipped with the newest of earth-moving and rock-drilling equipment, some publicly owned and some hired. The advantage he found was that such a method of construction can be organised quickly, without detailed survey and design, and it could be commenced before purchase is made of all parts of the right-of-way. Above all, Gaglardi was always in a hurry!

This practice led to some criticism, especially about the widespread use of equipment owned by Prince George contractor Ben Ginter. At the time it was said that the highways were being built by the "Three G's Construction Company—Ginter, Gaglardi, and God." In fact, Ginter bid on and won many contracts; he became extremely astute in the bidding process even though he was not easy to deal with. It was necessary, when hiring his equipment by the hour, to look into the buckets of the motor scrapers regularly to make sure they were not moving about half full! When this powerhouse of the north was properly controlled, he achieved exceptional results.[4]

One reason Ginter and the Ministry did not fall into constant warfare in the last half of the 1960s was the good nature and common sense of Dudley D. Godfrey, who succeeded Fred Brown as Chief Engineer between 1964 and 1969. Although he was English by origin, Godfrey came from a career as a railway engineer in South America to positions as Divisional Engineer at Prince George and Regional Highway Engineer at New Westminster, before he became Chief Engineer in Victoria. A true "gentleman" in the original sense of the word, he was renowned for his geniality as well as for his recreational skills as an alpinist and skier even in his retirement years. In long and frequent meetings with Ben Ginter in Victoria, Godfrey demonstrated endless courtesy and patience, but he did not always overlook the constant criticism of Ministry field personnel that Ginter was prone to make. In one legendary meeting with Ginter and Gaglardi, he earned the nickname "tiger" for his spirited rebuttal of one accusation.

However, after a few years of jungle warfare, Dudley decided that the advantages of being at the top were far outweighed by the lack of skiing facilities near Victoria, and in 1969 he returned to the lower mainland to his previous position as Regional Highway Engineer. He was one of a number of excellent men who found the regions a preferable location to headquarters!

The program that Gaglardi accelerated and generally completed before he left office included practically the entire Interior two-lane highway system. (Four-laning in the Interior came after Gaglardi left, except for rare sections such as the Prince George bypass and the north approach to Kelowna.) The program also embraced the creation of a basic multi-lane highway system for the Lower Mainland. Gaglardi was the father of the Peace Arch/Tsawwassen/Deas Island Tunnel/Oak Street Bridge route into Vancouver, and he proclaimed his proposal for a ferry terminal on the sand flats near Tsawwassen and a tunnel under the river to be a triumph of vision over cold engineering fact.

The estimate, bid price, and final cost correlation of the Deas Island Tunnel was not without incident. Gaglardi had indicated to the Premier and to Cabinet that the cost would be $9 million, and when it finally came out at $16 million he was somewhat slow in advising them, especially Bennett. The latter became furious, and assessed every Ministry 5 percent of their year's estimates to finance the overage. It is reported that Bennett's emissary to the Highways Department was far more severe in the reduction of its funding.

One round Gaglardi did lose was the battle with Vancouver over a freeway system to its centre. However, he gained the satisfaction of building the Port Mann Bridge and B.C.'s first urban freeway through Burnaby right up to Vancouver's border before swinging into North Vancouver by the Second Narrows Bridge.

Of course, his riding of Kamloops was Gaglardi's first priority, and when public criticism of the number of contracts there became highly vocal, a popular but untrue tale in the Department surfaced that Gaglardi answered this by saying, "What's unfair! It's even-stephen—half to Kamloops and half to the rest of the province!" Be this as it may, it was the highway from his riding towards Vancouver that gave him his first major challenge: the rebuilding of the Trans-Canada Highway through the Fraser Canyon.

The Trans-Canada Highway Agreement signed between Ottawa and Victoria in 1950 was extended, let lapse, and then renewed again in 1962, with adjustments for the interim period. Throughout the term of the agreement, the highway was completed to two-lane standard throughout the Interior—from the Fraser Canyon to Revelstoke and on to Golden by the Rogers Pass, and then by the Kicking Horse Pass to Alberta, the sections through the National Parks being undertaken solely by the federal government. It was also substantially completed throughout the Lower Mainland and Vancouver Island. The last payment was made in 1970.

Ottawa agreed to pay half the cost of a two-lane highway, with the additional sweetener that the federal government would pay 90 percent of the cost of 10 percent of the mileage. British Columbia repeatedly urged that, in view of the difficulties of road-building in the province, Ottawa should relent on the two-lane rule and contribute to half of four or six lanes wherever traffic demanded such increased capacity. Disagreements about work done on the Second Narrows to Horseshoe Bay section without prior agreement resulted in the Province never being recompensed completely by Ottawa for its share of that costly urban construction. Much of B.C.'s bitterness was due to concessions given in Central and Eastern Canada, concessions that never got as far west as British Columbia.

Of course, the section of greatest interest to Phil Gaglardi was the one from Hope to Monte Creek, the end of his electoral district, twenty miles east of Kamloops. Reconstruction of this 190-mile section commenced in 1947, before the Trans-Canada was a national project, simply because the need was so great. In the twenty-year period to 1967, within which it was substantially completed (to two lanes at least—truck lanes and four-lane passing sections coming later), a grand total of $82 million was spent on it, an average cost over twenty years of $432,000 per mile.

The section in the Yale electoral district, from Hope to Spences Bridge, was the most difficult, comprising in cost $71 million out of the $82 million total, or $780,000 per mile. Both sections of highway had expensive structures built within them. The most notable in the Fraser Canyon was the third version of the Alexandra Bridge located a few hundred feet downstream from its predecessors. This crossing is 1600 feet in length, and its deck level is 220 feet above the low water level of the river. However, the Ministry had not much reason to be overly proud of this third version of the crossing as serious problems developed within its foundations, and the bridge's completion was about two years late. Fortunately, it did not delay the highway, but the final cost was almost twice the bid price.[5]

Other structures nearby, just as high, were the crossings of Nine Mile Creek and Anderson River; they were bridges to be proud of as the terrain challenged both bridge designers and builders. All of these structures removed narrow, winding, and steep crossings of creeks and rivers in favour of good roadway alignment and gentle grades. Farther up the route, the Thompson River was again crossed at Spences Bridge by a graceful new bridge with slender single-column concrete piers. This was part of a complete rebuilding of the difficult section from Lytton eastward, which included replacing Pat Philip's timber cribbing with modern steel binwalls.

Unique features of the road between Yale and Lytton were the tunnels. The first two were let to contract in 1956, and by 1963 there was a total of seven open to traffic, with the largest being the China Bar Tunnel. At more than 2000 feet in length, it came complete with its own electric generating plant to power its lighting, fans, and carbon dioxide monitoring plant. The smallest was the Hell's Gate Tunnel close to it which was just over 300 feet long. The total length of two-lane highway tunnelling was in excess of 6000 feet.

The obvious section to select for the 10 percent of the Trans-Canada mileage that was to be 90 percent a federal responsibility was the China Bar to Hell's Gate section: four and a half miles long including four tunnels and an overhanging concrete retaining wall called the Hell's Gate Structure, 250 feet in length.

The most expensive part of all was the China Bar Bluffs, 1.18 miles in length, which was bid at $2.2 million, and ended up costing a total of $5.4 million, probably the first ever two-lane highway construction costing in excess of $4.5 million a mile in Canada.

Structures of interest on the Revelstoke to Golden section included the graceful 950-foot-long suspension bridge at Revelstoke over the Columbia River, completed in 1961 at a cost of slightly over $3 million, and the two Albert Canyon bridges. There were also three snowsheds constructed by the Province, which naturally also ended up being selected for the 90 percent mileage claimed. These were located between Revelstoke and the Glacier National Park west entrance. There were eight similar snowsheds built by Canada within Glacier National Park.[6]

The 92-mile Rogers Pass route between Revelstoke and Golden was opened on July 30, 1962. The traffic immediately increased tenfold from that on the rough and dusty Big Bend! The cost in round figures was $50 million, or $540,000 per mile (compared to $780,000 per mile for Yale to Spences Bridge).

All of this stretched out in time from 1947 right through to 1962. Including $34 million for the 130 miles between Kamloops and Revelstoke, the Province paid out a total of $166 million ($260,000 per mile), for an excellent highway from Hope to Yoho National Park Boundary, a distance of 372 miles (not including Glacier Park mileage), of which money a good proportion came back; an achievement that would have given much amazement and a great deal of satisfaction to Sir Joseph Trutch had he been there to see his dream come true.

At the same time as all this was taking place, another large road-building program was under way about 130 miles farther south, also progressing from west to east. The Southern Trans-Provincial Highway between Osoyoos and Crowsnest Pass lies on the map along the United States border just like a knotted, twisted length of rope. Following the lakeshores and rivers, it makes its way over the eastern part of the Okanagan Highlands, then through and over the Monashee, Selkirk, and Purcell Ranges before passing through the Rockies by the Crowsnest Pass. (See map, "Highways, Mountains, and Summits," in the Introduction.)

The knots, which are usually at division points, are the towns and small cities along the way: places such as Greenwood, Grand Forks, Rossland, Trail, Nelson, Cranbrook, and Fernie. Tag ends give access south, and much less frequently north. In fact, this area has one of the closest trans-border relationships with the United States anywhere in the country, with ten border crossings at an average of twenty miles spacing. In contrast to this, the outlets north to the rest of the province are sparse, even today.

The first major postwar revision on this line of Coast Connection was started in 1949 from the eastern shore of Osoyoos Lake eastward to where Rock Creek flows into the Kettle River at a village of the same name. Climbing up out of the Okanagan Valley to the eastern half of the Okanagan Highlands, it took the traveller over a spectacular escarpment called Anarchist Mountain, the same mountain barrier that had forced HBC clerk and trailblazer, John MacKay, to circle south below the 49th parallel in 1830, and the same one that Dewdney had bypassed in his trail-building of 1865 when he started east of it.

The Southern California Automobile Club Road Bulletin of June 1, 1927 described the old road that originally had been built up the mountain in 1893, and no doubt had been improved by the time the description was written:

> A fair sandy road climbs over Anarchist Mountain (elevation 3800 feet) thence fair to good natural gravel road down through Kettle Valley to Midway.

A climb it was indeed, from about 920 feet above sea level at Osoyoos Lake to 3800 feet of elevation at Anarchist Summit all in ten miles (an average ascent of 288 feet per mile or 5.5 percent). By the old road there were eighteen switchbacks, later reduced to three with the new construction. While the auto club bulletin described it as a "fair sandy road," twenty years later, with traffic ten times as dense, its narrow washboard surface choked the driver in summer dust and terrified him in winter's snow and ice.

In the high plateau in the midst of this section lay Rock Creek Canyon, over 300 feet in depth and about 1000 feet wide. The Rock

Creek Canyon bridge spanning the canyon brought miraculous relief when it was completed in 1951. A 940-foot-long steel deck truss, its 740-foot main span was supported on two 90-foot high steel towers founded with great difficulty in the steep canyon slopes. At a cost of $1.1 million it seemed at first to match the highway as a bargain for the money at $45 per square foot, compared to the Alexandra Bridge at $120 per square foot. However, a few years later the concrete deck was found to be faulty and had to be replaced, which rather took the icing off the cake.

Bridging the Gaps

One of the favourite Ministry stories was the attempt to fill in the holes on the Savona Bridge near Kamloops on the Trans-Canada Highway route. This bridge had an open steel grid deck, rather like an egg-crate, with a multitude of openings about two inches wide by three inches long. Of course, these were no problem for vehicles, and there was a sidewalk for people to walk over the bridge as well, but the holes made this crossing totally impassable to herds of sheep.

In the late 1950s, the price of beef went down and local farmers turned to wool and mutton as a substitute income. They demanded that something be done to allow them to drive their flocks back and forth to pasture on either side of the bridge. Orders to comply were issued at the highest level, but the Bridge Branch was adamant that nothing could or should be done to the bridge for structural reasons. Staff suggested that the sheep be trucked across.

This was not acceptable locally, but from some still-mysterious source came the idea of using blocks of wood shaped to fit the holes in the grid, and hammered into place. The matter was complicated by the fact that the holes were not rectangular but oval in shape.

In short order, thousands of wooden blocks were ordered and delivered to the Kamloops Highways yard, an action which set up a loud protest from the engineers in Victoria who announced to all and sundry that the blocks would inevitably crack in winter and fall out in the hot, dry summer because the co-efficients of expansion for wood and steel are so different.

After this well advertised revelation, nothing further was said or done. The mountain of blocks remained, unshaped, in the Kamloops yard to the wonderment of visiting engineers for some time to come.

British Columbia was fully into its golden age of highway construction, and the resulting wide pavements, high-speed alignment, easy grades, and excellent bridges were a delight to the residents who had coped with the rough gravel roads and narrow timber bridges for so many years.

The survey and design of the initial work on the Southern Trans-Provincial Highway immediately after the war was to a remarkably high standard, for which the Province was to be grateful to its surveyors and engineers. Often supervised by ex-railway engineers forced out of retirement by the postwar decline of their investments, the young highway surveyors shared in an immeasurable pool of expertise and grassroots "know-how" under these veterans. Working alongside these penny-pinching graduates of the Depression, they also learned to be sticklers for accuracy. A typical individual was John Lillico, retired from the Southern Pacific Railway before the war and working for the Department until well over seventy years of age. While based in Kamloops, his idea of a Sunday afternoon stroll was to Tranquille and back, a return distance of about twenty miles.

It was a time of bright promise for any enterprising contractor capable of taking full advantage of the new highway-building equipment increasingly available from the revived postwar industry of the United States. Earthmoving was possible in volumes previously unthinkable, with larger tractors and bulldozers, and especially with the new rubber-tired motor scrapers first used widely in British Columbia on the Anarchist job.

The road surveyors on the Southern Trans-Provincial Highway in the 1950s were happy men—there was a joy and a freedom in the outdoor work in that beautiful countryside. Running line through the undisturbed forest among the trees, the bushes, the occasional wild flowers, and the vistas of mountainside and lake, they sometimes saw a deer, very occasionally an elk, and very very occasionally a black bear—never a grizzly, which was just as well as the men never carried rifles.

Little noise came from the small survey crew, two men with machetes and hand axes, followed by the chainmen, one either end of the hundred-foot-long "chain," actually a metal tape. They seldom needed to shout, the routine was so regular. The instrument man packed his fifty-pound transit and heavy tripod, set it up over the freshly re-set wooden hubs, and directed the lead man with hand signals. The lead man held the brightly striped picket and moved it side to side until he received a signal that it was on line; then he drove the stake on the spot.

The clearing contractor came next with his expert tree fallers, always moving ahead. The bucker skillfully trimmed off the springy boughs and sized the tree trunks into logs. The air smelled of fresh-cut timber—fir pitch, the tang of pine or spruce, the subtler smell of cedar—and the sharp, smoky smell of burning brush. Snorting and roaring machines brought the bright flash of a huge steel blade against the dark earth. Alongside their clattering machines, the stance of the rockdrillers was eery and sentry-like—grey-green men covered by the pall of dust their work produced. The sudden jar of the klaxon horn of the blasting crew warning of an impending blast, then a strange silence was broken by the mournful final cry of the powderman, "Fire, fire!" The crack and thump of the blast was followed by the sharp smell of the spent dynamite and shattered rock.

These hardy men even expressed a liking for the dust on the long, hot summer days. It made the icy-cold beer taste better in the small country beer parlour after work, especially on a really hot day after a dip in a quiet Kettle River pool. The comradeship of the evening meal in camp was followed by a read of a newspaper—usually a week old—or the *Saturday Evening Post* before sleep. Often, with no union contract to dictate otherwise, the men would put in a few hours of unpaid evening work preparing survey notes for the day ahead.

There was great joy, seldom expressed, in watching the roadway coming into shape, the fills and cuts reaching final grade. Strangely, it was always a surprise when the final form of the sweeping road grade became clear. The drone of the grader as it spread the windrow of crushed gravel like a long wave of surf unrolling on a beach; the road rollers, the packers, the water trucks, and then the light spray of asphalt to hold the "fines" in the gravel—it was a good life.

On the southern route, the activity moved steadily eastward, following Dewdney through Midway and Greenwood, then circling the mountain spur with the remains of the old mining centre of Phoenix, with its abandoned railway roadbeds, to follow the 1893 wagon road rather than Dewdney to Grand Forks.

The provincial engineers could not wait to get at the major challenges in mountain range crossing which lay ahead. The first went over the Monashee Range, lying between Grand Forks and Rossland, where the old wagon road took a southern route closer to the border than the route Dewdney had chosen. This was the section of road described by the California automobile enthusiasts in their 1927 Road Bulletin:

> Winding over easy grades through a mountainous country to Grand Forks and Cascade from where good two way natural gravel road is used to Rossland and Trail.

Anyone using that road in the early 1950s, or riding in a Greyhound bus over it, would have debated heatedly the accuracy of the term "two-way" or the existence of "natural gravel" on something that was mostly natural rock, with nothing good about it. For extra interest—or apprehension, depending on the traveller—after climbing up and over one summit, with grades in excess of 12 percent and numerous hairpin bends, and then up again to Rossland on the steepest of all climbs, the weary motorist passed through an old minehead centre, which was sometimes being worked and which provided the very minimum of clearance for the roadway between the buildings.

In winter the snowfall was usually much heavier here than in the Rock Creek section, making the journey even more hazardous. The cautious and informed tourist, like the locals, always turned right at Cascade and entered the United States to circle round by Kettle Falls and Northport, where there was a ferry over the Columbia. Even at more than twice the distance, it was the best way to go. The major drawback to this escape route was that Canada Customs closed at 8:00 p.m.

The Northport ferry in the early 1950s was sometimes quite an adventure as well. The Columbia ran swiftly at the ferry's location, making a cable crossing out of the question: the vessel was always swept well downstream and had to beat its way up to its landing. If the engine faltered, the ferry sometimes had to beach itself until it recovered. The area was subject to dense mountain mists, and in this pre-radar period the captain at times could not find his landing. The Northport ferry mysteriously burned to the waterline one week before a new bridge opened to replace it.

At this time I was the District Engineer in Nelson, and I experienced for myself the dangerous conditions often faced by travellers who were forced to cross on the Canadian side of the Monashees in winter. One mid-winter evening I dallied too long while on a visit to my colleague in Grand Forks. Having missed the Customs south of Cascade, I could not return via the United States. There were two inches of snow on the road and it was snowing lightly as I started up the west slope of the Monashee Range.

Nine miles farther on, at the first summit, there were ten inches of snow on the road and it was snowing heavily. Expecting the westbound bus to pass by about that time, and recognising that it was difficult for vehicles to pass each other with the high snowbanks alongside the narrow road, I pulled over at a wide spot by the deserted public works road shed to wait for the bus. While waiting I decided to put the chains on, and as I had no gloves and it was freezing cold, I could do this only by working a few minutes then repeatedly going back into the car to warm my hands over the heater.

Midway through this process the Greyhound bus came along, and the driver stopped to check on a fellow traveller, as all motorists did in those days. He had me get in the bus and really warm up while he put on his gloves and finished the job on the chains. Then we wished each other well and went on our way.

As I descended to Sheep Creek I found the switchbacks filling with drifting snow and very difficult to negotiate even on the down grade. The trick was to go fast enough into them to avoid bogging down in the snowdrifts, but not so fast as to be unable to get around the sharp curves: in other words, controlled sliding. Things were complicated by an increasingly cold air temperature that caused the snow to freeze to the windshield and made it necessary to stop frequently to scrape the glass. Twenty miles on and an hour and a half later, I was profoundly relieved to safely reach Rossland. Before I fell into bed, I phoned the local road foreman and advised him to close the road. Snowplowing was seldom attempted in those conditions.

With such winter hazards to contend with on their only route to the lower mainland within Canada, the local southern Interior residents found themselves in a somewhat similar position to that of the miners of the Kootenays in Governor Douglas's time. They much preferred dealing with the Americans, and as a result they kept on going south to Spokane to do their shopping, rather than face the risks of travelling west within the province. Something had to be done.

The solution was a complete relocation of the highway. Cutting straight across the mountains to Castlegar and bypassing Rossland and Trail, the line was much closer to that chosen by Dewdney, but farther north. Residents east of Rossland and Trail greeted this idea with enthusiasm, as it relieved them not only of the bad road from Rossland to Cascade but also of the steep hill from Trail to Rossland along with the traffic congestion of the smelter and fertiliser plants on either side of the road.

Almost as an afterthought, the government built a connecting link to Rossland from the summit of the new highway, nineteen miles in length. As a bonus this link road provided better access to the Red Mountain ski area, the home of one of Canada's expert world skiers. In her honour it was named the "Nancy Greene Highway." At Kinnaird, near Castlegar, a magnificent new bridge was constructed over the Columbia River to bypass a ferry crossing en route to Nelson. This led in turn to a fine new bridge over the Kootenay River at nearby Brilliant, which replaced an existing single lane suspension bridge that had served the Doukhobor community.[7]

The total length of highway constructed was about eighty miles, including the connections to the new bridges and improvement to the highway from Castlegar to Taghum near Nelson. As well as the Kinnaird and Brilliant structures, during this period there was also a four-lane bridge built over the Columbia River at Trail to replace an older two-lane structure. Near Sheep Lake and the summit—which is at an elevation 5036 feet and became known as Bonanza Pass—the McRae Creek gorge was crossed by a high steel arch.

Construction started in 1956 on the main link of the new route, with seven contracts over the fifty-four miles from Christina Lake to Castlegar. In 1960 an additional four contracts were let from Sheep Lake to Rossland, and one connecting to the new Trail Bridge en route from Trail to Salmo, in preparation for an entirely new route eastward. Work went well on the roadway to Castlegar, and the road was completed by 1962 with overruns not in excess of 18 percent, which was quite acceptable in such untried country. (In calculating overruns of the final cost of a project over the bid price, an addition of 20 percent is first made to allow for engineering costs, materials, contingencies, and normal right-of-way acquisition costs, and it is not included in the overrun. This was never understood by the press, nor the NDP opposition, in their much later calculation of Coquihalla overruns.)

From Sheep Lake to Rossland, it was rather a different story when it came to completing the work on time and within cost estimates. That nineteen miles was not finished until 1966, with contracts overrun by an average of 68 percent, which was excusable to some extent as there was much more rock to excavate than expected, and it proved to be very difficult material. Two contracts of the four resulted in total expenditures of twice the initial bid.

At the same time as this was going on, work started on the longest trans-mountain cut-off of them all, from Salmo to Creston over the Selkirk Range. Here the modern surveyors did not follow Dewdney on the western side, taking Stagleap Creek instead of Lost Creek, but they did accept Dewdney's choice of Summit Creek as the route down from the 5820-foot Kootenay Pass to the flats of the Kootenay River Valley at Creston. To reach the flats, a new crossing of the Kootenay River was built (replacing a ferry), and an even longer structure was put in across the old floodway called Kootenay River Channel. This route also required quite a large bridge to be built over Summit Creek.

Construction of this Kootenay Skyway commenced in 1957 and was complete by 1966, featuring at 5820 feet the highest summit in British Columbia's highway system. Providing an alternative to the forty-minute ferry trip across Kootenay Lake, the new cut-off left the existing Nelson-Nelway Highway at Burnt Flat Junction; forty-two miles of new work were required before it rejoined the existing Southern Trans-Provincial Highway at Creston.

It was not until 1976 that the final cut-off from Castlegar to Meadow Siding, a point midway between Trail and Salmo, was opened, to put it all together and to reduce the distance from Castlegar to Creston by twenty miles for trans-provincial highway travellers. When the new connection between their communities was opened to traffic in 1963, the important immediate benefit to Nelson and Creston residents was the saving in time: an hour and twenty minutes by the new route, as against an average of four hours by the ferry, assuming there was not a long ferry wait to add to the time.

In fact, the first pressure to build the Salmo-Creston cut-off had come as far back as the summer of 1951, when the Creston and Salmo Boards of Trade organised a trek across the mountains to promote the project. Led by Frank Rotter, a veteran logger from Salmo, the party included six pack horses, numerous local luminaries, and both the Divisional Engineer (H.T. Miard) and the District Engineer (myself) from the Nelson office of the Public Works Department. None of these modern day pioneers were experienced in any way with packhorses, and it took us three hot and sweaty days to cover the forty-five miles.

On the west side we started up an existing logging road by the South Salmo River; then we took to unopened country and broke trail up Stagleap Creek to Summit Lake. From there we followed the old Dewdney Trail itself down Summit Creek to the flats, overnighting in an ancient, rat-infested cabin en route. Unlike the fur brigades on other interior trails, we did not have to worry about forage for the animals along the way. Frank Rotter had thoughtfully arranged for an air drop of horse fodder at Summit Lake.

We two highway engineers brought up the rear, measuring distance by pacing, determining altitude by aneroid barometer, and taking voluminous notes and many photographs. We certainly experienced the worst aspects of horse-packing, and learned something of what the Hudson's Bay men endured in their everyday existence. In any event, the effort achieved its objective within a reasonable time: The start of work on the new highway only took another five years. Unfortunately, Mr. Rotter did not live to see its completion.

It was the Creston-Salmo Highway that first introduced the Department of Highways to really serious problems in avalanche control. The experience gained there, as well as in Rogers Pass, proved that a highway could be maintained year-round in avalanche slopes with relative safety. This was despite the loss in January 1976 of three people unwise enough to attempt the winter transit of an avalanche-prone highway in a convertible without the use of seat belts. The avalanche control crews rescued a baby thrown from that car and successfully resuscitated the child. The experience strengthened the vigilance of the crews who expertly close and open the road as avalanche conditions dictate. No further fatalities have occurred to date.

Almost the total length of the Southern Trans-Provincial Highway from Osoyoos to Crowsnest Pass, over five hundred miles including all the various links, was reconstructed and paved to good two-lane standard during the postwar period and the Gaglardi years from 1947 to 1967. All this very difficult highway-building cost the Province close to $80 million, or an average of $160,000 per mile; many have thought these were some of the best dollars ever spent by the government.

The work was evenly spread in location and time. The Southern Trans-Provincial was built steadily, without scandal, without fanfare, and generally without any of the recognition given to the Trans-Canada Highway or to the Hope-Princeton Highway, which triggered it. It was a Coast Connection for those along the southern border of the province, but it never became a trans-provincial route from the Coast to Alberta. Aptly nicknamed "the roller coaster route" for its many summits and valleys, this highway has provided a major transportation artery to the little towns and cities along its length.

On the Okanagan Highway, and particularly along the west shore of the lake, the benevolent attention of Premier Bennett from 1952 onwards ensured that a steady but prudent level of improvement was maintained, and from 1947 to 1967 a total of $5 million in contract work was put out on these thirty-nine miles; there was also a great deal of work done by day labour. This meant the two-lane road was well kept up but was not at all spectacular, which was exactly as Bennett wanted it.

Nevertheless, traffic counts increased steadily at Westbank, rising from 3740 vehicles per summer day in 1962 to 9100 in 1967 and to a dramatic 26,400 in 1981.[8] It was obvious that the panacea of providing a good paved two-lane highway had outlived its usefulness in that area: multilaning became the growing need of the 1970s.

In 1958 the B.C. Toll Highway Authority constructed a landmark floating pontoon bridge across Okanagan Lake, at a cost of over $10 million. This structure of reinforced concrete with rock causeways at either end is 2400 feet long and has a lift span to allow a full-size railway barge and tug to pass through. A bridge designer from the United States refused to contemplate such a floating design because of the potential for drifting lake ice. Drifting ice would be the only serious test under winter conditions but in thirty-four years it has not threatened the structure.

Broad Beans in a Sea of Rice Grains

The break-up of winter's ice on Canada's northern rivers is always unpredictable, often educational, and occasionally very expensive. In the 1960s, the oil and gas industry in northeastern British Columbia developed a new gas field, requiring a bridge to be built across the Sikanni Chief River near Fort Nelson. The industry convinced the Department of Mines and Petroleum Resources that Bailey bridging such as used by the army would suffice, with 60-foot-long spans making up a total length of 900 feet. The Department of Highways was recruited to execute this project, driving piles through the ice in winter even while expressing some doubt about the choice of such small distances between the wooden piers.

In the spring the ice around the bridge melted without incident. One bright sunny day, a rancher who was flying his light plane upstream of the bridge realized that he was witnessing the sudden breakup of a five-mile stretch of river ice into thousands of floes. He later reported that from 5,000 feet the larger floes looked like broad beans in a sea of rice grains flowing down a child's play channel on a sandy beach.

While he was admiring this, he spied the Bailey bridge downstream about to receive some of these broad beans, which appeared to be larger than the pier openings. Circling over the bridge, he described it as a matter of seconds before the force of the ice and water swept away 900 feet of bridging like a hand brushing off a cobweb.

By coincidence, this same day a regional conference of the Department of Highways was winding up in Prince George. The closing dinner featured the District Superintendent responsible for the Fort Nelson area giving a talk about the new Bailey bridge that his team had recently completed. As he was concluding his speech, he was advised that his bridge no longer existed, a fact he had to share with the audience before he left the podium.

Seventy percent of the bridging was recovered, and the following year the bridge was rebuilt with spans three times wider than before.

Before leaving Highways as a result of a disagreement with Premier Bennett over his use of government aircraft, in July 1965 Phil Gaglardi presided over the opening of the Richter Pass Highway between Keremeos and Osoyoos. This provided a very welcome short-cut, which saves the traveller to the Boundary region seventeen miles between these points. Construction by day labour had dragged on since 1956 on the western slope to the pass but real progress was only made when a contract was let in 1964 for the heavy rock work necessary to obtain an acceptable grade on the climb out of Osoyoos on the eastern side.

The public goodwill that Highways should have built up by its good work from the end of the war to the 1970s was offset in many quarters by discredit brought upon itself by its own officialdom. This was to seriously affect the Department staff and their successors in later years. Ironically this often came to pass from too much scrupulous observance of the law and Departmental regulations, when it would have been to everyone's advantage to have bent both of these occasionally.

The first self-administered black eye came from the way the Department acquired right-of-way; the second from the manner in which it controlled the subdivision of land outside of municipalities in the land boom of the 1960s and 1970s; and the third from its often ill-advised granting of access to the new high-speed paved highways that it was building throughout the province.

After Gaglardi's departure in 1967, and after a few months with W.A.C. Bennett himself holding the post of Minister, came the genial generalship of Wesley Drewett Black, the member for Nelson-Creston, whose term of office ran from 1968 to 1972. A dedicated supporter of the Premier, and loyal to the core, Wes Black was a wonderful sedative to everyone after the pressures and strains of Flying Phil, and the Ministry settled down to work under a man with whom they felt more comfortable.

Black, of course, was assisted in restoring tranquillity to the Highways Ministry by the support he got from Premier Bennett, and this brought him much popularity with his civil servants. Bennett wanted nothing more than a quiet, uneventful highway administration after the turbulence of Gaglardi. However, paternalism was on its way out in the B.C. civil service of the early 1970s; the change from employees' association to union made any resemblance to a family shortlived. Progress always exacts a price.

Noted for his kindness and consideration, Wesley Black was a remarkable public servant who probably lost his seat in the 1972 election for not leaning on the Department to complete projects in his own riding more speedily. He was Bennett's willing workhorse, assuming not only the heavy burden of Highways but also retaining other portfolios at the same time.

During his term in office, Wesley Black presided over the completion of the 200-mile-long North Thompson Highway; this project had been a continuing favourite of Gaglardi until it extended beyond his electoral district. The highway was notable for the number of bridges on it—twenty-five in ninety-three miles. Between Kamloops and Valemount alone it crosses the North Thompson River four times. The only highway section in B.C. with more bridges is between Terrace and Prince Rupert, where there are thirty-seven in ninety-eight miles. During Black's term many fine highways were also built in northern parts of the province, which, together with Vancouver Island, had definitely lagged under Gaglardi.

Unfortunately, officialdom, in such a happy state as it was in Highways from 1967 to 1972, consolidated itself, and entrenched procedures that it believed were for everyone's good. Such methods, developing from a single, rather narrow perspective, proved extremely dangerous to overall government policy. In fact, it was in land development regulation that the potential for disaster was created at that time, although it took fourteen years for the complete results of this complacency to come to light.

The first major annoyance to the public was one that had existed from the very early days. When the pre-emptors took up land, the first need was for road rights-of-way, traditionally sixty-six feet in width. On the flat prairie areas of B.C.'s neighbouring provinces where the land was laid out by straight lines to form exactly square sections, the practice was to retain a strip thirty-three feet in width along each quarter-section boundary for road allowance.

British Columbia's early legislators came to the conclusion soon after Confederation that this amounted to setting aside 5 percent of the original Crown-granted and pre-empted land area; they also realised that B.C.'s mountainous terrain did not lend itself to laying out square sections with the edges dedicated to road allowances. At the time, it seemed a simple solution to rule that everyone must dedicate one-twentieth of their Crown-granted acreage to roads.

As it turned out, however, their successors did not stop at assessing the original Crown-granted area: they interpreted it to mean that if the original grant were subdivided, and if one-twentieth of the acreage had not been taken before that, then the onus of dedication still applied to subsequent parcels no matter how far the subdividing carried on. Thus was created B.C.'s infamous one-twentieth rule, so dear to the Province's right-of-way negotiators in later years.

Section 14 of the Highway Act came from the Province's first Ordinance in 1870. It required the Minister to compensate landowners only for "improvements on the land taken" but not for the land itself except that taken "over one twentieth of the original Crown grant" or "where the original Crown grant has been subdivided into two or more parcels the taking shall be proportioned among these parcels."

There is nothing more likely to infuriate a landowner in Canada than a civil servant informing him that a government agency intends to expropriate a piece of his land and to pay him nothing for it. His resentment is lasting and is even more intensified when he learns that for a long period of time after that, sometimes many years, he has paid taxes on the expropriated land, because the process of removing it from the tax roll was too complex.

Only later in the seventies did the Department properly and severely reduce its use of the one-twentieth provision. The potential friends lost over many years before that were legion, and many were the enemies gained. One notable and longlasting opponent of the Department was Arthur Lymbery, owner of the Gray Creek General Store, which occupied an idyllic location by Kootenay Lake. First antagonised by the expropriation of a road allowance along the foreshore of his property in the 1930s, he was further infuriated by the extension northward of this intrusion in the 1940s when the ferry terminal was moved from Gray Creek to Kootenay Bay. A retired court official from London, England, reportedly from the Old Bailey, he fought the Minister's expropriation powers in a polite but relentlessly damaging manner for over twenty-five years. While Lymbery proved unsuccessful in shifting the highway, his efforts without doubt led to better expropriation procedures being put in place.

The next manner in which the Department acquired adversaries, particularly from 1965 onwards, was in the control of land subdivision in the unorganised areas of the province. In its excessive zeal to exercise its power to require subdividers to dedicate land for roads in their subdivisions and build the roads to ever-increasing standards within them, the Department also pushed developers to build and improve roads outside the land being subdivided.

Some of these regulations a reasonable person could understand—why should the public pay for something bringing profit to an individual? But the extension of the regulation to require improvement—and in some cases the complete rebuilding of public roads outside the subdivided parcel—was much less easy to accept.

During Wes Black's term of office these impositions against the long-suffering patience of the public grew rapidly, as the bureaucrats found fertile ground in the protective shade of Minister and Premier. Sadly, the effects of the regulations often fell upon innocent landowners, either due to their owning land in the path of a highway, or wanting to subdivide in a very small way, such as for family, or for a much-needed addition to a modest agricultural income. Yet the original intent of the regulations had been to frustrate freewheeling land speculators.

It was often very difficult to convince a developer about to spend millions of dollars on a sometimes risky venture that as well as building a roadway to serve his own lots, he should also spend large sums on public roads built to lesser standards by previous subdividers. It was even more difficult to convince him that it was fair to be required to provide additional rights-of-way from his land for the improvement of these roads, without any compensation, all of this simply because his subdivision might increase the traffic.

As if the foregoing were not enough, the Department developed a third surefire method of antagonising not only the landowners and developers but also the municipal politicians. In 1960 the Province introduced the "Controlled Access Highways Act," later consolidated with the Highways Act; in 1964 it extended its scope to give the Minister of Highways sweeping powers to control land development within municipalities in respect to the layout and access arrangements to nearby provincial highways. This legislation also gave the Minister the power to grant or refuse approval of rezoning in any municipality "within a radius of 800 metres of the intersection of a controlled access highway with any other highway." If there was anything guaranteed to frustrate, enrage, and permanently alienate a municipal politician, this was it, especially if he thought that the use of this power was to the detriment of his municipality; or even if it simply made it necessary for him or his colleagues to renege on assurances given previously to the electorate.

This legislation was passed with the best of intentions to ensure the orderly development of land, particularly in unorganised areas surrounding the new highways. Initially, it was a gradual application of authority, as in the late sixties such development was steady but not out of hand. Gaglardi applied it paternally, and he was sufficiently sensitive to ensure that it never upset the political or bureaucratic balance too much.

Wesley Black also applied it discreetly, always maintaining the best of relations with the Union of B.C. Municipalities, at times a mutual admiration society for politicians. However, throughout Black's tenure the strength of the highways bureaucracy engaged in the approval of land and business development adjacent to provincial highways greatly increased. Particularly dangerous in this legislation were the powers given to provincial highways bureaucrats vis-a-vis municipalities, especially in zoning approval. The danger became even more pronounced after 1965 when the new Regional Districts entered the arena of land development control.

Things were definitely heating up in the Ministry when an election in 1972 brought a political change of guard. With the election of B.C.'s first socialist government a radically different set of philosophical groundrules were unveiled. And W.A.C. Bennett, the steadfast champion of highways and steadying influence in control of the Cabinet, had departed from the political scene forever.

"Rogues" Gallery

R.W. Bruhn—1929-32, 1941-42

H. Anscomb—1942-1945

E.C. Carson—1945-1952

P.A. Gaglardi—1952-68

W.A.C. Bennett—1968

W.D. Black—1968-1972

R.M. Strachan—1972-73

G.R. Lea—1973-75

A.V. Fraser—1975-86

Above is a "Rogues Gallery" of Public Works or Highways Ministers in office in British Columbia during the years indicated. (Having served for a short period only, both John Hart and E.T. Kenney have been omitted deliberately.) Despite the term used, the primary virtue of these men was honesty. Few, however, did not suffer from the sin of expediency that politics often demanded of a difficult job.

Photos courtesy of the British Columbia Ministry of Transportation and Highways

Two Highways of the 1950s

The Hart

The picture on the left shows the highway shortly after it was opened on July 1, 1952. The first snow has fallen on the Hart Ranges of the Rocky Mountains to the north. The car is parked at the Pine Pass summit, 195 dusty kilometres from Prince George.

The valley of the Pine River takes the road on to Dawson Creek, which is 217 km distant. The Pine Pass is the lowest pass through the Rocky Mountains, at 869 m elevation.

The Crowsnest

The climb up the west face of Anarchist Mountain is 880 m in elevation in sixteen km of road length. It involves several sweeping curves similar to the one below. This is the International Viewpoint between Osoyoos and Bridesville. The mountains in the background are the Okanagan Range of the Cascades as seen from the west, directly across Osoyoos Lake, and the part of the lake on the left of the picture straddles the Canada/United States border.

162

CHAPTER SEVEN

1972–1975

The province acquires its first "no-blacktop" government, which finally rushes through many paving contracts near the end of its term. The weather and terrain of the Coqui-halla route are studied, and the railway's ex-perience suggests there should be numerous countermeasures against the snow. Land de-velopers encounter many problems.

*T*HE NEW Democratic socialist government of Premier David Barrett was not as great a disturbance to the province as was Simon Fraser Tolmie's Conservative government of forty-four years earlier, but it came close. From the opposite end of the political spectrum, Barrett proved that the public of British Columbia can become just as exasperated by over-indulgence in social programs and the expansion of government, as they were with Tolmie for exactly the opposite.

A social worker from Port Coquitlam, "wee Davie" was an accom-plished political street fighter, a raconteur with a ready wit, and a genial and at times charismatic host to public discussion in the pres-ence of the media, a skill he went on to demonstrate in a later ca-reer as a radio host. However, he was not the best of administrators.

Barrett fell into the party leadership with the defeat at the polls of Thomas Berger in the election of 1969, and in 1972 he inherited a mixed bag of elected but inexperienced Members with which to form a Cabinet. Some of those he chose—Ernie Hall and Norman Levi, for example—turned out to be the most voter-generous Cabi-net Ministers that British Columbia has ever had in office.

Barrett's failure to properly control his Ministers in their opening of the government coffers to the public service unions and to the recipients of social assistance defeated him within three years. Ironi-cally, the private industrial trade union movement, which had so strongly supported him at the polls, administered the final death blow by striking for higher wages, on the entirely logical premise that if so many others were to get so much for so little, then they certainly should get more for continuing to work.

The horror felt by the average British Columbian when Human Resources Minister Norman Levi naively admitted in legislative debate that he had "misplaced" $100 million remained just as strong when the N.D.P. next went to the polls. In fact, politicians have "misplaced" many times that amount both before and since Levi's gaffe, (W.A.C. Bennett did so in the fiasco that was his B.C. Railway Dease Lake line, for one), but for so much money to go on greatly increased and often doubtful welfare payments, which were Levi's major creation for the province, was too much for most citizens to bear.

An early victim of Barrett's uncertainty was Robert Martin Strachan, who had been the leader of the party previous to Berger and who became the first N.D.P. Minister of Highways. Strachan had been a carpenter foreman and for many years an M.L.A. representing the Nanaimo district. He was a kind man of good character, as the staff in Highways quickly discovered when he became Minister. However, the next-to-impossible task of instantly organising publicly-owned automobile insurance for B.C. citizens dropped on him by Barrett left him little time for managing the Ministry, despite there being no work put to tender. Some detractors said Barrett wanted to keep Strachan too busy to challenge the leadership, but whatever the reason it was only a few months until this heavy work load led him to change portfolios to Transport and Communications.

When the Insurance Corporation of B.C. showed a loss of $34 million in its first year, the battering that this sensitive and not-too-healthy man took from the media proved too much. In October of 1975 he resigned from Cabinet to become the Agent-General for British Columbia in London. Of course, I.C.B.C. has since been recognized as a boon to British Columbia drivers, and the same media has loudly protested its suggested privatisation.

Robert Strachan was a good Minister to work for, despite his habit of calling in his Assistant Deputy Minister (Operations) first thing every Monday morning and loudly describing something he had seen or heard over the weekend, all the while bouncing up and down with rage in his chair. (Alex Fraser, years later, always waited until after lunch to perform this ritual on his Deputy Minister.) Both Strachan and Fraser were invariably prepared to accept a reasonable explanation, honestly given, and my meetings with both of them usually ended with a smile.

Strachan's successor as Minister of Highways was Graham Richard Lea, a radio announcer and sometime taxi-driver from Prince Rupert. Although many said that all Lea achieved in his short stay in the position was a ferry route between Moresby and Graham Islands in his home riding, Lea did eventually bring a measure of tranquillity to Highways, a not inconsiderable task in the continuing turmoil of his party's controversial administration.

Graham Lea's initial gross offence was the replacement of the revered career Highways Deputy Minister, H.T.(Tom) Miard, by an engineer from outside the civil service. After the N.D.P. government was defeated, Lea did not remain a member of the party for very many years as he was not basically a left-winger. His success in re-election was in fact due to the support he received from the small businessmen of the Queen Charlotte Islands as well as from the unionists on the mainland.

Unveiling the *Kwuna*

Civil servants sometimes find themselves in a position of having to help a Minister gain re-election; however, this usually involves more of a risk to reputation than to life and limb. The following marine adventure offers an example of testing in both areas. Thankfully, the story has a happy ending.

In 1975 Graham Lea achieved a major goal for his northern coastal riding: the installation of a government ferry service between Skidegate and Alliford Bay in the Queen Charlotte Islands, joining Graham and Moresby Islands across Queen Charlotte Inlet. The ferry, named *Kwuna*, was built in good time in Victoria, arriving in the Charlottes ready to go by late summer. With its long landing aprons jutting from either end, and in silhouette against an evening sky, the vessel suitably resembled a Haida war canoe, reflecting the native tribal area through which it runs even to the present day.

Two things held back the ferry's inaugural run. First, the landing ramps were not yet paved. These are similar to big boat-launching ramps and are necessary because the very large tidal range in that area makes normal piled wharves difficult and expensive to operate from. Second, the necessary channel markings and lights on the new route were not yet in place. However, the Minister was very keen to have a preliminary sailing to show off his new toy to the voters, especially with an election looming in a matter of months.

Despite being told that the ferry could not sail in darkness, he planned a trip he felt confident could be carried out during daylight hours between the terminals on Graham Island and Moresby. An afternoon banquet was arranged for Alliford Bay with most of the population in attendance and several special busloads of guests arriving on the ferry as well.

The first mishap occurred when the rear bumpers of the buses dragged on the gravel ramp trying to negotiate the change of grade from the landing onto the flat ferry apron. Jacks and timbers had to be used to assist the buses onto the ferry with a predictable delay in departure time of an hour. The banquet at Alliford Bay was a roaring success, running on past scheduled departure time despite the attempts of anxious Department staff to nudge events along.

Daylight was fading when the fully loaded buses arrived back at the ferry ramp, but the Captain assured his passengers there would be no problem. Using the brand new searchlight on his wheelhouse roof, which had a handle in the ceiling to operate it from inside, he could easily see any reefs even if it did get dark. The sea was dead calm, if a bit foggy, as the ferry pulled away.

When the vessel approached the reef area, by now in relative darkness, the Captain confidently grasped the searchlight handle. It came away in his hand. Someone in the Victoria shipyard had forgotten to tighten a vital screw which, having loosened and fallen somewhere in the wheelhouse, could not be found anywhere. Desperate attempts to replace the handle proved futile, and attention was turned to getting through the reef area by other means.

The Associate Deputy Minister and the Services Engineer of the Ministry of Highways sat on the wheelhouse roof, spelling each other by heaving back and forth with borrowed welding mitts the very heavy and hot searchlight, all the while communicating by walkie-talkie radio with the Captain, and through him the helmsman, to guide the ferry safely along its path. The final leg of the trip was made very slowly but without further incident. The Minister stayed behind in Sandspit for the night, thus missing the foggy crawl home.

Premier David Barrett did not in any way endear himself to the senior bureaucrats in Government during his short spell in office. One major reason for this was his insertion of politically appointed Deputy Ministers into the hierarchy. The Barrett government made eighteen appointments at the Deputy Minister level; only five of these were career civil servants. It also demoted nine long-term Deputies to a new "Associate Deputy Minister" status, and one of these was Miard.

In many eyes this was the start of the decline of the professional civil service in British Columbia, which until then had been based on the British system of a permanent nonpolitical bureaucracy. Unfortunately, Barrett's successor, Bill Bennett, continued along this path and in the first two years of his premiership made twenty-three appointments, of which only nine came from the civil service. By the end of 1978 only four of the eighteen deputies appointed by the N.D.P. were still in office. W.A.C. Bennett very seldom appointed Deputy Ministers from outside the civil service, a policy that probably came out of an early experience when he declined to confirm an appointment by his predecessor, Boss Johnson, to make Johnson's executive secretary Deputy Minister of Railways.[1]

Barrett started off his policy on highways by declaring that his was not to be a blacktop government, and he seemed anxious to underline this by advertising for tender a total of only five new highway-building contracts in his first full fiscal year in office, a record low up until that time. His expenditure on highways dropped to 9 percent of the total budget for the Province from an average of more than 20 percent, another all-time low. He increased to fifteen new contracts the next year, but then in 1975, his last year as Premier, he reverted to the astoundingly low number of only three new highway grading contracts. In paving contracts his government suddenly let a total of sixty-seven late in its term of office (three times the yearly average), after the penny finally dropped that something had to be done to maintain B.C.'s road network.

There is little doubt that the N.D.P's "no-blacktop" highway policy found its roots among its citybound and less affluent supporters. They finally rebelled against thirty years of highway building with tax dollars they begrudged as more to the benefit of the businessman, particularly those in the Interior of the province. Of course, there was much truth to this, and it would be unfair to criticise Barrett for what was in this case the fulfillment of a pre-election promise.

Even the twenty-three road-building contracts that were let to a hungry construction industry in the years 1973 to 1975 were an ill-conceived collection from a political point of view, with only three located in the southern Interior. Two of these comprised a rather reluctant start to the Castlegar-Salmo cut-off, and the other was located in Kimberley. Only when it was too late did Barrett realise that without a progressive highway program votes evaporate in the Interior of British Columbia. This is probably a major reason why B.C.'s first "road-neutral" premier lasted such a short time.

Ironically, it was to be during this government's term in office that an event of the greatest importance to the future highway system of the southern Interior and to its Coast Connection was to get under way. However, neither the Honourable Graham Lea nor the Honourable David Barrett were even aware of it.

In the early 1970s Highways officials became concerned about the Fraser Canyon section of the Trans-Canada Highway. There were two reasons for this concern: First, traffic was rising steadily, and congestion on the long summer weekends was becoming intolerable; and second, there were stability problems in the cliffs surrounding the highway, especially in the historic "Hell's Gate" section.

Instability in the high rock bluff alongside the Ferrabee Tunnel between Hell's Gate and China Bar was first detected during the widening of the highway in 1964. The Ministry expanded the work at that time to include the drilling in of rock bolts and the placing of pre-stressed rock anchors. This did not solve the problem, as showed by the ongoing monitoring of the rock for movement, and so a contract was let for the removal of thousands of cubic metres of loose rock lying mostly above the troublesome bluffs in order to "unload" the rock face to lessen its instability.

Finally, a large area of the rock face was "shot-creted," a process in which stucco-like concrete mix is sprayed against the rock face and held in place by wire mesh. This was some of the most difficult and dangerous work ever undertaken by the Ministry. The instability, however, has not been solved, and it is unlikely that it ever will be. The movements still take place, the water still runs through the myriad of fissures, and freezing and thawing causes further cracking, as it has for millennia. At the level of the highway, the canyon is less than three thousand feet wide and a large failure of the rock bluff could feasibly block the valley and wipe out the highway as well as the two railways.

Planners forecast that by the mid-1980s the highway—bottlenecked at two lanes in many places—would be at more than capacity to handle the traffic on it. With the challenges of terrain, four-laning throughout would be impossible, certainly at Hell's Gate. Moves were also afoot to double track at least one of the two transcontinental railway lines sharing the Canyon with the highway; there was obviously not enough room for all between the steep slopes. As a result of this, in 1973, the Department started looking for a new route between Hope and Kamloops. The obvious one was through the Coquihalla Pass.

Late in 1973 Department staff produced a report called "The Proposed Divided Highway from Hope to Merritt." It followed a proposal that had been under consideration for many years by Department staff on a route using the Coquihalla River Valley as far as Boston Bar Creek and then by that creek's valley to its summit, across to the head of the Coquihalla River, from there to the headwaters of the Coldwater River, and down the valley to Merritt. With only two exceptions, the final design and construction followed this report's recommendations. The exceptions were two-laning some areas initially and dividing the highway on opposite banks of the rivers in some other locations.

Acknowledging concerns expressed in the report regarding avalanches in the Boston Bar Creek Valley, the Department instituted a program of meteorological and snowfall measurement in 1973, continued up to the present time, which has been invaluable in dealing with the avalanche threat.

Thus, in that year, under the supervision of the most reluctant highways-building government of all time and totally at the instigation of the civil servants, the stage was set for the most spectacular Coast Connection in the history of British Columbia—one built in the footsteps of A.C. Anderson and George Landvoigt, in a straight line from Hope to Merritt following the Coquihalla and Coldwater Rivers across the Hozameen Range of the Cascade Mountains. The Province was poised to tackle the most difficult terrain and the most hazardous climate that it had ever had to deal with in its building of roads. It is a good time to pause in our story and take a close look at that terrain, as well as the potential effects of the climate in that region.

The Cascade Mountains of British Columbia are only a small part of the main body of mountains of this name extending up into British Columbia from Washington State.[2] There are three ranges, the centre one of which, the Hozameen Range, extends much farther into the province than the other two. These consist of the Skagit Range on the western side of the Hozameens, and the Okanagan Range on the eastern side. All lean toward the northwest as do their accompanying sierra, the Coast Mountains, the Columbia Mountains, and the Rockies. (See map this chapter, "Landforms of Central and Southern British Columbia.")

The base is about 185 kilometres wide and stretches from Chilliwack to the point where the Similkameen River enters the United States. The Hozameen Range extends almost 110 kilometres to Lytton, the Skagit Range ends at Hope, and the Okanagan Range at Keremeos. The Skagit and the Hozameen Ranges are divided from the Coast Mountains by the Fraser River.

The great body of the Cascade Range, about 1100 kilometres long, lies in the United States, stretching throughout Washington and Oregon and extending about 250 kilometres into California. It is a major feature of the Western Cordillera of North America, and probably one of the youngest of the mountain masses in geologic terms. It features much more pronounced volcanic activity than the neighbouring Coast and Rocky Mountains, as it showed dramatically on May 18, 1980 when Mount St. Helens exploded.

The mountains were named for the cascading waters or rapids of the Columbia River where it breaks through the mountain barrier between Mount Hood and Mount Adams, the Columbia being the only river to flow through the range. These rapids, which have now been dammed out of existence, were a particular torment to the immigrants to Oregon in the 1840s, who had to put their wagons on rafts upstream of the rapids and float them down the Columbia with considerable hazard.

The by-pass road built by Samuel Barlow and located south of Mount Hood crossed Barlow Pass at 1300 metres above sea level. It was the first toll road through the Cascades (the Coquihalla being

Landforms of Central and Southern British Columbia

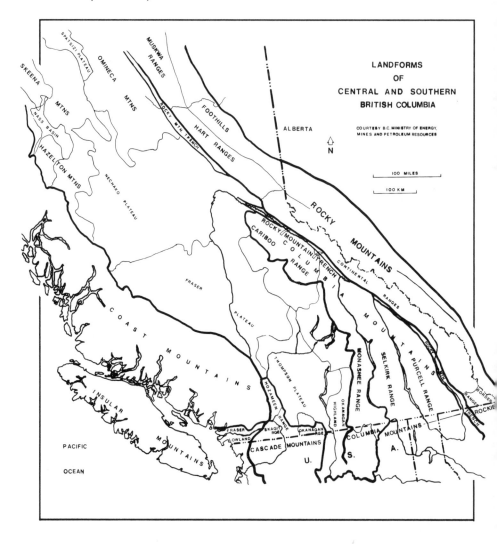

the second), and Barlow regained his investment in two years, 1846 and 1847, by charging five dollars per wagon and ten cents per head of stock on its 145-kilometre length. The annual total reached $3660 in one year.[3] By way of comparison, the Coquihalla Highway returned $150 million in tolls annually as of 1992.

The geology of the Cascade Mountains within British Columbia is extremely complex. It includes plutonic, volcanic, and sedimentary rock, with the upward intruding ancient plutonic rock (essentially granodiorite and quartz diorite at the Coquihalla summit) partially bared in places by the erosion of the overlying softer and newer layers of sedimentary rock. All of this was drastically and sometimes spectacularly altered by the effects of intense alpine glaciation.

The many serrated peaks, high sharp ridges, and cirque basins were confined to the higher levels by the action of the Cordilleran ice sheet. This reached as far south as Puget Sound in the last ice age and finally receded some ten thousand years ago. At its maximum the ice reached a thickness of between 1800 to 2100 metres. Advancing and retreating, this huge ice mass caused by its grinding action rounded dome-shaped mountains below its elevation and left the "Matterhorn type" peaks and ridges remaining above that level.

The numerous valley glaciers left over after the main ice sheet had melted probably caused the most notable effects by their movement, and by the resultant melt-water erosion as they disappeared. The most visible of these are Dry Gulch and Box Canyon, both melt-water channels, and the upper and lower Coquihalla gorges, all probably due to drainage blockages and subsequent outbreaks. Mantled with glacial till, the terrain today is a mixture of clay and boulders eroded and eroding in an always unpredictable form. The glaciers have almost totally disappeared in the Canadian Cascades, with only minor evidence of them among the higher peaks of the Skagit Range.

British Columbia did in fact have a "mini-Ice Age" about five hundred years ago, reverting to a warming trend three hundred years later. It was probably the advance and retreat of the glaciers during that time that led to the statement that the Coquihalla River valley is one of the "youngest" valleys in Canada: It was likely altered quite radically by these events.

Of course, the glaciers were not all bad in their effects on the terrain. Alluvial deposits of glacial lake-borne material provide sand and gravel in generous quantities in many places. The Shylock Landing area is the largest of these in the Coquihalla River Valley. It bore one of the largest glaciers in the Cascades reaching a depth of 1500 metres. This tremendous weight of ice caused massive forces and compression on the underlying strata, which even now is still "rebounding" or gradually rising, a geologic abnormality that many people find hard to accept. It also resulted in the rock being fissured and layered, leading in turn to difficulties of drilling and blasting, and in places even more troublesome problems from the rock carrying water through its fissures and causing instability.

All this applies only to the western side of the mountains leading to the Coquihalla summit. From that point the Coldwater River follows a wider, more shallow, and gentler-sloped valley within the Thompson Plateau.[4] This valley represents the division between the plutonic belt, described as the Needle Peak Pluton, and what is known as the Princeton Belt, comprising volcanic and sedimentary rock. As the valley widens out, alluvial fans and terraces occur, frequently containing sands and gravels and marred only by the occurrence of fine-grained lacustrine silts, mostly on the river banks. This material is particularly notorious in road use for causing frost heaves. (Place names in this and following paragraphs are located on the Strip Map in Chapter 8.)

Throughout the route there is a very wide range of climate: from the wet and temperate Fraser Lowlands to the drier and more extreme Interior Plateau, there is a world of difference in winter conditions. Hope receives an average of 1.5 metres of precipitation yearly, and Merritt only 0.3 metres (all water equivalent). Within a distance of twenty-four kilometres in the Coldwater River Valley, the annual precipitation varies from 400 mm down to 100 mm The highest annual precipitation recorded is 1524 mm in the Skagit Range, incurred primarily in storms in October and November.

From Ophelia in the Coquihalla Valley to Coquihalla Lakes at the summit, the route passes through a topographic and climatic area which is highly prone to avalanches for up to seven months in an average year. Of course, the intensity of the avalanche activity varies greatly from year to year depending on the amount of snowfall and the temperature variations, which in turn govern the type of avalanche to be encountered.[5] In this part of the continent, considerable seasonal fluctuations occur as the weather comes directly upon the Cascade Mountains from the Pacific Ocean. Within this avalanche prone area, a total of 108 avalanche paths have been identified. Of these up to 67 may be of danger to any use of the valley if triggered.

The avalanches of highest intensity and frequency in the Boston Bar Creek Valley are named the Rhodes-Janus group. This group has a history of 116 avalanches in the six years 1973 to 1979. The next highest is Great Bear, which had 97 in the same period. Unfortunately, these two groups are located directly opposite each other on either side of the valley and therefore are much more likely to completely block both the pass and the highway; hence the snow shed at that location. All these avalanche groups are mapped and described in a *Snow Avalanche Atlas* prepared by the Department between 1973 and 1979. Measurements and data recording have continued.[6]

The incidence of avalanches in British Columbia history dates back to the first settlements, and even before that, to the time when the fur traders were moving throughout the province. It is possible that Simon Fraser's son was killed by an avalanche while he was asleep at a camp below Manson's Ridge. However, there is some mention in the history books that his death might have been from a tree felled with murderous intent by a member of his crew.[7] With or without him in the statistical record, there were seventy-five lives lost in avalanches between 1860 and 1900.

Snowed In

The motor grader was the work horse for the Ministry both for smoothing gravel roads and for clearing snow (including avalanches). Rather like a mechanical insect, it wore its skeleton on the outside—a metal frame with wheels at either end and a cab and motor mounted at the back. With four-wheel drive and four-wheel steering, the motor grader could track its front wheels differently from the rear and go down the road like a crab. The motor grader also had a peculiar ability to slant over its front wheels, an arrangement that helped the underframe grading blade to "bite in." This phenomenon led to regular phone calls from observers who had noted that the front wheels were falling over on some of our equipment!

For snow plowing, the grader often had a large vee-plow mounted at the front and two rather strange-looking attachments on either side; these, in fact, were steel blades protruding outward like wings. The blades could be adjusted in height and angled to sweep the tops off the snow windrows thrown up by the vee-plow. Known as "winging back," this process was designed to prevent the snow from falling back or later drifting in.

One very snowy New Year's Eve, a graderman (Don Young of Creston) was plowing the main road when he received a message that a fruit rancher had phoned in to say he had a sick child and needed to be plowed out. With two miles of narrow winding road to the ranch house, the operator knew this was really a job for a bulldozer, but he gave it the priority such an emergency deserves. He could not turn the large machine at the end of the road and would have to back out the last half mile.

When he finally reached the house, he learned that the child was better, but the rancher indicated that he and his wife would follow him out anyway, both dressed in their best clothes and with a babysitter standing by. The graderman returned to his machine without a word, raised the vee-plow high and extended the side wings. In their reverse position, they neatly swept the excess snow back into the cleared roadway, filling it in with snow as the grader backed out.

The party-goers went nowhere that night!

Profile of an Avalanche Path

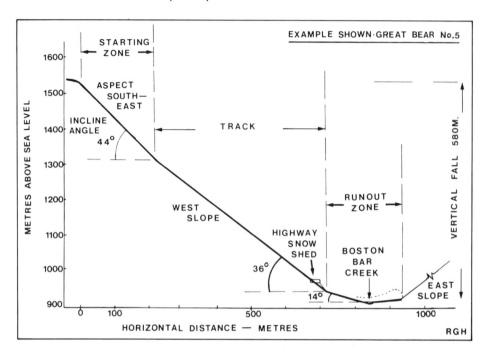

The above is typical of many avalanche paths in the upper Boston Bar Creek valley. This particular path had a frequency of twenty-six avalanches recorded in eight years between 1972 and 1979. Obviously, a roadway should not be located within the track or runout zone of any avalanche, but in this case another avalanche shared this runout zone, bringing snow from the other side of the valley: hence the need for a snow shed. Although it is huge in size, the snow shed appears puny in this view with the vertical scale distorted.

The question of what is an exceptional year and what is not is an interesting one in respect to snowfall on the Coquihalla route. Quite comprehensive records were kept by the Kettle Valley Railroad from 1915 to 1961. In that period much greater snowfalls occurred than have been recorded since the Department of Highways started to keep records in 1973. One major cause of this is a higher temperature trend: in every month of winter in recent years there has been a measurement of precipitation in the form of rain. This seldom was the case in the winters prior to the last war.

The valley lies in a northeasterly inclination so it lines up exactly with the movement of the majority of the weather systems which enter British Columbia from the Pacific. Both the Coquihalla and the Boston Bar Creek watersheds have this same alignment, and both end abruptly against the steep walls of Zopkios Ridge. This assembly of more than a dozen peaks and ridges rises to more than 1800 metres above sea level, and the sudden rise to the water-laden clouds usually causes heavy precipitation. Of course, in winter at this elevation the result is snow, with an average of thirty storms each winter season.

Zopkios Ridge seems to be a magnet for snowfall, exposed as it is to direct flow of air from the ocean. In contrast, Allison Pass to the south of it has considerably less snowfall. The reason for this is thought to be the large group of mountains, containing Silvertip Peak, which lies directly to the west of Allison Pass and thus shelters it from much of the onslaught of moist air flow. Silvertip Mountain group is one of the few areas of the Canadian Cascades glaciated at present.

The snowfall in the Coquihalla Pass is, on average, about twice that experienced in the Allison Pass, and five times that of the Fraser Canyon area. The maximum officially recorded annual snowfall is 16.38 metres, which fell in the winter of 1955-56, but the railwaymen claim that in the winter of 1915-16 the snowfall reached 20.4 metres. They say that the drifted snow at some places reached forty feet in depth during that winter.

It is remarkable that the construction of the Kettle Valley Railway between 1913 and 1916, and its subsequent operation in this same area until 1959, did not see more people killed by moving snow. A number of crew members of that railway died as a result of slides knocking trains off the track, but no passengers were killed.[8]

There are, of course, many other avalanche prone areas surrounding provincial highways. One of these is where Highway 16 crosses the Coast Range using the valley of the Skeena River. An avalanche here in the early 1970s brought down snow on a roadside restaurant killing six highway travellers and a waitress near Terrace. This event spurred the Minister of Highways to create an avalanche task force, whose report led to an avalanche management program that the Department has been undertaking ever since. The major areas of activity originally were those parts of the Rogers Pass maintained by the Department and the Hope-Princeton and Salmo-Creston sections of Highway 3.[9]

The Department has based its avalanche management program on three basic points. First, it is absolutely necessary to try to forecast the onset of conditions that might trigger avalanches. Second, the travelling public must be warned in good time. And third, the highways must be closed before the avalanches occur. Of course it is also important to know when to re-open the highway to traffic and this is a difficult decision, for the natural tendency is to be ultra-cautious.

The Department set up three unmanned weather stations in the Coquihalla Pass area in 1973. The weather stations recorded snowfall quantity, rate of snowfall, rainfall, maximum and minimum temperatures, water content of the snow cover, atmospheric pressure changes, and the amount and direction of the wind. We also set up radio-operated weather or satellite stations on various mountain tops; these were less accessible to human observers visiting on a regular basis.

The mountain-top weather stations did not provide nearly as much data as the visited ones, but they did give temperatures and pressures from above the 1800-metre level—vital information for predicting avalanches. The best way that regular visits could be made was by helicopter, but as the winter wore on, the pilots had to employ rather unusual methods of landing. The helicopters' skids did not act very well as snowshoes when the snow was soft and fluffy, and the machine would then go right down and sit on its belly. The aircraft could not stay too long in this position as it would freeze in and not be able to take off. Because the snow cover in late winter was as deep as nine metres, the instruments that had to be read were mounted on towers at least ten metres high. These towers all but disappeared from sight in a heavy winter.

For the Ministry of Highways in British Columbia, the Coquihalla Highway posed challenges relating to geology, terrain, and weather to a degree seldom equalled anywhere that a freeway style highway had been proposed. The Department commenced an intensive pre-construction examination not only of the avalanche situation, but also of the general environmental and animal habitat problems. The Design and Survey Branch, the Planning Branch, and the Geotechnical Branch of the Department all participated.

Just how much these matters concerned the ruling politicians it is hard to tell, but one novice in the world of B.C. politics was vitally interested. William Richards Bennett, son of W.A.C. Bennett, was elected M.L.A. for Okanagan South on September 7, 1973. He was also a prominent member of the Kelowna Chamber of Commerce, which had been intrigued with the Coquihalla corridor as a Coast Connection ever since the Kettle Valley Railway had vacated it in 1956, and the oil and gas companies had occupied it in the early 1960s as a quick pipeline route through the mountains.

But while the Department investigated the possibility of a new route, the N.D.P. government, and specifically their Minister of Highways, apparently had different ideas for solving the growing problem of the increasing traffic on the Fraser Canyon and Hope-Princeton Highways. Congestion at that time was primarily pinpointed to be a problem on long summer weekends, when Lower Mainland holiday traffic clashed with Albertans moving to and fro in their campers, and with the ever increasing numbers of large recreational vehicles and cars from the United States. The delays, although as yet short in duration, were of growing concern to the heavy interprovincial truck traffic that had built up in the Fraser Canyon corridor. Both these vehicle flows came together at Hope.

It was during his first summer in office that Minister of Highways Graham Lea made his widely publicised—and deplored—statement that American recreational vehicle drivers were not welcome in British Columbia. By his assessment these visitors purchased only gas; they brought all other supplies and accommodation with them and they filled up his Department's overnight camping areas. Lea was no doubt responding to complaints from his Prince Rupert constituents, based on their observations while driving to the Coast, and there was some truth to his statement, but it was seen as just one more blow administered by his government to the growing provincial tourist industry. In fact in the next fifteen years, the tourist industry was to challenge the mining industry as the second largest revenue producer, after forestry, in this province.

Early in 1973 the N.D.P. government introduced its Land Commission Act and also in that year established its controversial Environment and Land Use Secretariat. This supra-ministerial agency supported by powerful legislation and controlled by its own Cabinet committee started a trend in the reduction of powers of individual Ministers, a trend that has been enthusiastically pursued by Barrett's successors and is still under way. (Bill Bennett, after some hesitation, abolished the Secretariat because it became so unpopular, but he substituted the powerful Cabinet Committees of Environment and Land Use, Social Services, and Economic Development, all under the Planning and Priorities Committee, which he chaired. He also took up Barrett's lead by appointing his own super civil servant as his "deputy." These innovations were all borrowed from Canada's Liberal Prime Minister, Pierre Trudeau, and the B.C. equivalents in personnel were imported from Ontario.)

177

In the Annual Report for the year 1973-74, a special mention was made of a program to control rezoning applications that would generate high traffic volumes on provincial highways. It was noted that "these were carefully examined and often refused." The report also described another program wherein the Department was designing minimum street networks within municipalities to ease main highway traffic. There is no doubt that this applied to Kamloops and Kelowna, where Premier Barrett, in an unprecedented action, imposed amalgamation on two satellite communities created in the land boom by developers, the Kamloops one being the infamous Dufferin.

Even before the Agricultural Land Commission came into existence, the urgent need of the new government to interfere with land development was indicated by an Order-in-Council passed in December of 1972 freezing the sale of all agricultural land in the province. This draconian measure cost many people dearly in respect to land that was only marginally agricultural, and in many cases not at all feasible for cultivation. The Department of Highways, prominent as it was in land regulation, found that with the freezing of agricultural land, it was to fall further into a morass of public disfavour, even with a Commission to whom it could deflect many subdivision decisions.

One major problem was described in *New Concepts in Highway Development*, a booklet issued in November of 1973 by Graham Lea. This booklet was to place the Department solidly and unmistakably in the forefront of an area of controversy that should have been only peripheral to its primary responsibility of building and maintaining roads.

The logical and traditional way for land settlement to expand in the province—and B.C.'s Interior population in 1973 was expanding everywhere—was from the established centres outwards. If, however, the centre of settlement were surrounded by developed or potential agricultural land as many of the Interior towns and cities were, the total ban on agricultural land development created many serious problems. The developers, who were desperate for land on which to build, rushed to pick up nonagricultural land areas, often far removed from access to such services as water, sewer, and adequate roads. To offset any need for improved road access, the most sought—after of such areas were those close to primary provincial highways, particularly at intersections. This was exactly the type of development that the Controlled Access Highway Act was designed to forbid.

In October 1974, Lea wrote an article for the *Road Runner*, the quarterly published by the Ministry for the staff, in which he conveyed his, and presumably his government's, philosophy toward highways and land use in the province. The flavour of the article is evident in the following excerpt:

> As you know, the Department of Highways holds two important keys to land use—the control of access to highways and the supervision of subdivisions in unorganized areas. If you know anyone who recently tried to establish a gas station on a highway or subdivide his farm, you will be well aware that we are exercising this control very stringently. We are demanding that developers prove to the satisfaction of our planners that their projects are consistent with sound land-use policy. This is one of the more sensitive areas of our duties; much pressure is put upon our staff to bend to commercial considerations. But I am proud to be able to report that our Planning Branch, which I consider one of the bulwarks against the misuse of land, is not bending to that pressure.

Such an emphasis on obstruction of most proposals in such a wide range of uses, unfortunately brought Highways even more into the position of being the opponent of land development, not only in the eyes of the public but also of elected municipal officials. In later years this was to have disastrous consequences for all Highways staff, including their next Minister.

On November 3, 1975, exasperated by the forest industry union's defiance, Premier Barrett surprised his own followers almost as much as everyone else in the province by announcing a provincial election to be held on December 11. During the one thousand days of N.D.P. rule in British Columbia, which ended with the party's defeat at that election, the investigation and preliminary design of a Coast Connection to top them all got firmly under way. It required only a "pro-roads" Premier, with vision and a solid link to the southern Interior to put matters in gear. The election that returned the Social Credit party to power put just such a man on centre stage.

The Taming
of the Rock Bluff—

The answer is to drill down from the top . . .

The photograph on the right shows air drills downdrilling from a flat bench prepared in advance. The downdrill is about 40 feet.

And then . . .

Shear it Clean by Microsecond Delayed Detonation

This is the way to blast the least amount of rock, and it is made necessary because modern road design has increased quantities so massively.

The view on the left is the shear rock face resulting from the drilling shown above. This method works well provided the rock is reasonably uniform and has a degree of structural integrity. It is not effective for crumbling rock, or rock with other material interspersed, or with voids or excess moisture.

The work is on the Coquihalla Highway, Phase I, west end.

CHAPTER EIGHT

1976–1986

A new Social Credit government comes into power. The ultimate Coast Connection is built, but its completion does not end the story.

*I*N MID-DECEMBER of 1975, when most citizens of British Columbia were preparing for Christmas, William Richards Bennett, forty-one years of age, was planning his new Social Credit Cabinet. After a stunning victory at the polls on December 11, with the N.D.P. losing twenty seats and the Social Credit party gaining twenty-five—including David Barrett's own seat—Bill Bennett faced the greatest responsibility of his life.

For his first and only Minister of Highways, he chose 59-year-old Alexander Vaughan Fraser, M.L.A. for Cariboo since 1969 and former Mayor of Quesnel. With a father active in federal politics much of his life, Alex Fraser seemed to be born to politics, so much did it become a part of his personality and the overwhelming interest of his life. He was a kind man, an excellent Minister in many ways, and quite remarkable for the affection he generated among his friends and associates.

Early in his new job as Minister of Highways and Public Works, (the Department now became a Ministry), Fraser suffered a telling humiliation at the hands of his fledgling Premier. When twice in six months he attempted to remove his N.D.P.-appointed Deputy Minister, Bill Bennett's initial insecurity at the helm nearly defeated him. The first time these politically appointed Deputy Ministers got wind of Fraser's intention, they banded together and threatened to quit en masse. On that occasion, Bennett gave in and retained them all. It was months before the new Premier fully realised that in every

181

Ministry the senior staff could quite well have replaced the Deputy in the short haul, and that he could have called their bluff and let all the Deputy Ministers go immediately. That is certainly the action his father would have taken.

In fact, these Deputy Ministers, most of whom left within a few months after receiving a substantial separation payment, certainly ill-served their successors, especially those who came from the ranks, because Bill Bennett never lost his distrust of anyone who served in that position. For his part, Fraser hereafter was always wary of introducing any proposals at all to Cabinet, and that wariness grew in time to an unfortunate reluctance to change the status quo in any way. One legacy of this caution was his reluctance to change Highways' contract documents.

However, an important area where Fraser's inherent caution was to serve him well was in his meticulous observation of personal propriety and in his unswerving respect for the responsibilities of his elected office, both within the Legislature and in public life. His record was an admirable one, as he soon realised in the face of relentless disclosures of unethical behaviour against many of his cabinet colleagues over the next few years.

The first of these disclosures was the Jack Davis affair, where a Rhodes scholar and a professional engineer, formerly a federal cabinet minister, was found to be manipulating airline tickets.[1] Davis was ejected from Cabinet and Bill Bennett, most unwisely, added the portfolios of Transportation and Communications to those held by Fraser, who already had his hands full with Highways. The additional workload included two extremely onerous Acts to administer: Motor Vehicles, which was prominent in the public eye; and Motor Carriers, which was very important to the trucking industry.

It is alarming to note that one more B.C. Premier saw fit to grossly overload his Highways and Public Works Minister in this way. Dave Barrett had done it to Bob Strachan, W.A.C. Bennett to Wes Black, and many years before, Sir Richard McBride had loaded down Thomas "Good Roads" Taylor with the deadweight burden of Railways as well as Public Works.

All suffered as a result of this load, with Alex Fraser destined to bear more than any of the others. Fortunately, in 1979 Pat McGeer took over the portfolio of Communications, thereby reducing this unmanageable portfolio from the Ministry of Transportation, Communications and Highways to Transportation and Highways. No one ever got the former name right, particularly Bill Bennett.

No matter how willing, no one man could handle the burden of complexity imposed by the huge program of road-building that the Province carried through the 1970s and into the 1980s, combined with the day-to-day detail of the legislative responsibilities of motor vehicle administration. For Alex Fraser, the price in the end was his health; and the acknowledgment of his efforts was minimal.

Alex and Gertrude Fraser were legendary in the Cariboo for their humanitarian concern, as evidenced by their adoption of numerous foster children. On one sad occasion when an immigrant Scottish doctor and his wife died in a road accident at Quesnel, the Frasers cared for their two young children for months. When the paternal grandparents, lairds of an isle in Western Scotland, invited the Frasers to the funeral, all expenses paid, Fraser had two surprises he liked to recall: one was his surprise when their plane could not leave Glasgow until the tide was out at Barra, where a beach landing was the only way on to the island; the other was the herd of wild, black-faced Scottish sheep roaming about the cemetery.

Fraser's consideration occasionally overflowed into his work, as well. One time in late November of 1978 when he and I (his Deputy) attended a regional meeting in Terrace, we witnessed one of the worst floods in the history of that flood-prone area. After weeks of work restoring the roads and bridges were over, the Minister insisted that at each centre in each District affected, a dinner and evening's entertainment be arranged at Ministry expense, where he personally made the rounds to thank the men and women of the Ministry for their dedication.

Alex Fraser was particularly concerned about the Kitimaat Indian Village, which had suffered severe damage with only a minimum of complaint from the residents. After much care and attention to the rehabilitation of the area, he received a cake baked for him by the ladies of the village. Fraser always got along well with the native people: he liked them, and the feeling was mutual. In one notable interview with the Nisga'a nation from Greenville, he promised them a bridge over the mighty Nass River. Despite the dismay of his staff, he made good on his promise. Prior to that, the crossing to Greenville was by boat from the logging road, a particularly hazardous method when ice was forming. Drownings were fairly regular. The Nisga'a never believed the Minister would build them a bridge, even when the contractor laboured for most of a year building piers two hundred feet apart. Then one foggy morning an armada of tugs and barges appeared out of the mist, each barge carrying two huge steel beams two hundred feet long and fourteen feet high. At high tide each barge was placed between two piers and by low tide the bridge was complete. Then they believed.

Ministerial Bloopers

Ministers of Highways were not always right, no matter how devoutly some of them believed in their own judgment. They were guilty at times either of acting impetuously before knowing all the facts or of heeding questionable advice, very often fired by the imaginative and unique quality of the idea for which they wanted to take credit.

Phil Gaglardi's blooper was due to impetuosity in his early days as Minister. On a sunny morning, very early, he was driving from Kamloops to Merritt when he noted with great satisfaction that one of his first projects was well under way: the relocation of a part of the road over which he was travelling.

After initial clearing of the route, the re-fencing of the right-of-way had been started, but at this hour he was appalled to see the fencing crew idling their time away. Gaglardi stopped and sallied forth in their direction, asking the first man he met to direct him to the foreman of the crew. When the new Minister had introduced himself and demanded an explanation for the crew's inactivity, the foreman seemed remarkably unresponsive as well as unimpressed. Gaglardi then informed him that he was relieved of his duties pending a full investigation by the Senior Road Foreman back at district headquarters. The Minister returned to his car feeling that he had taken a regrettable but necessary step.

When he reached Merritt, Gaglardi immediately advised the Senior Foreman of his action and was informed that the only fencing crew out on the highway that morning was employed by the Douglas Lake Ranch, which had chosen to do its own re-fencing.

Alex Fraser listened to Cariboo advisors a lot, and the results soon became part of Ministry folklore. Fraser's friends convinced him that the solution to dusty summer roadways in the Chilcotin was to spread on them material that would pack down, and they recommended for this purpose a kind of clay shale found in the local area. Headquarters staff argued staunchly against it, but Fraser would not be deterred. He even went so far as to give the orders himself to the local foremen, who dutifully covered several miles of gravel road with this shale. The material compacted beautifully, and the result was a dust-free road for several months, with Fraser announcing far and wide that this was his doing and his alone.

When autumn rains fell—and fell, and fell—the clay surfaces became so slippery that no one could drive on them without a high risk of accident, and they soon became known as "Fraser's long, long skating rinks." The clay had to be graded off and hauled away at considerable expense.

A vital area where Fraser's political instincts seemed to let him down, as had Wes Black's before him, was land use control in the province. The basis for the government's unpopularity has already been discussed in the previous chapter; however, when the effects of the real estate boom of the late seventies and the early eighties became fully evident Fraser found himself really under the gun. With very little effort, he acquired a highly dangerous adversary in Cabinet!

In 1947 William Nick Vander Zalm had emigrated to B.C. from his native Holland at the age of twelve. After a very successful career in commercial gardening he tried his hand at politics and won election as the Mayor of Surrey in 1967. Following a spell with the Liberal Party, he joined the Socreds and was swept into office with Premier Bill Bennett in the 1975 election.

Bennett was never really happy with Vander Zalm, whose exuberance and personal charm won him a large following in the party. Bennett was especially unhappy when, as Minister of Human Resources, Vander Zalm gained widespread publicity by exhorting the welfare recipients to get themselves shovels. Transferred to the less controversial post of Minister of Municipal Affairs in late 1978, the firebrand from Surrey now became fully involved with the Highways Minister in the onerous task of regulating land developers, mostly of their own Social Credit party, who were then swept up in pursuit of their greatest chance to make money in a land market gone crazy.

Vander Zalm's solution to Highways' conservatism in land use control was to draw up a proposed Land Use Act, which intended nothing less than the handing over of control of all land use in the province, including all lands in provincial or municipal ownership, to one Minister of the provincial Crown: the Minister of Municipal Affairs.

This was not a commonplace statute devised to address one or several issues. It was an Act that proposed to delete large sections of many statutes of great consequence to the province and to place them within itself. It set out to diminish the Land Act, the Forest Act, the Land Titles Act, the Land Registry Act, the Municipal Act, and last but not least, the Highways Act. Of course, it proposed to diminish correspondingly the powers held by the various Ministers administering these Acts, with the conspicuous exception of the Minister of Municipal Affairs.

In Highways' case, it would have left the Minister almost completely without powers to acquire additional land for expansion or construction of new highways, and it would have removed any control he had over the development of lands surrounding them. It was hardly a mystery why Fraser and his staff were the first to speak out against the proposal in Cabinet Committee. It was also no coincidence that Bill Bennett, who was equally appalled by it, chose Alex Fraser and his Ministry as the instrument to shoot it down. In an attempt to give the appearance of Cabinet solidarity to outsiders and staff, Bennett kept his participation and Fraser's well concealed: the task of opposing the Act in committee was given to Fraser's Deputy, namely me.

The proposed Act proceeded slowly, but it did proceed, and

Vander Zalm rather unwisely anticipated its passage and appointed directors in his Ministry for its future administration. The Act's eventual death on the Legislative Order Paper in July of 1982 was therefore particularly embarrassing to him as well as disappointing. His feelings were not too well controlled as proved by an outburst to the press: he described his Cabinet colleagues, (and presumably also his Premier), as gutless for not passing it. Alex Fraser recalled that it was Grace McCarthy who consoled Vander Zalm with W.A.C. Bennett's old maxim for political infighting—"Don't get mad, get even." The disappointed Minister did not forget that advice.

In the short run, Vander Zalm swallowed his pride, stayed with the Cabinet, and moved on to the Education portfolio. He refused to run under the leadership of Bill Bennett in the 1983 election, at which time he temporarily retired from politics, except for an unsuccessful try at the mayoralty of Vancouver. His day of glory was to come in 1987.

Meanwhile, the road construction industry of British Columbia, after the spectacular achievements of the Gaglardi years, forged steadily onwards into the 1970s, first under the cheerful and energetic leadership of Chief Highway Engineer, Jim Dennison, and after his tragically early death, under the guidance of Ray White and Norm Zapf.

From Dennison's long Ministry experience wearing many engineering hats in different parts of the province, he acquired a more comprehensive knowledge of B.C.'s roads than probably anyone ever before or after him. Typically, the staff would meet with Fraser after the Minister returned from a weekend in the Cariboo, and the failings of some particular area of his constituency would be the subject. Dennison, completely unforewarned, would go to the blackboard and draw a rough plan of the road at the exact point of discussion. He would then go on to give an expert opinion, carefully reasoned, why it would be most difficult if not impossible to "straighten out" or radically alter in some way, the piece of road Fraser was citing. He was also quite likely to propose an attractive alternative. Only occasionally was Jim Dennison unable to do this, and his capability was much admired and highly valued by Fraser and Wesley Black before him.

On the Coast Connection from the southern Interior, the Ministry's work mostly consisted of more four-laning on both the Hope-Princeton and Trans-Canada Highways, as well as continued improvement to the Okanagan Highway, and further conversion to freeway on the Vancouver to Hope link.

Most of the new highway-building in the 1970s was centred in northern and central B.C. and in the northern part of Vancouver Island. A new version of the highway between Revelstoke and the Mica Dam was unveiled to suit the new Revelstoke Dam and its reservoir (the second of two rebuildings of that part of the old Big Bend Highway). Just as that drew to a close early in the 1980s, the North-East coal project started up, with new highways at Chetwynd and near the west coast port facilities at Prince Rupert. Both of these undertakings were financed by the megaproject itself.

Coming from the taxpayer's pocket rather more directly, the Highway Ministry's one and only mega-project got under way, albeit rather reluctantly, on the final and most high profile link of the province's southern Interior Coast Connection.

The Throne Speech delivered before the second Legislative Session of the Bill Bennett government on January 13, 1977 contained an extremely interesting paragraph for the province's road-builders, if they had time to look up from their busy schedules. In it, the Lieutenant-Governor intoned:

> I am advised (that) a new route is needed from the interior to the coast. The last major new highway route to the coast in the southern part of the province was the Hope-Princeton Highway, which was completed 28 years ago in 1949. For these reasons, my government has directed my Minister of Highways and Public Works to proceed as soon as possible with the design and construction of a highway from Merritt to Hope through the Coquihalla Pass. This will require the construction of 70 miles of new highway.

As the Deputy Minister of Highways and Public Works at the time, I was just as surprised to hear this as were the road-builders. Some weeks before, I had put forward my suggestions for the Throne Speech, as was normal, and no mention had been made of such an important new highway, for the very good reason that I had been given no indication of interest either from my new Minister or from the new Premier. The latter I immediately suspected to be the sponsor of this initiative. However, the Ministry lost no time in commencing design.

Snowfall record-keeping had been under way for the previous four years, so the Ministry was well aware of that particular challenge to road construction and maintenance. However, we also recognised the equally difficult task of protecting all parts of the sensitive environment in the mountain valleys from the effects of the proposed new highway construction. Even the very tentative examination to date was enough for both federal and provincial environment departments to demand that the highly valued fishery resources of the Coquihalla and Coldwater Rivers be protected completely. Never before had a summer-run steelhead trout river of such importance as the Coquihalla been so threatened; its preservation became a factor in every phase of planning.

Of course, neither the Coquihalla nor the Coldwater valley was virgin territory, as their history well indicates. The railway first threatened the fishery not only with its excavations and embankments but later with the fires caused by the sparks from its coal-fired locomotives. This was followed by the pipelines whose road construction opened up the country and brought in logging and mining. Survey work on the final line was started in 1978 and completed as far as Kingsvale by the end of 1982. During this time three highway grading contracts were let, the first from Nicolum Creek to Peers Creek, and the second and third near the Coquihalla summit. Some detailed survey work was accomplished elsewhere prior to the letting of these contracts, but design was far from complete in the Coldwater Valley. The survey work on that section was suspended at Kingsvale pending the outcome of negotiations with the Coldwater Indian Band.

From the time of the 1977 Throne Speech announcement to the end of 1983, only a token amount of work was done. Three contracts were let, totalling 18.5 kilometres, out of a length of 120 kilometres; these were for grading only with no gravel surfacing. After many months of disuse they looked rather pathetic with the two parts near the summit separated by a huge, deep unbridged ravine, called Dry Gulch, 200 metres wide and 100 metres deep.

When 1984 dawned, the most positive thing that could be said about the situation was that a decision had been made about the problem of the highway disturbing the Coldwater Indian Band. The roadway was to be rerouted high on the slopes on the right side of the river and would thus avoid entering the Indian Reserves altogether. As 1984 drew to a close, the picture was entirely different. What changed the equation was a decision made by the provincial Cabinet at a meeting retreat on the shores of Cowichan Bay in the spring of that year.

Flushed by the excitement of their resolve to undertake a world's fair in Vancouver in 1986, the Cabinet was well aware of the political desirability of carrying out similar megaprojects in parts of the province outside the Lower Mainland. With the Expo 86 theme of "transportation" at least in the initial publicity, such a state-of-the-art highway project seemed even more appropriate. The government also recognised the necessity of giving some boost to the civil engineering design and construction industry, which had largely been idle since the recession of 1982.

A decision was made to start construction of the Coquihalla Highway immediately. In fact, the express instructions to the Ministry of Transportation and Highways were to have the full 120 kilometre length of new highway built and paved from Hope to Merritt by May of 1986, the opening month of Expo 86.

This was an undertaking of rather staggering dimensions, but the Ministry did not flinch from it. On the theory that it is best to strike while the iron is hot, the bureaucracy not only accepted the challenge but also added a considerable amount of reconstruction work on highways leading into the Coquihalla, so that by May of 1986 the province would have a reasonably complete new highway route through the mountains. In retrospect, there is clear evidence that the father of this huge project was in fact Premier Bill Bennett, never an enthusiastic pro-roads Premier until this time, but now prominently front and centre in that distinguished company.

Construction of the Coquihalla Highway commenced in the fall of 1984 with clearing, grubbing, and burning of the brush and trees preceding roadway excavation. At the same time work got under way on the various bridges and other structures, all following the calling and awarding of contracts for the various items of work. The bidding went on all that fall and into the winter, with the last grading contract out of twenty-seven being called on February 8, 1985. Thirty-two bridge contracts were also called to tender within this period. These, of course, only provided for the Hope to Merritt section, the first of three phases of the new route.

In addition, a number of new or replacement sections of existing highways leading to and from the Coquihalla route were designed and put under construction including a long six-lane freeway section of the Trans-Canada Highway west of Hope.

At least until the bridge over it was completed, Dry Gulch turned out to be a natural barrier dividing the entire highway project into two parts. One side was linked to Hope and the other to Merritt; these centres supplied the contractors working on the two sections of the highway. A pipeline access road around Dry Gulch existed, but it was very steep and narrow. While it was used continuously during construction, it was never suitable for the hauling of heavy loads or the movement of gravel and other materials in large quantities.

In both the winters throughout which the work took place, this ravine was also a division point in climate. Dry Gulch easterly was within the interior plateau weather regime, much colder and drier than Dry Gulch westerly, which had more coastal weather. The division was clearly defined by the two grading contracts either side of the gulch already completed when the accelerated program started.

Strip Map of the Coquihalla Highway
Phase I—Section from Hope to Brookmere

This strip map has been abridged to show only the place names and features mentioned in the text. This alignment was used by the historic cattle trail built in 1876, except that it followed the Coquihalla River from Coquihalla Lakes to Portia. The railway supplanted the trail forty years later, lasting for another forty years. Since 1960 the alignment has been used by an oil pipeline and a gas pipeline with a joint access road using the abandoned railway grade in places. The gas line, owned by Westcoast Transmission Company, follows Boston Bar Creek from the summit to Portia. The route now accommodates the highway and both pipelines and access roads. Shakespearian place names used by the highway designers are from the railway days. The distances shown are in kilometres; they have been subsequently altered and are, therefore, not exact.

The revision in alignment to avoid the Coldwater Indian Reserve is obvious in the section of the strip map on the extreme right. This relocation put the highway high on the valley slope and across some very deep gullies which required large fills and extra length pipe culverts. Kwinshatin Creek, for example, is carried in a pipe 3060 mm in diameter and 162 metres in length.

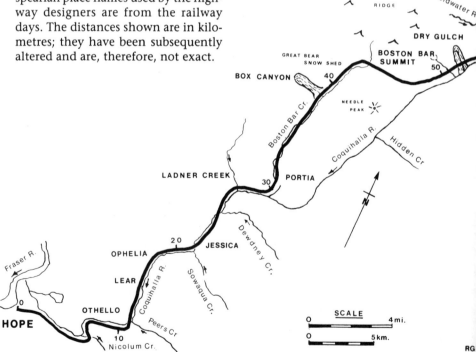

190

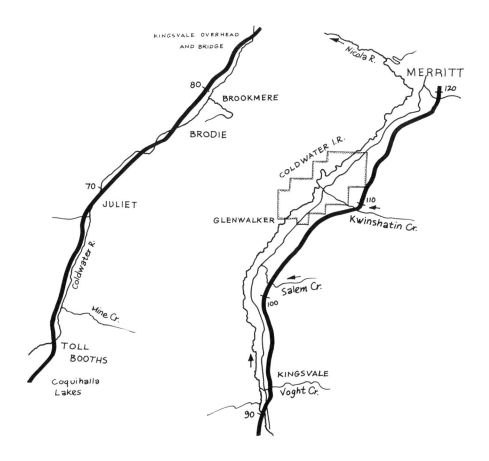

Description of the Roadway

Phase I of the Coquihalla Highway is basically a four-lane freeway with 3.7 m-wide paved lanes. Truck lanes of similar width are generously provided where adverse uphill grades require them as well as on extended downgrades, where there are also runaway lanes. The highway has an 2.4 m-wide centre median with a concrete barrier except where there is a 8.0 m-wide grassed centre median. There are 1.6 m-wide paved safety shoulders throughout with guardrails where necessary. This excellent roadway width is carried through on all structures, some of which are very large. The highway alignment is for 110 km/h operating speed. With such standards, it is one of the finest highways ever built over a major mountain range.

191

The first contract on the west side of this dividing point was at the head of Boston Bar Creek and over that summit in the warmer but wetter climate. The first contract on the eastern side started at Mine Creek, nine kilometres from Dry Gulch, and all within the colder interior weather regime. It was in a deep freeze from November onwards, and no grading work took place from then until well into the spring. On the west side, the work went on throughout both winters, and this turned out to be the key to meeting Premier Bennett's dictate that the highway be opened by mid-May 1986, (although it also proved to be the key to a Pandora's box of criticism of the project after its unveiling).

As work progressed in the upper Boston Bar Creek Valley, it became quite clear that this was to be the most difficult section of the entire highway. It was soon dubbed "the ugly section." Close behind in difficulty was the section around Ladner Creek and south of it, where instability problems in soil and rock substrata came to light. However, the Ladner Creek area did not have the higher elevation and longer lasting snow cover that plagued the contractors in the ugly section, even allowing for two of the mildest winters on record in 1984 and 1985. In the first winter the two valleys recorded only three metres of snowfall—for an area that has often recorded five times that amount!

The challenge in this rugged terrain was to build a grade that was twenty-four metres wide as a minimum, yet high enough above the surrounding valley bottom so that it would not be totally buried in the winter snows. From their experience the designers knew that they would have to use borrowed material, that is, material excavated in addition to the local cuttings needed to build up the highway grade.

After consultation with the avalanche experts, they decided to kill two birds with one stone—the borrow pits to get the material could be placed at the runout areas of the avalanches and become avalanche containment basins, huge in area and volume to accept the avalanche debris and prevent it spilling onto the highway.

It seemed like a good solution to the problem. The one thing overlooked was that it is very dangerous to designate any area as a borrow pit, especially one for hundreds of thousands of cubic metres of fill, unless you are absolutely sure that the material in it is exactly what you want, and that it is usable—not only in summer, but in winter and spring as well. Unfortunately, much of the material proved to be unsuitable. This turned out to be a major miscalculation in the design, due mostly to a lack of time for thought and investigation of subsurface conditions. In addition, there was much more unusable overburden in many areas than was expected. All of this led to very large quantities of suitable quarried rock having to be hauled in, which contributed substantially to the large cost overruns on these contracts.

In the Boston Bar Creek Valley, where the ancient glacier had carried all before it in its relentless journey to the sea, the Ministry encountered difficulties that quickly threatened to bring the project to a grinding halt. The only answer turned out to be a process known as "fast-tracking," a cumbersome term meaning to cut corners in every conceivable way. This was done by adding unforeseen. work to existing contracts instead of re-bidding. Building a highway in certainly one and probably two years less time than normal is a highly risky business at best, especially when subsurface soils investigation is far from complete.

Inevitably, foundation problems developed in both the highway and structures— notably the Great Bear snow shed—problems that led to delays and more cost overruns. In the Ministry's administration of the snow shed contract an accounting shortcut was also taken in order to save time, for, amid all the frantic productivity, time was the one commodity that could not be created at will. The overruns and the administrative juggling in turn led to a potentially devastating embarrassment to the Ministry when such revelations eventually came to light, and the Pandora's box revealed its contents.

The situation in the fall of 1985 on the snow shed project could best be compared to a man building a house who has completed the main floor with expensive carpeting before the roof is built. He is then told by the roofing contractor as the rainy season approaches that the work will not be done unless payment is made in advance. Of course, he has to find the funds in a hurry.

Due to unforeseen subsurface conditions, completion of the foundation of the snow shed in the summer had been delayed. The Ministry rushed the erection of the shed in an attempt to have it complete before the oncoming avalanche season. The contractor could not handle the increased cash flow and requested accelerated payment. Inexperienced Bridge Branch staff in the Ministry, uncertain of procedure and fearing the additional paperwork would delay the work, issued what they dubbed "over-progress estimates," that is, advances against submitted invoices not yet fully checked. When these invoices were fully approved, final payment was made with a deduction for the advances, and eventually all was in order. This was exactly what the R.C.M.P. told the next Highways Minister eighteen months later when he ordered them to investigate the matter, and the police recommended no further action.

On the plus side, the goal of the provincial Cabinet to generate work and business within the provincial economy was certainly met on this highway megaproject. The statistics of individual commercial enterprises involved are impressive: sixty-six separate consulting companies were employed on highways, bridges, specialised and environmental design; ninety-one contractors and sub-contractors worked on clearing, grading, paving, and bridges; and a total of eighty-six supply companies filled the huge list of materials required.

Thanks mainly to the extraordinarily mild winter, the progress made by mid-summer of 1985 was outstanding. While the slowest progress was generally in the ugly section, the Boston Bar Creek Valley, even these projects were close to the half-way mark in their heaviest dirt-moving sections by August due to the fast-tracking. By this time, grading jobs farther down the Coquihalla River were 75 percent to 80 percent complete. The only exceptions were sections where summer traffic on the highway out of Hope eastward complicated matters.

On the Coldwater side an early spring saw grading off to a good start. The dirt flew on the long sidehill cuts and fills as a warm sunny season with little rainfall made the contractors smile. All that was needed was a good Interior Indian summer, and once again nature cooperated. Paving contracts were let late in the summer, and with many supplies of paving aggregate already stockpiled, much of the road was surfaced with base course paving, if not the final coating, by the end of 1985.

Difficulties still lay ahead for the early months of 1986 in the higher altitudes, and last-minute efforts to complete the final paving were strenuous, but the promises were met and the highway was opened to traffic on schedule on May 16, 1986. While the opening ceremony did have an unmistakable air of "vintage corn" about it, there was a genuine exhilaration to the event, intensified by the wide, sweeping pavement, the elegant bridges, and the wondrous snow shed. A Highways truck burst through a paper barrier followed by an open convertible carrying the Premier and his wife plus the Deputy Minister, Tom Johnson. The row of snow plows on display resembled a line of shield-carriers while the tracked avalaunchers with their artillery-like gun barrels stood at attention ready for war against a snowy menace. There was none of the lyrical prose that characterized the opening of the Big Bend Highway, but the new road was much the better one in every respect.

A hundred and one years had passed since the opening of the CPR at Craigellachie; seventy years had passed since the Kettle Valley Railway opening in this same mountain pass. The Coast Connection opened in 1986 with the logical assumption of automobile supremacy over the iron horse, at least for the present time.

The difference between the Coquihalla Highway and the Hope-Princeton Highway as regards quantities is impressive: for rock and dirt excavation combined, the figures are Coquihalla 27.5 million cubic metres, Hope-Princeton 3.76 million cubic metres. Of course the Hope-Princeton section was only two lanes with narrow shoulders, but it was several miles longer.

Making some historical comparisons, it is interesting to look at the highway construction and the railway building at the time each stood close to completion in the fall of the year prior to their opening. The spread of time is exactly seventy years. On the highway, the trouble spot was near Ladner Creek in late 1985. On the railway work in the fall of 1915, the tracklayers were stalled by a partly built 560-foot wooden trestle across the same creek.

Disaster was not long in striking the railwaymen as winter set in. Instead of the long Indian summer that the highway builders enjoyed, the railroaders had the wettest September on record, and in late October a rock slide completely demolished the Ladner Creek bridge crew camp. Fortunately, no one was hurt as they were all out working on the line.

The setback with their camp only spurred on these hardy men. Early in December, after superhuman efforts, they completed the Ladner Creek structure and laid steel on it. Later that month after supply trains fought steadily through increasing snowfall to keep the tracklayers supplied, a massive slide came down ten miles west of the summit dumping a fifty-foot depth of snow on the track and trapping a thirty-five car work train. The workers hiked out, and the whole section from west of Ladner Creek to the summit lay deeply covered in snow until March of 1916.[2]

Reaching even further back into B.C.'s pioneer history, it is interesting to reflect on the pathbreaking dreams of Chief Trader Donald Manson of the Hudson's Bay Company in 1851. What would he think of huge trucks, each one carrying three times the combined load of the largest fur brigade through the same mountain passes from Hope to Merritt in one hundredth of the time it took his men to make the same journey on foot?

Or what of the hardworking sapper, Sergeant James Turnbull, surveying the mountains east of Hope in 1862, conscientiously noting down the evidence of "fearsome snow falls in the defiles of the Coquihalla." Undoubtedly he would have shaken his head at the helicopters placing steel towers high in the mountains above these same defiles to support an aerial ropeway carrying explosive charges to be set off close to the snow surface. With the snow buildup thus dislodged, its fearsome qualities become manageable.

The story of the Coquihalla should end here. The ultimate Coast Connection had been completed under an almost superhuman timetable, and a magnificent highway it was. But it was not the Ministry's fate to bask in the glow of such a worthy achievement. There was an epilogue, and just eighteen months after the opening of the Coquihalla Highway, there was a very different Ministry.

The Coquihalla Route

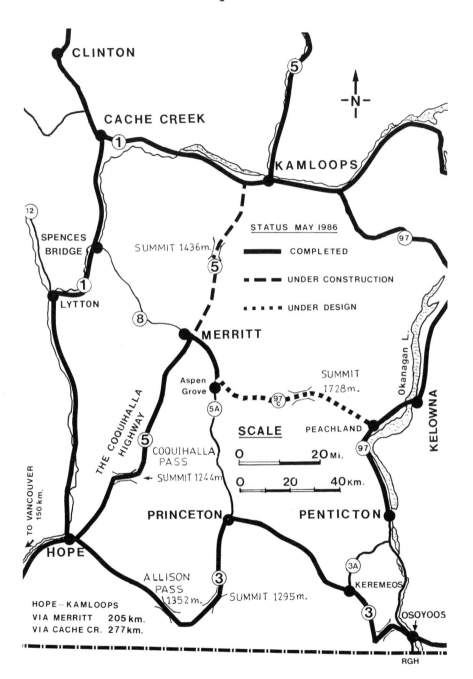

CLINTON

CACHE CREEK

①

KAMLOOPS

⑤

–N–

12

SPENCES BRIDGE

SUMMIT 1436 m.

⑤

STATUS MAY 1986

COMPLETED
UNDER CONSTRUCTION
UNDER DESIGN

97

①

LYTTON

⑧

MERRITT

Aspen Grove

5A

SUMMIT 1728 m.

97C

Okanagan L.

KELOWNA

97

THE COQUIHALLA HIGHWAY

⑤

COQUIHALLA PASS
← SUMMIT 1244 m

SCALE

0   20 Mi.

0   20   40 Km.

PEACHLAND

97

TO VANCOUVER 150 km.

PRINCETON

PENTICTON

HOPE

ALLISON PASS 1352 m.

③

SUMMIT 1295 m.

3A

KEREMEOS

③

OSOYOOS

HOPE--KAMLOOPS
VIA MERRITT   205 km.
VIA CACHE CR. 277km.

RGH

197

The Trouble with "Other Material"

In road builder's parlance "other material" is anything that is not good, sound, solid rock. Many of the fraternity become convinced that solid rock is much easier to deal with than some forms of other material.

A case in point— the hillside above

R.G. HARVEY COLLECTION

This hillside, located close to Dewdney Creek, was part of the Coquihalla Highway under construction in Phase I. The slope is almost exactly thirty degrees to the horizontal, very close to the sliding point of gravel or boulders when dry. The roadway is a temporary haul road, and an access road for the major excavation necessary later to create a four-lane highway in this difficult terrain. The embankment will be built up from the bottom in layers, and the upper slope will be stabilised.

Massive Fills Mean Massive Culvert Pipes

As a part of the construction of the Coquihalla Highway Phase I the site below requires a fill of massive proportions. A huge multi-plate galvanised steel culvert pipe has been installed to carry a small creek underneath.

The difference between the Hope-Princeton and the Coquihalla in quantities is immense. Despite two lanes against four, distances about the same, the Coquihalla was 27.5 million cubic metres, rock and dirt, and the Hope-Princeton 3.76 million.

R.G. HARVEY COLLECTION

198

CHAPTER NINE

1987 & Following

Questions about the Coquihalla bring an inquiry and its aftermath, and an answer to the conundrum why those who built this great modern Coast Connection received so little recognition.

*I*T IS unfortunate that this story cannot end with the triumph of the previous chapter. However, events since the opening of Phase I of the Coquihalla Highway have necessitated that some points be made concerning the aftermath to the initial construction project.

On May 22, 1986, after the opening of the Coquihalla, Bill Bennett announced his intention to step down as Premier. At a party convention in July, the reins of Social Credit leadership passed to Bill Vander Zalm, who also assumed the role of Premier. Premier Vander Zalm's leadership was confirmed later that year by the electorate in a province-wide election won by the Social Credit party. The stage was now set for some actions that would not only have serious and long-lasting implications for the Ministry of Transportation and Highways but also for the reputation of the province as a whole.

On July 31, 1987, the Vander Zalm Cabinet passed an Order-in-Council setting up a full Commissioner's Inquiry under the Inquiry Act to:

> inquire into . . . and report on the costs of construction of the Coquihalla Highway, to compare the total costs incurred on the project and each phase of it, (Phases I & II), to determine the rationale for any differences where they may occur and report on the justification for those differences, and without limiting the generality of the foregoing, but as an aid to the investigation, the commissioner is authorised and directed:

(a) to inquire with respect to any other recent highway construction project that appears to have had any significant variation between the actual and estimated costs of construction and to report with comparisons, and

(b) to examine the standards and practices adopted by officials of the Ministry of Transportation and Highways in costing projects, to investigate the procedures followed by that Ministry in the administering and reporting on such projects, and to make such recommendations for such change as the commission considers appropriate in the circumstances.

The Commissioner appointed by this Order-in-Council was Douglas L. MacKay, P.Eng. He submitted his report on December 21, 1987, and shortly thereafter it was made public. The Commission held public hearings in Kamloops, Vancouver, and Victoria with Ministry of Highways and other government officials being cross-examined at the Victoria hearing.

The major allegations which evolved during the Inquiry were that Phase I of the highway had been grossly underestimated by the Ministry, and that there was concealment of the excess expenditure, over that reported to the Legislature by the Minister on numerous occasions. Further, it was alleged by the Commissioner that this misrepresentation was achieved by the manipulation of special warrants in amounts of many millions of dollars authorised in secret by Treasury Board, misleading the Legislature in the process. The format used for the Inquiry was quite extraordinary to say the least. Accused of major transgressions, the Ministry was, in fact, tried in the wrong kind of court.

The only recent precedent to the Commission of Inquiry into the Coquihalla and Related Highway Projects was the British Columbia Railway Inquiry established under Justice Lloyd MacKenzie and two other justices in March of 1977 by Bill Bennett. This was called to investigate the British Columbia Railway (B.C.R.) under the regime of his father, and that only after the most extreme pressure by the public as well as the Opposition.

Upon examination there is little similarity between the two, for the circumstances greatly differed. The B.C.R. was in massive financial distress. Their Dease Lake line had been literally left to rot miles from anywhere, and two contractors had threatened to sue for fraud. These contractors were bought off by multi-million dollar settlements, and permitted to leave the work unfinished. The Fort Nelson line was supposedly complete when the contractors left, but it was virtually unusable: the ballast under the tracks was supported on sheets of plywood laid over the soft clay beneath. This 210-mile project was fully comparable to the Coquihalla Highway in its impact on provincial finances. It originally had been estimated by the engineering branch of the railway to cost $80 million, a figure that was reduced on Premier W.A.C. Bennett's order to $68 million. It finally ended up costing $235 million.

Unlike the Dease Lake or the Fort Nelson lines of the B.C.R., the Coquihalla Highway from Hope to Merritt had recently been opened in triumph, was fully completed in record time, and was a delight to its users. There were no contractors threatening suit or abandoning their contracts (there were also no contractors proven to have reaped great profit), and although there was evidence of serious divergence of final cost from estimate ($250 million as against $409 million)[1], this paled in comparison to the B.C.R. figures, which had to be dragged into view by an inquisitor. The Coquihalla figures had been fully and openly detailed in a report rendered to the public and not demanded by anyone.

The Coquihalla Inquiry followed questions in the Legislature midway through July by the Opposition New Democratic Party concerning the Great Bear snow shed contract. Then Highways Minister Cliff Michael stated that the R.C.M.P. had investigated allegations of wrongdoing, made by a union source, and the police had not recommended any further action, a matter already outlined in Chapter 8 of this book. With the privilege of hindsight, both MacKay and a junior representative of the consultant at the hearing were very critical of the decisions, secure in the knowledge that the previous winter had brought no avalanches and that it would have been safe to have left the shed unfinished that fall. Of course, neither the Commissioner nor the consultant had borne the responsibility for decision-making and action two years before. They stood in much more comfortable shoes than the Ministry staff.

The N.D.P. had also questioned the reported overall costs of the highway following the publication of the Annual Report by the Ministry of Transportation and Highways for fiscal year 1985-86, which showed substantial overruns from the estimated total cost of $250 million for Phase I, as reported to the Legislature by Alex Fraser. Fraser was not reappointed Minister after the 1986 election despite Premier Vander Zalm's assurance to him during the election campaign that he would be reinstated.[2] However, in 1988 questions raised about the building of Phase I required Alex Fraser to defend his actions in the Legislature.

As Social Credit M.L.A. for Cariboo, Alex Fraser made a speech in the Legislative Assembly on a motion of privilege on Wednesday, March 9, 1988. The speech was quite an ordeal for him as he had lost his voice box to throat cancer by that time, and he used an electronic device attached to his throat to communicate. He had only a year to live. In his speech, Fraser claimed that he had never knowingly misled the House concerning the estimated cost of Phase I. He believed the estimate to be true, based on the information he had been given. All costs related to the building of the Highway were recorded in the Public Accounts, and he assumed they had been audited by the Comptroller-General and by the Auditor-General of B.C. "I agree with the Auditor-General," he emphasized, "that the MacKay Commission did not know what they were talking about when they reported that the Legislature was avoided...and misled by the documents presented to it." Fraser concluded, "What expertise and knowledge has Mr. MacKay about the procedures of the B.C. Legislature? I suggest to you none whatsoever, and he should not be considered a proper critic of what takes place in the Legislature." Despite the exhausting physical effort, Fraser felt it was important to defend himself and the actions of the Ministry from what he perceived to be very unfair treatment.

At the time the inquiry was announced, it is probable that the N.D.P. would have accepted an investigation by a joint committee of the House such as the Public Accounts Committee, comprised of Members from both sides. However, the question that many informed observers asked themselves was why, quite suddenly, had the Government decided to stage a full scale investigation of itself, and one which excluded members of the Legislature. In our system of government, the last point is particularly puzzling because the situation primarily concerned matters vital to that institution and there has always been a tradition of handling such investigations internally.

What was remarkable about the terms of reference was the virtual exclusion of anyone other than officials of the Ministry of Transportation and Highways to be investigated. In a huge highway construction project such as the Coquihalla Phase I, there are predictably five major groups involved: the responsible Ministry of Transportation and Highways, other involved Ministries (particularly Finance), the contractors, the consulting engineers, and the suppliers.

The latter group was not relevant to this inquiry, but very definitely the others were. The Commissioner, to his credit, went somewhat outside the terms of reference to include officials of the Ministry of Finance, including the Minister, in the interrogation of witnesses at the Victoria hearing. No contractors appeared at that hearing, and the questioning of consultants was limited entirely to the snow shed affair.

What was even worse from the point of view of the unfortunate officials of the Ministry of Highways who were told to be there, was that they were denied vocal defence counsel support, despite being grilled by an obviously well-experienced prosecuting attorney representing the Commission. While the inquiry was skillfully and legally conducted, and the Commissioner went to some lengths to attempt fairness in his handling and in his reporting, it cannot avoid the label of a kangaroo court, if only because of the interrogation procedure.

What really sealed the fate of the Ministry was the performance by the media, electronic and print. Before, during, and after the hearings they tried the case daily, and for the Ministry the news was all bad. Headlines and comment were sometimes accurate, sometimes not, but they were never favourable. When the official report at last came out, the reporters skimmed through it, took out the juicy adverse material, and wrote the epitaph of the Ministry with a flourish.

In his final report, the Commissioner severely criticised the Ministry for its global estimating, its contract documents, and for its project management and cost control, including the addition of extra work not bid upon, especially on those projects fast-tracked on Phase I. It found the Treasury Board of Bill Bennett's Cabinet guilty of misleading the Legislature, but did not report any individual wrongdoing. MacKay was acclaimed for his work, both by the media and by Vander Zalm's Cabinet. Little was heard from the Socred backbenchers at the time, except from Alex Fraser, who bitterly refuted and condemned the Commissioner's findings.

The Report was not totally adverse to the Ministry of Transportation and Highways by any means. For those who cared to look at the Report and not just at the media coverage, it not only contained some very complimentary remarks, but also excluded the Ministry entirely from responsibility for some of the most serious of the allegations. For example, in the Summary, page xii, relative to the misleading of the Legislature by the manipulation of the special warrants, the Report reads:

> The Commission's terms of reference directed it to inquire into estimates and costs and into the Ministry's practices and procedures in administering and reporting projects. This it has done and is satisfied that the reported irregularities did not originate within the Ministry of Transportation and Highways.

Global cost estimating was the subject of comment by the Commissioner on page xv of the Summary of his report:

The root causes (of the difference between global estimates and actual costs) are both the failure of the government to demand such things, and the failure of the Ministry to supply them.

When considering this rather puzzling comment, it must be understood that the term "global estimating" as it applies in Highways usage means only the estimating of the cost of projects spread out over more than one fiscal year's duration. Historically, the Ministry has been reluctant to estimate more than one fiscal year ahead[3], both because it is not part of its regular system of operation, which is to estimate by fiscal year independently, and because it is a risky business at best to come up with accurate costs over a longer period of time than one year in such a variable construction environment as B.C.'s mountains, and especially before the final soil surveys and complete designs have been done. Such estimating is only prepared at the specific request of the Minister or Treasury Board.

The following excerpts from the Report are a remarkable acclamation for the Ministry. On page xii of the Summary, the Commissioner states that:

.... The Ministry has a reputation for high morale; it has "gotten things done"; it has a record of accomplishment which is publicly visible everywhere in the Province.

On page 40 of the Report, the Commissioner further acknowledges the Ministry's accomplishments without qualification:

Suffice now to say the construction of the Coquihalla Highway was a remarkable achievement. The fact that the highway—a major, complex, and fast-moving construction project—was completed in 24 months using this project management process and the existing contract documents is in the Commission's view close to a miracle. The staff's long experience has been referred to many times in the evidence and is testified to by the final results. Without their experience and dedication the project would never have been completed on time.

And finally, and of particular interest to road engineers and others in the business, is the comment again on page xii of the Summary:

A financial investigation was carried out by the Commission's accounting expert into 15 selected contracts on the Coquihalla and other recent projects. His detailed review compared the Ministry's financial records with those of the contracting companies. This revealed:

• the Ministry's records were corroborated in all important respects,

- there was no evidence of excess payments made to contractors,
- the prices bid and the profits made by the contractors were not excessive.

No mention of even one of these favourable comments can be found in Vancouver newspaper files. Due to the barrage of negative media coverage throughout the fall of 1987, there remains a strong and widespread perception implanted in the public mind, particularly in the Lower Mainland, that there was a gross waste of public funds and a serious failure of trustworthy conduct by public officials on the Coquihalla project.

Unfounded rumours have long been the bane of road-builders in B.C. and, of course, the Coast Connections have not been immune, certainly not in two prime examples. The Hope-Princeton project long suffered from the rumour that it was estimated at three million dollars and cost twelve (see Chapter 5). Similarly the Coquihalla Highway is now widely thought to have been estimated at $250 million and to have cost a billion. There is some consistency here: the factor of exaggeration in both is four! The one great difference between the two is that in 1949 the builders gained widespread and lasting public acclaim for their achievement, something denied to their Coquihalla counterparts in 1987.

In reality, on the Hope-Princeton project the $3 million was the sum of the first grading contract bids between Hope and Princeton, and the $12 million was the total cost, including improvements and paving, right through from Hope to Kaleden Junction. To this was also added the Okanagan Highway down to Okanagan Falls.

On the Coquihalla the $250 million was the bare estimate (without embellishments) on Phase I, and the media's $1 billion was in fact $771 million, the cost of all three phases together. Phase I actually cost $409 million, of which $59 million was for additions, all encouraged by support of the project at every level including the very top.

Additions to the original concept of the highway were listed on page 11 of the Report as "Scope Changes." These were:

a) Greater access to Hope and Merritt,
b) Addition of chain-up areas,
c) Addition of snow shed,
d) Construction of toll booth (which also involved re-grading several miles of roadway),
e) Addition of runaway lanes,
f) Locating at higher elevations in Coldwater Valley to agreed move out of the Indian Reserve,
g) Addition of truck passing lanes,

h) Addition of lighting at the summit (which required a power line from Merritt),

i) Provision for a median wider than eight feet,

to which I add:

j) Overhead variable message signs on all highways approaching the Coquihalla, such being interconnected and computer controlled,

k) A shortwave car radio broadcast system,

l) Concrete median barriers throughout,

m) Additional width to all bridge decks,

n) Addition of debris torrent protection,

o) Additional environmental protection (a huge item),

p) Avalanche protection, including two explosive delivery tramlines,

q) Provision of a maintenance depot and a permanent work camp site at the summit.

While the Commissioner did include a sketch map locating many of the scope changes, he did not cost them out in his report. Neither did he include the last eight additions listed above even though they were brought to his attention in time for him to add them to his list. In this he was remiss, as he had the resources in his million dollar assignment to do so. The Premier's Office is believed to have approved most of these additions: certainly they gave "carte blanche" for other ministries (such as Environment) to make widespread charges to Coquihalla projects for a host of inspectors and consultants who initiated endless and costly refinements. No fewer than nineteen environmental consulting companies were paid to submit reports on Phase I of the Coquihalla Highway! I have estimated the total cost of all changes listed above at $59 million, a task which was really quite simple as these costs are all contained within the brief to the Commissioner's Inquiry prepared in September 1987 and presented to Mr. MacKay by the Ministry. The brief was subsequently released to the public.

The Coquihalla Highway's adverse publicity has certainly produced destructive fallout. It has damaged the reputation of the province for being a place where things are done well. It has damaged the reputations of all the road and bridge consulting engineers of B.C.—and they are some of the finest in North America—who could have used credit for this wonderful highway to sell their services abroad.

Further lasting damage was done to the Ministry by the sudden departure of hundreds of the best experienced and most knowledgeable technical and professional staff, something also brought about by the Vander Zalm administration as part of its early retirement and privatisation program, for which the Highways Ministry was particularly singled out.

A full-page advertisement was placed by the Government in all B.C. newspapers in October, 1987—the Victoria *Times-Colonist* of October 24 carried it. "AN INVITATION TO INDIVIDUALS, CORPORATIONS, SMALL BUSINESS, CONTRACTORS, INVESTORS AND PRESENT PROVINCIAL EMPLOYEES TO PARTICIPATE IN THE BUSINESS OF GOVERNMENT" read the headline. It then went on to describe how any of the above could bid on the private contracting of over $200 million of provincial road, bridge, and other structure maintenance operations starting with the Highways operation on Vancouver Island. The full privatisation of all B.C. road and bridge maintenance then followed—a first for a provincial or state government in North America. Highway design, planning, and contract supervision were also widely privatised.

Even a casual observer would recognize that the Ministry of Transportation and Highways was not by any measure Premier Vander Zalm's favourite organisation. The saddest note, however, is that on June 29, 1988, the Vander Zalm government presented and passed Bill 36, amending Section 49 of the Ministry of Transportation and Highways Act, revising W.A.C. Bennett's cherished concept that all highway contracts must go to open public tender and be awarded to the low bidder. Some of these contracts may now be negotiated.

Contrary to public perception, Lady Luck very often favours, in the long run, those who do not stick their necks out. The brave souls in the Highways Ministry who accepted the challenge of building 120 kilometres of rural freeway in just twenty-two months, through the most difficult of terrain, subject to extremes of winter weather, should ponder this. They had a good run at controlling all the elements involved, except for one: their political masters.

With the passage of time, accomplishments often rise up to speak for themselves. The Coquihalla and all the Coast Connections of this province are the product of a great deal of dedication and expertise in a part of the world where transportation challenges have been a daily fact of life for 150 years of settlement and expansion. When traversing their many miles for business or for pleasure, travellers should not take for granted the roads beneath their wheels. Great sacrifices and stalwart achievements have brought these highways to their present standard.

Route Map of the Connections to the Highway through the Coquihalla Pass

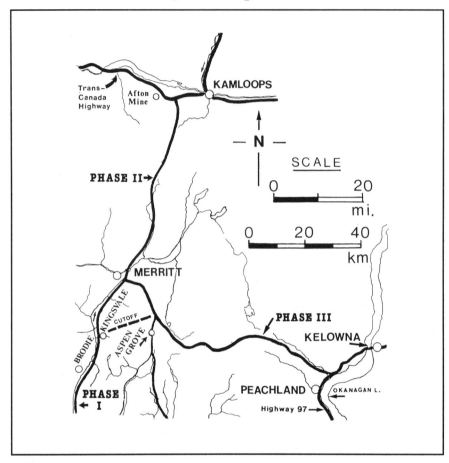

Phase II of the Coquihalla opened in September of 1987. The 80-km section included eight bridges and six underpasses with only one large river crossing at Merritt. Phase III finally opened in October of 1990. Called the Okanagan Connector, this 108-km section has no major structures on it. In some places the Connector is a modified route rather than brand new construction. South of Merritt one infamous hill remains of sufficient grade to cause truck radiators to boil over. The total cost of the 308-km system was $771 million (409, 137 and 225 millions respectively), an average of $2.5 million per kilometre. The Aspen Grove/Kingsvale cutoff shown in dotted lines will eventually be built as Kelowna becomes the major Interior centre that the highway is making it. The Aspen Grove/Kingsvale route would cut off a combined climb westwards and eastward of 700 metres vertically, which is vital to economic trucking.

NOTES

Fuller details of works cited in short form in the Notes are given in the Bibliography.

Chapter One, 1793–1864

1 Morice, *The History of the Northern Interior of B.C.*, pp. 103-119.

2 Akrigg and Akrigg, *Chronicles, 1874-71*, pp. 12-l6.

3 Report on a Journey of Survey from Victoria to Fort Alexander by Lt. Henry Spencer Palmer, R.E., published in November of 1862, p. 13. PABC.

4 Akrigg and Akrigg, *Chronicles, 1847-71*, pp. 12-16.

5 Ormsby, *A Pioneer Gentlewoman in British Columbia: Recollections of Susan Allison*, p. 10.

6 Noel Robinson and the Old Man Himself, *Blazing the Trail through the Rockies. The Story of Walter Moberly and his Share in the Making of Vancouver.*

7 DPW File 3464. Leighton is confirmed by Walter Moberly in the book by Noel Robinson. The first six miles were built by the R.E.s; the next seven from Chapmans Bar to Boston Bar by J.W. Trutch; followed by Thomas Spence who contracted the 32 miles to Lytton in partnership with George Landvoigt; then Oppenheimer, Moberly, and Lewis who joined G.B. Wright coming south from Alexandria but who only completed 30 miles.

8 DPW File 3464.

9 Trutch went back to England in 1876 but returned four years later as Dominion Agent for the CPR construction. (See footnote (2) in Chapter 2 re: tolls.)

10 The Imperial Government offered Col. Moody's services at £1200 per year, and the other officers at one-third and one-fifth that amount. Governor Douglas' resentment of Moody surfaced with the reply that he was not worth it.

11 Hill, *Sappers. The Royal Engineers in British Columbia.* pp. 123 to 144.

Chapter Two, 1865–1899

1 Akrigg and Akrigg, *B.C. Chronicles 1847 - 71*, p. 104.

2 According to "Notes on the Road History of British Columbia" by H.L. Cairns (see note 16 below), the road toll on the Yale-Cariboo Road was one cent per pound of freight levied at Lytton and another cent per pound levied at Clinton. The toll house was shortly moved from Lytton to Yale. There were also toll houses at Lillooet, Hope and Port Douglas, no doubt to tap other routes. In addition there were tolls on

the Alexandra and Spences Bridges. Trutch charged one-third of a cent per pound of freight; Spence half as much. Both Trutch and Spence charged a quarter for each draught animal, half as much for other animals, and a quarter to two dollars for vehicles, dependent upon the number of animals hauling them. Spence also got twenty-five cents for foot passengers. (Trutch, for example, collected about forty dollars for a wagon hauled by ten mules carrying a full load of freight.) The government also levied three dollars per ton on waterborne goods en route from New Westminster or Victoria to Yale. All in all, it was estimated that the average total charged on one long ton of freight from New Westminster or Victoria to the Cariboo was $56.53, a sizable sum with the dollar valued at ten times what it is today.

3 R.C. Harris, "The First Alexandra Bridge, Fraser Canyon, 1863 to 1912." *B.C. Historical News*, Fall 1982. pp. 8-14.

4 "Overland Coach Road." Minute of the C.C.L. & W., dated February 10, 1868, and published in full in the *British Colonist*, April 14, 1868. PABC.

5 Ormsby, *British Columbia: a History*, p. 239.

6 A report in DLW File 449/81, dated May 25, 1881, shows that legendary stagecoach driver Steve Tingley had no patience with delay. Although stopped for clearance of rocks that had been dislodged by railway surveyors working up above, Tingley went on ahead and tipped over his coach. Nick Black got harsh words on that from Commissioner G.A. Walkem, who was also Premier at the time.

7 R.C. Harris, "A Good Mule Road from Semilkameen," *B.C. Historical News*, Spring 1981, pp. 8-14.

8 *The Rossland Miner*, June 30, 1905.

9 Letter from Walter Moberly to Edgar Dewdney, DLW File 286/65, April 10, 1865, PABC.

10 *British Colonist*, December 23, 1869, PABC.

11 Wooliams, *Cattle Ranch. Story of the Douglas Lake Cattle Company*, p. 16. (This volume gives a complete history of the ranch.)

12 DLW File 2000/76.

13 DLW File 1335/77.

14 Ormsby, *A Pioneer Gentlewoman in British Columbia: Recollections of Susan Allison*, p. 67. Besides describing the lives of John and Susan Allison, these well edited recollections also contain a series of single page or less biographies of individuals familiar to the reader, contributed by the editor and very well researched. These include James Douglas, Edgar and Jane Dewdney, Richard Moody, George and Mary Landvoigt, William Teague, Walter Moberly, the Trutch brothers (Joseph and John), Stephen Tingley, John Robson, F.G. Vernon, and A.C. Anderson.

15 Ormsby, *British Columbia: a History*, p. 318-24. See also lists of Premiers and Administrators.

16 Cairns, MS "Notes on the Road History of British Columbia (From an Old File)." January, 1953. DPW Archives (as provided by E.C. Webster).

17 Report by Chief Commissioner of Lands & Works to the Provincial Assembly, 1875. PABC.

18 DLW File 1441/76. Letter of June 30, 1876.

19 DLW File 1401/76, Letter of June 26, 1876.

20 Report of the Operations of the Lands and Works Department, 1874. PABC.

21 Ormsby, *British Columbia: a History*, p. 307

22 Ormsby, p. 314.

23 DLW File 5113/99, (DPW 1643, Sect. 1).

24 DLW File 5309/99, (DPW 1643, Sect. 1).

Chapter Three, 1900–1917

1 Cairns, "Notes on the Road History of British Columbia."

2 In 1903 the first annual licence fee for an automobile was set at $36. In 1907, 175 motor vehicles were registered in the province, with a licence revenue of $6500. By 1918 the registration total had risen to 15,370 with a revenue of nearly $1,800,000, a surprising total which indicated that the average fee per vehicle had tripled to $115. Also by 1918 the government had received a bonus from the province's pioneer motorists and truckers in the form of $783,751 in gasoline taxes, a much better application of the "user pay" theory than is found today. By 1929 the vehicle count had risen to 94,300, a 600 percent increase in ten years.

3 *Victoria Colonist*, December 19, 1900.

4 Information on Thomas Taylor as well as some of the previous Roads Ministers is available in the Provincial Archives of B.C.

5 Ormsby, *British Columbia: a History*. p. 345-48.

6 Ormsby, p. 365.

7 DPW File 3464-18.

8 The negotiations took place between 1910 and 1926. The final settlement was $1000 each for 26 crossings, $12,000 for four miles of roadway wiped out between Lytton and Spences Bridge, $4000 for a crossing wrongly filled in, and $3000 for "casting damage." In addition, they built a subway at Lytton. In return the CPR obtained seniority and exclusion from all crossing charges in future, maintenance of all overhead crossings for all time by the Province, and return of all road right-of-way not required in any future highway design. They even obtained a concession to get their $1000 back if in future a crossing were re-

moved. Regarding precedence, the CPR used it resolutely against the CNR by refusing to let them use the same bank of the river between Cisco and Lytton. Because of this, the CNR had to bridge the Fraser River twice before reaching Lytton. The CNR did petition Ottawa but on July 28, 1911 a notice in the *Lytton Daily News Advertiser* closed the matter: the CNR withdrew its petition on the basis of an engineering report which ruled that the CPR embankment would be adversely affected. (DPW File 3464-17)

9 DPW File 3464-1.

10 *Manual of Provincial Information* (up to 1929), Legislative Library.

11 T.W. Wilby, "Motoring across Canada," *Motor Magazine*, 1913. PABC.

12 *Victoria Daily Times*, May 30, 1916; *Victoria Daily Colonist*, July 9, 1916.

13 Ormsby, *British Columbia: a History*. p. 377

14 Ormsby, p. 383.

15 One of the more intriguing footnotes to Public Works history is Thomas Taylor becoming the Traffic Superintendent of the Department during the later years of the B.C. Conservative Government in 1932 and 1933, a position similar to that of the present Superintendent of Motor Vehicles. His name appears in the 1933-34 Annual Report and in fact he is believed to have contributed to much of the original traffic control legislation for the Province. It is not known if he worked under R.W. Bruhn as Minister, (1930-33), which would certainly have been a reversal of their previous roles.

Chapter Four, 1918–1928

1 Ormsby, *British Columbia: a History*, pp. 365, 408, 421.

2 DPW File 1643.

3 DPW File 212.

4 DPW File 1643.

5 British Columbia Legislative Assembly, *"British Columbia Clerk of the House Papers,"* 5th February 1920, *Report, W.K. Gwyer, District Engineer,* Legislative Library.

6 DPW File 3464-1.

7 DPW File 3880.

8 The report and analysis following is taken from DPW File 3464-31.

9 DPW. Various Annual Reports.

10 Little personal information is available on Patrick Philip, who departed the scene in 1933 or 1934, presumably to retirement. The lack of background on such fine men is due primarily to the unfortunate decision in the 1970s to destroy all old files on personnel. Philip, who moved

to Victoria from Kamloops in 1918, guided the Department through the difficult post-First World War years, through the recession and boom of the 1920s, and through the worst years of the Great Depression.

11 In October of 1924, Locating Engineer, H.C. Whitaker, wrote to Deputy Minister, Pat Philip (DPW File 3464-30), giving his address as "The Gorge, via Boston Bar," recommending that a cabin be built on the Fraser Canyon Highway project, "for the convenience of visiting officers." This was approved and a site was chosen on the CNR right-of-way in Boston Bar. In due course, a framed three room shed, 38 by 13 feet, was built at a cost of $400. Philip turned down any plumbing, saying, "A bucket and a basin will do." He also vetoed any bunks. This was not nearly as convenient as staying in the camp would have been, but possibly more acceptable to the protocol of those days.

12 DPW File 3464-7.

13 B.R. Atkins, Vancouver *Province*, Sept 20, 1925.

14 DPW File 5784-1.

15 Tulameen Pass is shown on the map in Chapter 1, "Trails from the Skagit to the Tulameen." The Skaist River/ Tulameen River/Princeton route was quite feasible for the road standards of that time and was seven miles shorter than by Allison Pass.

16 DLW File 151. Letter written at Hope, B.C. PABC.

Chapter Five, 1928–1952

1 DPW Annual Report, 1929-30.

2 Material and quotations from this correspondence are taken from sources in DPW File 292.

3 DPW File 292.

4 Material and quotations from correspondence on the Experimental Farm problem are taken from sources in DPW File 1643.

5 Entitled *Geological Hazards and Urban Development of Silt Deposits in the Penticton Area*, the report was prepared by D. Nyland and G.E. Miller. Miller was the Regional Geotechnical and Materials Engineer at Kamloops at that time and Nyland an Engineer-in-Training.

6 This was never published, and except for one copy held in the Bridge Branch office in Victoria, the locations of other copies remain unknown to the author.

7 Clapp, MS *The History of the Hart Highway*.

8 Mitchell, *W.A.C. Bennett and the Rise of British Columbia*, p. 182.

9 E.T. Kenney spent almost all of his short term as Minister of Public Works in a desperate effort to divert as much of the provincial treasury as possible to the roads adjacent to his riding headquarters at Terrace,

which admittedly had been neglected for years. When he left in the coalition breakup, Department officials stopped several rock crushers and paving plants en route to Terrace, and returned them and the designated funds to their previous commitment.

10 Paul St. Pierre, *Vancouver Sun*, September 30, 1949, p. 21.

11 Worley, *The Wonderful World of W.A.C. Bennett*, pp. 185-6.

Chapter Six, 1953–1972

1 A good accounting of the life and times of P.A. Gaglardi, published in 1991, is contained in the book *Friend O' Mine* by Mel Rothenburger. It includes an extensive cataloguing of the achievements of his regime, mostly related in direct quotations from the central figure, who is definitely not reticent to talk about them.

2 Rothenburger, pp. 63 to 65.

3 Mitchell, *W.A.C. Bennett and the Rise of British Columbia*, 1983, p. 277.

4 According to full-page coverage of his life story in the *Vancouver Province*, July 25, 1982, p. C1, following his death the week before, Ginter in his lifetime presided over road and railway building and pulp mill site grading contracts totalling $330 million.

5 The Alexandra Bridge was started in 1956 and not substantially finished until 1962. It was an 805-foot steel deck arch with a roadway 27 feet wide, costing out at $120 per square foot of deck—a very high figure for that period. In comparison the 480-foot arch of the Nine Mile Canyon Bridge cost $87 per square foot, and the new Thompson River Bridge at Spence's Bridge was $77 per square foot with a 698-foot length and a 26-foot-wide roadway. The Revelstoke Suspension Bridge with a total length of 950 feet, a 600-foot main span and a 24-foot-wide roadway cost $137 per square foot, proving that suspension bridges are always more expensive. The Dry Gulch Bridge on the Coquihalla Highway, an 879-foot steel deck arch similar to Alexandra but with a 60-foot-wide roadway cost $197 per square foot. The Alex Fraser Bridge main span cost $217 per square foot of deck area.

6 The largest of the snow sheds built on the Trans-Canada Highway by British Columbia was the Lanark Shed at 1036 feet in length, with a 26.5-foot-wide roadway and 32 feet total width. When finally completed in 1963, it cost $1.5 million or $45 per square foot. Twenty-three years later, the Great Bear Snowshed on the Coquihalla Highway cost $165 per square foot. Lanark was quite sharply curved and was described as being capable of withstanding snow travelling at 125 miles per hour.

7 The 1200-foot-long Kinnaird Bridge is a most handsome structure on slender Y-shaped piers with cantilevered spans crossing high above the Columbia River. Due to its height, the cost was $83 per square foot of deck area, exactly twice the cost of the new 950-foot-long Trail Bridge

214

built at the same time and designed by the Department. The Brilliant Bridge, with a slightly smaller arch of 420 feet at the main span and a 992-foot overall length with a 28-foot roadway width, came in at $46 per square foot.

8 Ministry of Transportation and Highways Publication, *Summer Traffic Volumes on Provincial Highways in British Columbia. 1979 to 1982.* Issued in 1983.

Chapter Seven, 1972–1975

1 Worley, *The Wonderful World of W.A.C. Bennett,* 1971, p. 98.

2 The Cascade Mountains in British Columbia have an area of 6700 square kilometres, 4500 of which drain into the Fraser and Skagit basins, and 2200 into the Columbia basin. They are separated from the Coast Mountains by the Fraser River. The total Fraser watershed is 233,000 square km, and the Columbia watershed in British Columbia is 102,000 square km.

3 Unruh, *The Plains Across.*

4 The western half of British Columbia's 191,800 square kilometre Interior Plateau comprises the Fraser, Nechako, and Thompson Plateaus. These are tablelands up to 1850 metres in altitude above sea level with basins for the Fraser, Nechako, Thompson, and Okanagan Rivers as low as 600 metres. The Quesnel, Shuswap, and Okanagan Highlands rise to 2800 metres.

5 Colin Fraser, *The Avalanche Enigma,* pp. 77-120.

6 Ministry of Transportation and Highways Publication, *Snow Avalanche Atlas - Coquihalla,* 1980.

7 Akrigg and Akrigg, *British Columbia Chronicles, 1847-71,* pp. 83-4.

8 A full account of the building and operation of the Kettle Valley Railway through the Coquihalla Pass is given in Barrie Sanford's excellent book, *McCulloch's Wonder.*

9 National Research Council of Canada. Technical Memorandum No. 98. November 1970. *Proceedings of a Conference, University of Calgary, 23-24 October, 1969. Ice Engineering and Avalanche Forecasting and Control.* Compiled by L.W. Gold and G.P. Williams. III.2. "Mining versus Avalanches—British Columbia," by J.W. Peck. pp. 79-83. III.3. "Problems caused by Avalanches on Highways in British Columbia," by J.W. Nelson, pp. 84-90.

Chapter Eight, 1976–1986

1 Persky, *Son of Socred,* pp. 260-64, and Allan White, "Bennett fires Jack Davis," *Vancouver Province,* April 4, 1978.

2 Sanford, *McCulloch's Wonder,* pp. 193-94.

Chapter Nine, Aftermath

1 It would have been quite unique if there had not been an overrun on the highway megaproject considering the past record. The B.C.R. extension, Peace River Dam, and the Columbia River Dam had massive overruns. In more recent times, B.C. Transit's SkyTrain in Vancouver ran over by a billion dollars, and in 1992 the Vancouver Island Gas Pipe Line project announced a construction overrun of 40 percent, the same as Phase I of the Coquihalla after cost for extras was deducted.

2 Letter from A.V. Fraser to R.G. Harvey, August 20, 1986.

3 Director of Construction for the Ministry, Norman Zapf, commented on global or conceptual estimating in a brief prepared for circulation in February of 1988: "Except for allowances for inflation and the competitive climate, the first time a conceptual estimate can be intelligently updated is when the engineering investigations and design are well advanced." The Ministry Planning Branch in 1984 had to confirm an estimate with very little investigation or preparation of engineering data.

Glossary of Terms

The following terms are used in the narrative and are defined here only as they pertain to roads and road construction.

ASPHALT—a tough, gummy mineral by-product of oil refining used for paving road surfaces.

BATTER—the form in which the face of a wall, pier, cribbing or other structure recedes and slopes upward.

BLACKTOP—asphalt, or a similar material for paving roads. It also refers to the surface so paved.

CAMBER—the convexity, or arching, of a road surface from the centre to the sides built for proper water drainage.

CANTILEVER—large projecting beam fastened at one end. A cantilever bridge is formed of two meeting but not mutually supporting cantilevers.

CONTROLLED ACCESS—a legal condition whereby the rights of owners or occupants near a highway are limited or controlled by public authority.

CORDUROY—a section of road constructed of logs laid tightly together crosswise and usually lashed together to form a crossing over swampy ground.

CRIBBING—A log cribbing as used on older roads is an earth retaining structure with shorter header logs right-angled to the facing logs and corner-notched together. It is usually built continuously horizontally and in courses vertically, being filled with earth or boulders as it goes up. The face is battered.

DAY LABOUR—This term is used to describe a method of road construction, or other work on a road, done by hiring men and machines at a daily or hourly rate of payment. This sometimes substitutes for contracted payment whereby payment is made on the basis of a whole completed project.

DEFILE—a long narrow pass between hills.

EXPRESSWAY—a divided arterial highway for through traffic with full or partial control of access.

FREEWAY—an expressway with full control of access and all level crossings eliminated.

GRADE—short for "gradient," which is the rate of ascent or descent of a sloping road, or the part of a road which slopes. Also used to identify the part of the road structure below the final surfacing. The verb "grading" or the phrase "building grade" means the construction of that part of the highway.

GUMBO—Found in western North America, this is a silty, fine soil which becomes very sticky when wet.

INTERCHANGE—a system of interconnecting roadways in conjunction with grade separations, the most typical of which is a cloverleaf, providing for the interchange of traffic between two or more intersecting roadways.

LACUSTRINE SILTS—fine sediments from lakes or former lakes.

PIER—a vertical support for a bridge consisting of columns, spread footings, or piles.

PILE—a heavy stake, beam, or pole of timber, or a pipe of concrete or steel, driven into the ground or bed of a river to support a superstructure or pier.

PREQUALIFICATION—In highway and bridge contracts this means the examination of potential bidders in advance to determine if they have sufficient resources to do the job, in the opinion of the authority putting out the work to tender. Financial sufficiency is always checked, but prequalification also includes assessment of experience, expertise, personnel, equipment, and plant. Successful qualifiers are then supplied with documents to tender. The process is supposed to prevent contractors from failing to perform, but in fact the record does not always support this.

RUNNING LINE—surveying the line of a proposed road and placing stakes at measured distances between them by transit sighting.

SAPPERS—Technically, those soldiers who produce "saps" or narrow trenches dug for the purpose of approaching an enemy"s position. In the British Army the troops who did this were called "sappers," which fell into use as a term for troops who do all engineering work.

SCANTLING—the thickness and breadth of a timber.

SPREAD FOOTING—a concrete or masonry slab, or a grid of heavy timbers upon which the pier footing or superstructure of a bridge may rest.

SUPERELEVATION—the sloping of a road surface in a curve by elevating the outer edge towards the centre to offset centrifugal forces.

SUPERSTRUCTURE—that part of a bridge above the piers or footings.

SURFACING—the material used to provide the top layer to a roadbed, or "grade"; gravel or blacktop.

TANGENT—the straight section of a highway.

TOTE ROAD—an unsurfaced road used for transporting materials and supplies, such as to a temporary camp.

TRACE—a track, path, or trail left by a person moving through the bush. In early days it was sometimes marked by blazing or slashing trees along its length.

TRESTLE—A trestle is a short-span bridge with the longitudinal beams resting on post or piling frames transversely and diagonally braced, and with the outer piles or posts spread.

TRUNK ROAD—In B.C. the term was used many years ago to describe a main road. For example, the Dewdney Trunk Road originally was the only road in the area, with other roads later springing from it. Now that roads develop into complex networks, the word "trunk" is outdated and has been replaced by the word "arterial."

WATERSHED—an area drained by a particular stream, system, or body of water.

Senior Civil Servants
in Public Works and Highways, 1875 to 1986

Year Started	Names and Titles
1875	Joseph A. Mahood, Chief Engineer, CE (Until 1877)
1899	F.C. Gamble, Public Works Engineer, PWE
1908	W.W. Foster, Deputy Minister, & J.E. Griffith, PWE
1913	J.E. Griffith, DM and PWE
1916	J.E. Griffith,DM, and A.E. Foreman, PWE
1921	J.E. Griffith, DM, and Patrick Philip, PWE
1924	Patrick Philip, DM and PWE
1929	Patrick Philip, PWE (It is assumed that there
1930	Patrick Philip, CE was no DM in this period.)
1933	Patrick Philip, DM and CE
1934	Arthur Dixon, CE. (No DM, apparently, until 1942.)
1942	Arthur Dixon, DM
1943	Arthur Dixon, DM, and A.L. Carruthers, CE
1947	A.L. Carruthers, DM, and H.C. Anderson, CE
1948	N.W. MacPherson, DM, and H.C. Anderson, CE
1949	E.S. Jones, DM, and H.C. Anderson, CE
1949	E.S. Jones DM, and N.M. McCallum, CE
1957	E.S. Jones, DM
1958	H.T. Miard, DM, and F.T. Brown, CE
1964	H.T. Miard, DM, and D.D. Godfrey, CE
1969	H.T. Miard, DM, and J.A. Dennison, CE
1973	H.F. Sturrock, DM, and J.A. Dennison, CE
1976	R.G. Harvey, DM Highways, & G.L.Giles, DM Public Works
1977	R.G. Harvey, DM Highways & Public Works
1983	A.E. Rhodes, DM, (Acting), and T.R. Johnson, Asst. DM
1986	T.R. Johnson, DM, and R.G. White, ADM

The longest serving Deputy Minister is H.T. Miard, 15 years.

(Note: When T.R. Johnson was transferred in 1987, Premier Vander Zalm broke a tradition in effect since 1908, by appointing to succeed Johnson a Deputy Minister who was not a Professional Engineer, and no Deputy Ministers since then have been Professional Engineers).

Chief Commissioners of Lands and Works
1858–1908

Year Started	Name
1858	Colonel Richard Clement Moody, R.E.
1863	Judge Chartres Brew (Temporary Appointment)
1863	Joseph William Trutch (Later Sir Joseph)
1871	Benjamin William Pearce
1871	Henry Holbrook
1872	George Anthony Walkem
1872	Robert Beaven†
1876	Forbes George Vernon
1878	George Anthony Walkem†
1882	Robert Beaven†
1883	William Smithe†
1895	George Bohun Martin
1898	Charles Augustus Semlin†
1899	Francis Lovett Carter-Cotton
1900	James Stuart Yates
1900	Wilmer Cleveland Wells
1903	Richard McBride (Later Sir Richard)†
1903	Robert Francis Green
1906	Robert Garnet Tatlow
1907	Frederick John Fulton

† Means also Premier in the same period.

The longest serving Chief Commissioner of Lands and Works was Forbes George Vernon, who held the office for ten years.

Ministers of Public Works and of Highways
1908–1986

Ministers of Public Works	Ministers of Highways
Year Started	**Year Started**
1908 Thomas Taylor	1955 Philip Arthur Gaglardi
1914 Charles Edward Tisdall	1967 William A. C. Bennett[†]
1916 Dr. James Horace King	1972 Wesley Drewett Black
1922 Dr. Henry William Sutherland	1972 Robert Martin Strachan
1928 Nelson Seymour Lougheed	1973 Graham Richard Lea
1929 Rolf Walgren Bruhn	1975 Alexander Vaughan Fraser
1932 Robert Henry Pooley	1986 Cliff Michael
1933 William Savage	
1933 Frank Mitchell MacPherson	
1939 Thomas Dufferin Patullo[†]	
1939 Charles Sidney Leary	
1941 Thomas King	
1941 Rolf Walgren Bruhn	
1941 John Hart[†]	
1942 Herbert Anscomb	
1946 Ernest Crawford Carson	
1952 Edward Tourtellote Kenney	
1952 Philip Arthur Gaglardi	

† Means also Premier in the same period.

Later name changes from Minister of Highways are ignored.

The longest serving Minister was P.A. Gaglardi, 15 years.

Early Chronology and Listing of Name Changes

1793	Alexander Mackenzie reaches the Pacific Coast overland.
1808	Simon Fraser travels the Fraser River.
1807-14	The North West Company creates New Caledonia and the Columbia route to the ocean.
1821	The Hudson's Bay Company takes over the North West Company.
1846	The Treaty of Washington establishes the international boundary.
1849	The HBC is granted a Charter for Vancouver Island.
1850	The Colony of Vancouver Island (V.I.) is created.
1851	James Douglas becomes the Governor of V.I.
1858	The Colony of British Columbia is created. James Douglas becomes Governor.
1862	The Cariboo gold rush.
1863	The Royal Engineers leave British Columbia.
1864	Governor Douglas retires.
1866	The Colonies of V.I. and B.C. unite.
1871	The Colony of B.C. becomes the Province of B.C.
1871	The Department of Lands and Works is created by the British Constitution Act.
1899	The Department of Lands & Works is split into two Branches, a Lands Branch and a Works Branch.
1908	The Department of Public Works is created by the Public Works Act.
1948	The Dominion Government of Canada becomes the Federal Government.
1955	The Department of Highways is created, and the responsibility for public buildings is removed.
1976	The Department of Highways becomes the Department of Highways and Public Works.
1977	The Department becomes the Ministry of Highways and Public Works.
1978	The Ministry becomes the Ministry of Transportation, Communications and Highways.
1980	Communications responsibility is removed. The Ministry of Transportation and Highways is created.

Bibliography

Atkins, B.R. *Columbia River Chronicles* 1976. The Alexander Nicolls Press, Vancouver.

Akrigg, G.V.P. and Helen B., *British Columbia 1847-1871 Chronicles.* 1977. *1001 British Columbia Place Names.* 1969. Both from Discovery Press, Vancouver.

Baynes, Raymond. *Frontier to Freeway.* 1971. Ministry of Transportation & Highways, Victoria.

Beautiful British Columbia Magazine. Special publication, "The Fraser River." 1983. Victoria.

Berton, Pierre. *The National Dream* and *The Last Spike.* 1970 and 1971. Both from McClelland & Stewart Ltd., Toronto/Montreal.

Butler, William Francis. *The Great Lone Land,* and *The Wild North Land.* 1968. Both from Hurtig Publishers, Edmonton.

Bryan, Liz. *British Columbia This Favoured Land.* 1982. Douglas & McIntyre, Vancouver/Toronto.

Cairns, H.L. *Notes on the Road History of British Columbia.* DPW Archives, Victoria.

Carruthers, A.L. *Bridges Fit Strong and Handsome.* DPW Archives, Victoria.

Clapp, Frank A. *Lake and River Ferries.* 1991. M.O.T.H. Victoria. Manuscript, *The History of the Hart Highway.*

Clerk of the House, British Columbia. *Papers 1921 II. Reports by Fred. J. Dawson, W.K. Gwyer, W.A. Cleveland, and G.H. Richardson on the Hope-Princeton Road.*

Craig, Andy. *Trucking.* 1977. Hancock House Publishers Ltd., Saanichton and Seattle.

Downs, Art. *Paddlewheels on the Frontier.* Volume Two. 1971. Foremost Publishing Ltd., Surrey, B.C.

Dunae, Patrick A. *Gentlemen Immigrants.* 1981. Douglas & McIntyre, Vancouver/Toronto.

Farley, A.L. *Atlas of British Columbia.* 1979. U.B.C. Press, Vancouver.

Francis, Daniel. *Battle for the West.* Hurtig Publishers, Edmonton.

Fraser, Colin. *The Avalanche Enigma.* 1966. John Munroe, London.

Fraser, Esther. *The Canadian Rockies.* 1969. M. G. Hurtig Ltd., Edmonton.

Frazier, Neta Lones. *Five Roads to the Pacific.* 1964. David McKay Co. Ltd. New York.

Gold, L.W. & Williams, G.B. *Ice Engineering and Avalanche Forecasting and Control.* Proceedings of a Conference held in Calgary, Alberta, October 1969. The National Research Council, Ottawa.

Guillet, Edwin C. *The Story of Canadian Roads.* Univ. of Toronto Press, Toronto.

Harris, R.C. Various Papers in the *B.C. Historical Review.* 1982 and following.

Hill, Beth. *Sappers. The Royal Engineers in British Columbia.* 1987. Horsdal & Schubart, Ganges, B.C.

Holland, Stuart S. *Landforms of British Columbia.* Bulletin 48. B.C. Department of Mines & Resources, Victoria.

Howay, F.W. "Work of the Royal Engineers in British Columbia." *B.C. Brigade Trails.* Prov. Archives & Records Service, Victoria.

Hutchinson, Bruce. *The Fraser.* 1950. Clarke Irwin & Co. Ltd.

Johnson, Robert C. *John McLoughlin, Father of Oregon.* circa 1935, poss. 1920. Binfords & Mout.

Kavic, Lorne J. & Nixon, Garry Brian. *The 1200 Days. A Shattered Dream.* Kaen Publishers, Coquitlam, B.C.

Kopas, Cliff. *Packhorses to the Pacific.* 1976. Gray's Publishing Limited, Sidney, B.C.

McGregor, J.G. *Overland by the Yellowhead.* 1974. Western Producer Book Service, Saskatoon.

MacKay, Douglas L. *Report of the Commissioner Inquiry into the Coquihalla and Other Related Highway Projects.* 1987. Province of British Columbia, Victoria.

Mantle, H.A. *Functional Report for Proposed Divided Highway from Hope to Merritt via the Coquihalla River - Boston Bar Creek - Coldwater River.* 1973. M.O.T.H. Victoria.

Merk, Frederick. *Fur Trade and Empire. George Simpson's Journal.* 1968. Belknap Press of Harvard Univ. Press, Cambridge, Mass.

Ministry of Transportation & Highways. *Preliminary Environmental Report Coquihalla (Hope-Merritt) Highway Corridor.* 1978 and *Hope-Merritt Highway Corridor Surficial Geology.* 1978. M.O.T.H. Victoria.

———. *Brief to the Commissioner Inquiry into the Coquihalla and Other Related Projects.* 1987. M.O.T.H. Victoria.

———. *The Road Runner.* House Organ. Various copies. M.O.T.H. Victoria.

———. *A Short Illustrated History of Roads in British Columbia.* 1980. M.O.T.H. Victoria.

Mitchell, David J. *W.A.C. Bennett and the Rise of British Columbia.* 1983, and *Succession. The Political Re-shaping of British Columbia.* 1987. Both from Douglas & McIntyre.

Moody, R.C. *Correspondence Outward April - December 1860.* Prov. Archives & Records Service, Victoria.

Morice, Rev. A.G., O.M.I. *The History of the Northern Interior of British Columbia formerly New Caledonia (1660-1880).* 1904, Toronto.

Ormsby, Margaret A. *British Columbia: A History.* 1958. The MacMillans in Canada.

————. Editor. *A Pioneer Gentlewoman in British Columbia. The Recollections of Susan Allison.* 1976 The Univ. of B.C. Press, Vancouver.

Persky, Stan. *Son of Socred.* 1979, and *Fantasy Government.* 1989. Both from New Star Books Ltd., Vancouver.

Reid, J.H. Stewart. *Mountains, Men and Rivers.* The Ryerson Press, Toronto.

Reigger, Hal. *The Kettle Valley and its Railway.* 1981. Edmonds Washington Pacific Fast Mail.

Robinson, Noel, and the Old Man Himself. *Blazing the Trail through the Rockies. The Story of Walter Moberly.* News Advertiser Printers and Bookbinders, New Westminster.

Rothenburger, Mel. *Friend O' Mine.* 1991. Orca Book Publishers, Victoria.

Royal Engineers, (B.C.). *Correspondence Outward. April 1859 - June 1863, and July 1861 - October 1864.* Prov. Archives & Records Service, Victoria.

Sanford, Barrie. *McCulloch's Wonder - The Story of The Kettle Valley Railway.* 1979. Whitecap Books, West Vancouver.

Spry, Irene M. *The Palliser Expedition.* 1963. MacMillan Company of Canada, Toronto.

Turner, Robert D. *Sternwheelers and Steam Tugs.* 1984. Sono Nis Press, Victoria.

Unruh, John D. Jr. *The Plains Across.* Univ. of Illinois Press, Chicago.

Wooliams, Nina J. *Cattle Ranch. The Story of the Douglas Lake Cattle Company.* McClelland & Stewart, Toronto.

Worley, Ronald B. *The Wonderful World of W.A.C. Bennett.* 1972. McClelland & Stewart, Toronto.

Zapf, Norman R. *The Coquihalla Highway.* 1988. Manuscript.

Index

231